STEALING TWILIGHT

A Psychic Justice Novel

ERIN RICHARDS

www.ErinRichards.com

STEALING TWILIGHT
Erin Richards

Print ISBN: 978-1943800025
Digital ISBN: 978-1943800032

Cover Designer: Robin Harper @ Wicked by Design

Editors: D'Ann Burrow and Laurie Larsen

PRAISE FOR
CHASING SHADOWS
Psychic Justice Book 1

"I loved this book and it never faltered from its action and suspense. The story line not only kept my attention but each chapter was suspenseful trying to find out what the kidnapper was going to do and how Juliana would deal with it." ~*Night Owl Reviews* (NOR 5-Star Top Pick)

"This story was masterfully written and illustrates just what a frightfully good imagination the author has to work with." ~*Fallen Angel Reviews* (5-Star Recommended Read)

"A whirlwind of emotions, twists, turns and rediscovered love will keep you breathless!" ~*Fresh Fiction*

"The suspense will keep you turning the pages... The characters are complex and well-developed and there is never a dull moment in the story. If you love your romance with suspense, this is one book you need to read! 5 stars all the way!" ~*The Romance Reviews*

BOOKS BY
ERIN RICHARDS

Psychic Justice Series
Chasing Shadows, Book 1
Twilight Rising, Novella
Stealing Twilight, Book 2

Wicked Paradise

Young Adult
Vigilante Nights
Dragonfly Nightmare

STEALING TWILIGHT

*To the baddest Unicorns in the whole freakin'
universe with your stabby horns and rainbow tails.
You color my world.*

CHAPTER ONE

Lily's hand jerked, scattering a fistful of soil onto the casket awaiting its final blanket. The deep rumble of a Harley Davidson shattered her illusion of serenity. She sighed, hiccupped. The splintered silence lent a momentary respite from the day's somberness. Bleary-eyed, she glanced up at a tall, black-clad intruder sauntering with a slight limp across the wet lawn toward the grave, peeling off his black helmet.

Vivid blue eyes stared at her from a sun-drenched face framed by dark, almost black hair. Rocker hair. It flowed back from a strong, smooth forehead, tied at the nape of his neck. Underneath the leather jacket and pants, immense power radiated off his muscled body in waves. He towered over her. An unexplainable potent charisma and an unknown promise transfixed her as they stared. Dumbfounded, she blinked rapidly as if to dispel a hallucination. *Nope. Grief overload.* He was as real as the humid air dampening her last happy vibe forever.

The stranger perused her for a long brazen moment before she mustered words in her desert-dry mouth. "Can I help you?"

He swept his gaze over the headstones peppering the lawn, some embedded flat in the grass, others rising out of the earth. "Sorry I'm a bit late, darlin'."

His southern drawl tingled across her shoulders. *A bit? The funeral ended hours ago! And who does he think he is, calling me "darlin'"?* Lily swiveled away on her sensible blunt heels. She studied the stargazer lilies covering the grave—her father's favorite flower—and counted to ten slowly. The heady scent wafted up and the tranquility of the cemetery blossomed into her senses.

Another unsettling change in the air stroked her bare arms in warmth, despite the damp pre-autumn chill. She chose to ignore the man and the inexplicable reasons why he suddenly exasperated her, captivated her. Arms folded tight over her chest, she wrapped herself in a cocoon while despair beat down the door to her heart.

Hundreds of her father's friends and acquaintances had long departed. After a brief appearance at the wake, she'd returned to the cemetery to view her father's remains in their eternal resting place. The cemetery landscapers would flatten the mound and add sod later, but she couldn't witness the final act of her father's internment. She'd already shed enough tears to overflow a river.

Yet, she had a rough time leaving and allowing the earth to claim her father after already devouring her mother and younger brother. She shot a glimpse at the twin headstones next to the new grave. Tears welled and fed that damn river again. Another stab of grief pierced her heart, a new forever ache. Quiet sobs racked her, and she sank to her knees onto the damp ground. A lump in her throat threatened to obstruct her airflow. *Get a grip, Falbrooke.*

"Lily," a husky voice whispered behind her. A heavy hand alighted on her shoulder and squeezed gently. Another large, tan hand proffered a cotton handkerchief. She accepted the square cloth to replace the sodden wad of tissues in her fist.

"Can I give you a ride home?"

She twisted around and pinned a glare on him. Tears glistened in his odd aquamarine eyes, and she sucked in a breath. "No...I—" she stuttered. "Who *are* you?"

He held out a hand and she grasped it, lifting herself up with his aid. She brushed loose dirt off her bare knees, and kicked a clod of grass off her right pump. Unable to prevent dusk's cool damp from reaching into her barren soul, she shivered violently.

He shrugged off his jacket and draped the leather over her shoulders. She melted into the warm weighty material, a welcome shield against her miserable life. A pleasant mixture of leather and spicy cologne teased her nose. Her grief shut down the wild thoughts threatening to unhinge her further, warming places within her body that had no right to thaw.

"I'm Jake McAllister."

McAllister? Numbness refused to allow her mind to stretch her memory. "Friend of my father's?"

"Something like that."

"I see." She wiped the handkerchief under her sore nose, fearing she resembled Rudolph. "Well, thanks for coming."

"Sorry I'm late. I was...on another assignment."

"I'm sure my father appreciated it, no matter what time you came." *Idiot, much? Dad would never appreciate anything again.* Reluctantly, Lily shook the jacket off. He stopped her and tugged it back over her shoulders.

"Keep it for now. It looks good on you." A smile splashed his sun-darkened face, and she realized how incredibly handsome he was, with his days' old stubble and rugged good looks.

Lily buried her asinine meanderings. *Not the time, not the place.* "I really must be leaving."

"Let me take you home," he blurted out.

She eyed the behemoth two-wheel cause of his unwelcome interruption. "On that?" she asked with as much scorn in her tone as she could drum up. "No thanks. I have a car and driver waiting." Legs listless, she plodded through the wet grass toward the parking lot.

The clomping of his boots followed at a discreet distance. When she reached the limo, she slipped off his jacket and held it out to him. "Thanks. My jacket's in the car."

As if he'd read her mind, the limo driver handed her a long black duster to match her silk sheath. Her crystal and emerald shamrock pin broke her head-to-toe black. *So much for four-leaf clover luck. She may as well toss her pin in the hole with her father. Worms might get lucky.*

"I'm truly sorry about your father." Jake McAllister shouldered his jacket. "See you soon, Lily."

She stepped into the limo and sank onto the plush leather seat. "Goodbye, Jake," she said into the air of graveyard loneliness.

It wasn't until the limo was on the road when she noticed she still carried the borrowed hanky. She unfurled the damp piece of rich cotton and smoothed her fingers over the silk-embroidered initials. *JRM.*

Why did a rocker-looking, hawg-riding man in black leather own elegant handkerchiefs? Who was Jake McAllister and how did he know her father?

The unseasonal rain had held off from dampening the earlier funeral, but had unleashed after the mourners departed for the wake, a fitting tribute to her father who loved the rain. Drizzle dripped again, increasing the jackhammer digging a trench through her head. Closing her eyes and mind, she shut out the world and leaned against the cool leather seat.

⋐ℛℬ⋑

Jake gazed longingly at the sleek limo until the vehicle turned the corner and absconded with the most enchanting women he'd ever met. He'd watched her from a distance all day and sensed something raw and engaging about her. When he'd neared her, she stole his breath away.

Lily Falbrooke wasn't beautiful in the classical sense. She was petite, elegant, poised, and underneath the glossy, fiery hair flowing halfway down her back was a pale, heart-shaped face and rosebud lips. An angel. Certainly not the type he usually went for—wild, voluptuous, leggy, tan. Pictures hadn't done her justice.

Desire so pure swept away the desolation destroying him since hearing the hellish news about Michael's accident. His hands wanted to caress her, his arms wanted to lend comfort and chase off her sadness. His lips wanted to kiss away her pain.

Heat slammed him, and he was thunderstruck by the depth of his emotions, especially when their origins escaped perception. Never in his life had he experienced such intense feelings at the mere sight of a woman. One who wanted nothing from him.

"What the hell? I'm losing my grip." Insanity didn't run in his family, yet who was he to forestall it from running amok within him?

Drizzle magnified the day's dreariness, dispelling the unnerving thoughts chasing through Jake's head. He slipped on his jacket, inhaling Lily's perfume—a dominance of honeysuckle—and zipped it up to preserve the bouquet close to his heart.

With heavy footsteps, he trudged to the grave to pay his final respects. Words from the Lord's Prayer from his Catholic school days resurfaced in his memory and he recited them. Time lost all meaning as he hunched down and grabbed a handful of moist dirt from the mound, bringing finality to the existence Jake had only recently embraced.

"Ashes to ashes." He tossed the dirt on the grave. "Dust to dust." Another sprinkle of earth followed the first. His broad shoulders heaved, his stomach knotted. He made the sign of the cross, leaving dirt trails on the black leather. Jake wiped his hands on his pants and reached into his rear pocket for the hanky he'd brought for the occasion. Empty.

Lily.

"Damn, Michael, what happened?" His throat constricted, and he swiped the back of his hand over his wet cheeks. One final look at the pile of dirt covering the body of Michael Falbrooke, and he strode toward his motorcycle, cursing the rain he'd have to slog through to reach home. Cursing the bastards who'd taken his friend, and the darkness that had set the invisible wheels in motion coercing his every move from that point forward.

"I will keep my promises, Michael. I'll keep her safe." A breeze floated his whispered words toward the grave. No matter what the future entailed, he'd not let his friend down.

The motorcycle growled to life. The engine's steady vibrations soothed him, dipped deep into his soul to assuage the deep-seated bleakness. He yanked on his helmet, steered the hulking bike out of the parking spot, born a part of it like a Centaur, and shadowed the long black limousine tugging on his heartstrings.

CRSO

The heady aroma of coffee filtered into Lily's fogged brain. Dad always had coffee ready in the mornings, black and sweet. She smiled and cleared the last vestiges of sleep from her head. As she lifted on her elbows, her neck creaked and stiffened. She'd fallen asleep on the couch in Dad's den. *What the what?*

The sudden vivid memory of yesterday dug a new hole in her chest, and she collapsed onto her back. Dad had always been there for her, through all her life's upheavals, including the summer that had haunted her for a decade. She had no one left now.

By the time she'd returned to the house where she'd spent her childhood after visiting the cemetery, another early autumn rain hammered the San Jose foothills in the final act showcasing the worst day of Lily's life. Instead of facing the reality that her entire family was gone forever, she'd downed a sleeping pill and passed out.

Hauling her mother's afghan up to her chin, she tossed around the idea of not getting up at all. But the heavenly aroma of caffeine continued to lure her out of her funk. Elizabeth must've let herself in. Lily wanted to thank her for making all the funeral arrangements, for caring for her father after Lily left town three years ago. She couldn't have crawled through the funeral and wake without her surrogate mother.

Rising, she dragged her fingers through her tousled hair. Her neck twinged again, and she crooked it from side-to-side to stretch the tight, aching muscles. Reining in her interminable grief, she slogged into the living room and pushed open the swing door to the kitchen.

"Elizabeth?" Dead still, she stood on the threshold. The loose raven-dark hair and wide-shouldered back of a tall muscular man threatened to disturb her temporary pocket of equilibrium. Fear raced down her spine. Lily eyeballed the butcher block of knives on the far side of the kitchen. *Too freaking far.*

The man spun around. A network of scars marred his

thick-muscled left arm. The gorgeous motorcycle man from the cemetery.

Alarm seized her intestines. She snatched up a pair of scissors sitting on the black granite counter next to the door. "What the hell are you doing here?"

Wry amusement veiled the darkness of his eyes, adding anger to her alarm. She held the scissors aloft to plunge them into his heart at the slightest provocation.

"Well?" she demanded, edging closer to the cordless phone on the wall inside the door.

"Whoa there, darlin'," he drawled in that sensuous voice which served to irritate her more. "Put the scissors down." He paused a beat. "I live here."

"You *what?*" Her eyes widened, threatening to rip her face from her skull.

Slow surprise spread across his face. "You don't know?"

"Know what?" She inched closer to the phone, her upraised arm holding the scissors turning leaden. "Tell me why I shouldn't call the police."

Jake leaned against the counter and crossed his ankles. "I'm sorry, I thought you knew. Your father rented the loft to me. I have a legal rental agreement." He nodded at her weapon of choice. "Now will you call off the dogs?"

"Oh, hell to the no." Astonishment wilted her against the doorframe. She lowered her arm to her side, the scissors poking into her thigh. "That's my mother's studio. My father would never rent it out."

His lips tightened. "Lily—"

"How do you even know me?" she cut in, warmth creeping to her cheeks. Something about him stirred something equally unknown in her insides, disconcerting and thoroughly inappropriate. She felt as if she should know him, but she'd never met him before yesterday. It left her on the edge of a Level-10 freak-out.

He shrugged. "I live in your house. I've seen pictures."

"It's my fath—" She blushed anew. It *was* her house now.

Sorrow held his gaze hostage, swept the travertine stone floor, and passed up her length, ending with a friendly release of empathy. He extended his right hand. "Can we start over? I'm Jake McAllister."

She pointedly ignored his hand. Confusion battled her every emotion. There appeared a lot her father had neglected to share.

"If I lay this egg," he held the egg up engulfed in his large hand, "on the counter, you going to stab me in the back?"

"You can set it down, but stay where you are."

Once he complied, he leaned his hip against the counter. His gaze raked her from scalp to toe, and she grew uneasy under his all too familiar scrutiny, as if he slurped her up often...and she liked it.

His deep, slightly raspy voice shattered the silence, "Let me make you breakfast. We'll talk."

Lily considered her options. She just wanted a cup of fuel and to hang alone. "If you're renting the loft, why're you in my kitchen?" The loft had a sink, microwave, and small fridge, more than enough for a man. She stifled a snort.

His lips edged up. "The lease includes kitchen privileges."

Her mind spun, knees watered. Before she fell into a stupid damsel-in-distress heap onto the floor, she slumped onto a chair. Leaning her elbows on the small, round dinette table, she buried her face in her hands. San Jose could dive into a fault line before she allowed herself to cry in front of the enigmatic stranger. "I appreciate your offer of breakfast. But please get out of my kitchen and leave me alone."

"O-kay," he said softly. "If that's what you want."

"Yes."

The hissing of the gas stove quieted, and he strode on bare feet to the back staircase leading directly to the second floor loft. As his foot hit the first step, she said, "Jake?"

He froze. "Yeah?"

"Next time you come down, leave the rental agreement on the table. I'd like to review my obligations for terminating the lease."

CHAPTER TWO

After a few sips of black ambrosia, Lily had to admit Jake made killer coffee. Despite the liquid fuel, her stomach rumbled. Would his omelet have lived up to his claimed fame? She grabbed a freckled banana out of the fruit bowl and headed to the den.

As she passed through the living room, muffled footsteps drifted off the front porch. A crash of pottery drove her heart thumping into a new rhythm from the ashes of her heartbreak. The banana thumped onto the rug. She rushed to the door and flung it wide open.

A pot of chrysanthemums lay on its side on the porch, soil spilling down the two steps to the walkway. Scanning the front yard, she crept down the walkway, the shadows of the hillside trees in the surrounding woods darkening the front yard, matching her mood. She walked to her rental car in the driveway. The driver's door hung ajar, and she knew she'd locked it after arriving from the airport before the funeral. No one had driven it in the days since. Lily spun around, spied a couple of boys riding scooters down the street past her long tree-shrouded driveway.

"Idiot," she mumbled as she spied her neglected smartphone on the front passenger seat. Nothing seemed amiss in the car, until she noticed her cheap sunglasses missing from the cup holder and her shamrock rearview mirror dangle gone.

Lily covered her hand with the bottom of her multi-colored splatted T-shirt and finagled the door open. The second she bent down to peer inside, fingers tapped her shoulders. She jack-knifed straight and narrowly missed banging her head on the doorframe. The hands pushed her off balance. Unable to curb her fall, she sprawled over the driver seat and her forehead slammed the center console, missing the gearshift by an inch. Pain stabbed her head, and her left side smarted from its collision with the steering wheel. Heavy hands held her forehead pressed to the center console. Panic sent goosebumps across her shoulders.

"I have a message for you," a male voice with an Italian accent said. "Stay out of the Guild. Stay away from the McAllisters, no guardians, no police. You tell no one about our little chat. You follow my directions and I'll let you live." He pressed her face harder into the console.

"What do you want?" The plastic surface of the console muffled Lily's wobbly voice.

"You have forty-eight hours to give me the twilight jewels or your ass and the ass of everyone you know is grass."

Twilight jewels? Was he attacking the right person? Had he mistaken her for another? Lily blinked back tears springing to her mashed left eye. "I don't know what you're talking about."

"Then you better learn right quick. In forty-seven hours, I'll check in with you. I want the entire collection including the chalice. Or you'll become my prison bitch until I get what I want, *capiche?*"

The pressure on her back let up and his footsteps quickly faded away. Her face ached and she lifted her head.

Before she realized the man had disappeared, she heard Elizabeth yell, "Jake!"

A flurry of motion surrounded Lily, and Elizabeth helped her upright. Lily balanced against the car door as Jake bounded out of the house.

"What happened?" Arm around her waist, he braced her against his taut body, steadying her shaky knees, calming her racing pulse.

The screech of a raven shattered Lily's bafflement. She shoved away from Jake and straightened her twisted T-shirt, contemplated how to respond in view of the threat. After mulling it over while gathering her scattered wits, she said, "Someone...pushed me into the car."

Elizabeth pointed into the greenbelt of the next-door neighbor's one-acre lot. "He took off into the woods." Elizabeth probed Lily's forehead. "You'll have a bump. Let's go inside and I'll fix you up."

"Why'd you come out here in the first place?" Jake traded nervous glances with Elizabeth.

"*Hello.* No one's keyed in on the fact that some jerkwad *pushed* me."

"Maybe you lost your balance. They didn't take anything. Your phone's sitting in plain view."

Lily threw up her hands and scoured the car's interior. Should she tell him about the threat? Would the man harm them if she did? "My sunglasses and my shamrock dangle are gone. Taken before I was *pushed.*"

"Were they expensive?" Amusement crinkled the corners of Jake's eyes.

"Bite me, McAllister." Lily left the hovering pair, her legs barely supporting her walk to the house. The second she set foot onto the first step of the porch, a light flickered to her left in a bed of spindly flowers. She seized her shamrock and the broken bead chain out of a patch of weathered petunias. She never drove a car without a lucky four-leaf clover inside it. "Did I toss this into the planter while I was licking the seat?"

Elizabeth wrapped her hand around Lily's wrist, like one scolding a bratty kid. "Let's go inside." Maybe grief and stress had propelled the stalwart Elizabeth into a tailspin. Didn't appear assault made an impact. "There are things you need to hear. You too, Jake."

Foreboding fluttered in Lily's ribcage, setting the stage for her exit to Crazy Town. "What's going down?"

"Do I need to call Niles?" Jake asked Elizabeth. "In the dark again. Un-fucking-believable." He slammed the car door shut and stalked toward them.

Elizabeth rounded on him, her petite body strung tight. "You've been gone. Things are escalating."

"What're you talking about?" Lily's head spun, wishing for a time machine to take her back to practicing corporate contracts law in San Diego. A long, hot shower to wash away the feel of the man's hands and give her some needed clarity was the next best thing. "I'm...I'm taking a shower first." She couldn't contain the fear from her voice. "Then I want answers." Then I want to know what on God's green Earth is the Twilight collection. She refrained from asking then and there, not wanting to tip her hand about the threat.

She finger-combed her hair until they caught on a bird's nest of knots, her one ragged purple-polished nail plucking strands of hair out of her scalp. In a daze, she hid in the second floor hall bath across from her childhood bedroom. The pale, haggard reflection in the mirror wasn't Lily Falbrooke. Dark circles hung under her eyes with a screaming plea to the makeup artists of Hollywood. She definitely needed to pull her act together.

Jake hiked up to the loft, wincing from the pain in his left foot where psychic Juliana Westwood had used it for target practice. He shouldn't have manhandled her as they both investigated the site of Michael's car accident. She had knowledge he needed from her psychic—telepathic—visions of Michael's death, and he hadn't meant to scare her when he pounced on her in his desperation. He had to know who'd killed his friend and mentor.

His phone's chirp intruded, and he took the last few steps at a lumbering run. He snatched his phone off the couch and thumbed it on. "Give me some good news."

"Chill, man." His younger brother's chipper 'tude made him want to jam the phone up Ric's ass, taking his foul mood for the trip. "How's the flower chick?"

"Devastated." Jake flopped down on the couch.

"Does she know?"

"I doubt she knows what day of the week it is."

"Does she know why you're there, dumbass?"

"No." Jake shoved his foot against the edge of the coffee table, sending the table sliding off the rug onto the hardwood. "The Psychic Guild's keeping it close to the vest. Elizabeth's ready to download some shit. Lily's asking questions. We'll all know what's going on by end of day. Hopefully it helps with the murder investigation." The surface of the leather couch grew frigid under his tightly strung body. "Any new intel?"

"Zippo. Michael's car's still in impound."

"Juliana Westwood delivered Michael's belongings to his office after her vision in the impound lot. Nothing there but case files. Can you snag and stash the car?"

"Got the wheels spinning. It'll be done EOD."

End of day. Perfect. They needed to tear the car apart and scour it for clues the police might have missed in their accident ruling. The cops had no idea the accident was the tip of a major shitstorm. The Psychic Guild tended to exact justice outside the parameters of the cop shop. Silence raked his nerves until Ric's next question pounded them to a pulp.

"Did you find a key? Anything?"

"Seriously? I just hit home a few days ago after being gone three weeks. Michael's funeral and wake wrecked me." He dug his hands through his loose hair, snagging on a tangle. Even his hair aggravated him.

"Where were you?"

"Completing my last assignment."

"In Mexico? Sun, tequila, and luscious Jillian?"

"I'm entitled to a vacation. Get off my back." Jake cracked his knuckles, wishing he were cracking them over his brother's noggin. The boatload of messages from the Protectorate—the protection arm of the Psychic Guild—echoed between his ears. "What's the word? I didn't get the new assignment until I hit the airport. They wouldn't tell me jack."

"Better you than me."

"Why didn't you take the assignment?"

Ric jacked up the heavy metal music in the background. "They didn't offer."

"Why? You're up next."

"You're First Guardian. The best, as you so often cram up my rear door."

What kind of assignment needed a First Guardian? There hadn't been a need for First Guardian protection of a Guild psychic—a catchall term for anyone with extrasensory perception—since he'd joined as a member thirteen years ago when he'd hit eighteen.

"Jake, man, can you keep Lily safe?"

What the hell's going on? Why all the secrecy? "I'm here, right?"

"Yeah, you are," Ric replied somberly. "Westwood

shoot anyone else lately?" He snickered to lighten the mood.

"Bite me." Jake poked at the bandage on his foot. "I practically tackled her, thinking she was going to use me for target practice. Guess I deserved it."

"Dude, she did use you for target practice."

"We're on good terms now. Even got her fiancé cop on our side."

"Hunt for a key or something. I gotta jet. Catch you on the flipside."

The line deadened. Jake had spent two weeks playing bodyguard to Jillian, to throw off card players in a Vegas poker tournament who'd learned she might have manipulated a game with telepathy. Their investigation ended with no charges to pin on her last week, and then after a quick trip home for business meetings, he'd spent the third week getting to know the lay of her nubile body in Cabo San Lucas at her invitation. No strings attached. His groin tightened and heat speared southward. A hit and run was about all he'd wanted with any hot, luscious female. It was usually all they wanted too, and he never led anyone on. He steered clear of the clingy, wedding, white picket fence types. Eventually, he'd settle down when he tired of the Guardian game.

Four days ago, he'd made the mistake of checking his messages to learn Michael Falbrooke had died in a car accident. When he'd checked in at the Protectorate, he'd received the riot act and the summons for his next assignment. Too soon, too suspicious. They usually allowed two weeks off between assignments. However, the Cabal, an underground group, luring Guild psychics into their ranks to execute illegal Cabal dirty work, had become too dangerous to the Guild. If a Guild member refused a Cabal "offer," he or she met the hard bottom of a six-foot hole in the ground. All hands were on deck at the

Protectorate.

The image of Lily hunched over her father's grave seeped into his mind. The last words she'd said to him downstairs chased the image away. A grim chuckle rumbled up his chest. Tough girl just like Michael had always proclaimed. Lily Falbrooke didn't strike him as a woman who needed guarding, an independent young lawyer living alone away from her family, having once suffered through trauma and death at a young age. Yet, something about her caused him to want to glove his body around her and shield her mind and body from anyone trying to harm her.

Forever.

The idea shook him to the core, and very nearly shattered him.

CHAPTER THREE

Mind clear, wearing yoga pants, a baggy sweater, and a layer of foundation to cover her gray tinge of sadness, Lily hopped down the stairs. She hoped Elizabeth had the answers she so dreadfully needed, including understanding the incident in the driveway and the mysterious Twilight jewels. Time was ticking. At least she'd have the weekend to digest everything until forced to join the living on Monday when she'd have to take the helm of her father's law firm. If the Italian didn't come collecting with a gun in hand first. She buried the thought into a black hole to pull out after her conversation with Elizabeth.

Thank God for her one-year internship at her father's firm before the temptation of practicing as a corporate contracts lawyer in San Diego enticed her away. *Right, that'll come in handy. Not.*

Elizabeth marched out of the kitchen balancing grapes, crackers, and cheese on a loaded tray. Lily's antagonism dissolved into gratitude. Why be mad at the woman who'd been a mother to her since her own had passed away? They entered her father's office—nicknamed the "den"—and Elizabeth's gaze darted around the room as if she expected burglars to jump her.

She'd never seen serene Elizabeth so freaked.

"Do you want wine, soda, water?" Elizabeth set the snack tray on her father's scarred mahogany desk.

"No, thanks." Lily turned on the Tiffany lamps scattered around the room. The cut-glass lampshades created colorful prisms on the walls and the floor to ceiling bookcases, chasing away the cloudy murkiness filtering through the open plantation blinds, coloring the soul of the room. Lily sat on the couch facing the desk while Elizabeth perched on the cushioned guest chair across from her father's conspicuously empty leather chair.

"I wanted to have this conversation years ago, but I agreed to wait until you were thirty." Elizabeth fanned her face. "Things changed and Michael planned to tell you at Thanksgiving." She sniffed. "Do you remember anything of what your mother told you about her family that last summer in Tahoe?"

Lily's mouth gaped and closed like a hungry trout. "Like what?"

"The Twilight legacy. *Your* legacy."

Lily's head took on movement of its own and she felt like a bobblehead. "What does this have to do with kissing the interior of my rental car?" Or the threat to turn all our asses into grass?

"Your father's done well in keeping the truth from you." Elizabeth's soft expression forgave her bitter tone.

"Hit the beginning." Lily clasped her arms across her middle, trying to stem a glacial awareness. "You're scaring me."

"I'm sorry. You need to fear for your life right now." She waved off Lily's biting retort. "I've guarded these secrets for ten years, wanting to continue where your mother left off." Elizabeth paused to gauge Lily's vacant reaction. "Your maternal family line is the rightful owners of the Twilight collection."

Since hearing about her father's death, she'd experienced more bits of old memories, like random puzzle pieces fitting into one corner to another in her broken mind. Little made sense, except one memory she'd squeezed out the night after her father had died. *OMG. Twilight jewels?*

"I don't know—" A sneak peek at jewels her mother had shifted from one hiding spot to another. Lily had once snuck out the locked box, her mother never knowing she'd spied on her and discovered her hiding spot. Wide-eyed, Lily had glommed onto the huge sapphires, precious gems, and icy diamonds in a necklace, earrings, and ring. The ring was exquisite, the center sapphire changing colors in the light from purples to blues to blacks. It appeared to imprison starlight in its center with diamonds setting twilight into daylight brilliance under the lamp light. Out of her few resurfaced memories, that one mystified her the most.

"You remember?"

"The jewels in the locked box."

"She...showed them to you?" Shock held Elizabeth's voice hostage, her hand gripping her neck. "You remember?"

"The memory recently emerged. I remember sneaking up on her once and watching her take them out. I figured they were baubles, the fashion jewelry she loved to wear."

"They are very real."

The ice forming inside Lily splintered into numbing shock. "Back the boat up." Lily stalked away from the couch. She brushed her fingers over a row of books on old world artifacts of Ireland, Scotland, and England. She pivoted around on her heel.

Elizabeth clasped and unclasped her hands on her lap. "They're ancient and beyond priceless. The collection has been in your mother's family for generations. Sapphires are the guardians of innocence, grantors of truth, and promoters of good health. Kings and highborn people wore them to ward off illness or for protection while traveling. The Twilight sapphires are believed to bestow fulfillment, joy, prosperity, inner peace, and beauty. The stones also ward off evil and bad luck and aid psychokinesis, telepathy, clairvoyance."

Whoa, what? Magic stones? Lily scoffed. It was enough to know that people actually held psychic abilities in this day and age. Psychokinesis was the ability to mentally influence external objects or events without the use of physical energy; telepathy was the ability to mind read or the ability to touch something and telepathically link to the owner of the object. Then there was clairvoyance—her own faulty breed of extrasensory perception.

Lily's disbelief became another dull ache within her skull. "Why don't I know about this Twilight legacy? Where are the jewels? What's the big deal about them now?"

Elizabeth rose and eased into Lily's personal bubble of space. "Your mother's family found a way to disassociate from them by changing the family's identity. In perpetuating the ruse, Michael also concealed your identity after your mother died. He wanted to protect you."

"My mother was Roselyn McKenna Falbrooke. McKenna's on her birth certificate." Lily had used her mother's maiden name and her own middle name— Lauren McKenna—when she was institutionalized at the Paranormal Institute of New York. Her father had committed her after her mother had died, for PTSD and loss of memory, loss of self...a self she had never regained and which still haunted her. A lost self she feared meeting.

"True. Your great-great-grandmother falsified genealogy documents, and the family maintained the deception. You're all descendants of the high kings of Ireland, the Kings of Tara, descendants of the *Tuatha De Danann*, the tribe that established Tara in the Boyne Valley of Ireland. Also known as the ritual inauguration and burial place of the Irish kings. The women in the McKenna line are known as the Flowers of Tara. The collection is one of the most sought after relics in the world."

Lily's insides froze. "I have no clue where the collection is. Why are you telling me this now?" *Why didn't Dad tell me years ago?*

"For your protection. It appears the cat's out of the bag."

Lily moved back to the couch, a maelstrom of dormant memories spinning, ready to explode. Nightmares had plagued her since the day her mother and fifteen-year-old brother died in a boating accident on Lake Tahoe ten years ago. Since then, her life floated in silence past the shuttered windows in her mind. Although she may not remember what had happened that fateful summer, the days after their deaths remained crystal clear. She'd accepted the tragedy and had known her mother and brother would never return. But what kept her from remembering? Would the knowledge destroy her? She'd grilled her father, and he'd told her she'd remember when she was ready. Same spin the doctors gave.

A soft knock on the door almost sent Lily jumping out of her skin. Her pulse quickened, and she hugged her knees to her chin to ward off the unknown circling her like buzzards over a dead body.

Jake entered the room, delectable in his snug jeans

and black T-shirt. His hair hung loose, giving him a dangerous edginess, and his tan, muscular arms were a feast for her eyes. She usually liked the clean-cut, man-in-a-suit look, but Jake exuded an undeniable aura of sinful, sexy mystery. *Ugh...why him?*

"Does your lease agreement include wandering privileges?" she snapped, rising from the sofa.

"She doesn't know, does she?" A frown drew down his full sensuous lips.

Lily scowled more at herself for drooling over his oh-so-fine lips than at him. "Know what? And what're you doing in my...part of the house?"

"My job." His legs spread in a defiant stance, and he hit her with his unnerving and downright mesmerizing stare.

"You're a stalker? Does that pay well?" So many emotions zinged through Lily her brain felt like a NASCAR event. She rubbed the sore bump on her forehead, belatedly remembering Elizabeth had invited him to this conversation earlier. Before she had a chance to retract her snippy words he unloaded his own snipe.

"Elizabeth, what the hell's going on? Niles isn't returning my voicemails or texts." He advanced and halted beside Lily, towering over Elizabeth seated in the chair. "Why did the Guild force me back from Mexico to guard *Ms. Falbrooke?*"

Guard as in *bodyguard?* "Well? Answer the man." She angled her body away from Elizabeth.

Elizabeth turned three shades of red. "Once I explain who Jake is, you'll understand." She tugged at the sleeves of her fine-gauge sweater, settled in the chair for the long haul. "Jake's a Guardian assigned by the Guild Protectorate to guard—"

"Guild *members.*" Lily flailed her arms. "You know I'm not a member. They can't just assign a bodyguard to me without my permission." People likened the Psychic Guild to the bar association in certain respects with its member rules, policies and bylaws. Not well known to outsiders, the Guild preferred to fly under the radar, not that it was a secret group. Most members were psychics. However, not all Guardians were, but they were family members of Guild psychics. Guild membership was voluntary, giving the members a sense of family, cohesion, and solidarity with like-minded professionals. *They can all drink the Kool-Aid together.*

"Who *is* she?" Jake clenched Elizabeth's shoulders in his sinfully large hands.

Elizabeth didn't waver in body or words. "She's the current descendant of the first Kings of Tara. She's the true beholder of the Twilight legacy, not merely the owner."

"Come again." Backing off, Jake tugged on his ear lobe, slid his hand into his long sexy hair. "I knew her connection to the Twilight legacy and the public info about it, but Michael never unloaded that."

"Apparently, *Michael* didn't unload much of anything." Lily did another arm-flailing dance to divert her edgy energy.

He wrenched his phone off his belt loop and stabbed a button, then commenced to chew on his fingernail. "I won't be part of this Guild conspiracy. This is insane."

Elizabeth knocked the phone away from his ear. Lily stood in mute horror watching her life take on a surreal existence. Bad enough her mind hid things from her, but others doing the same was enough to hurl her straight into a barrel of vodka.

"You'll do as you're told, Jake." Elizabeth thumbed the phone off and pocketed it, asserting her high-ranking position in Guild management. Did her empath skills— the ability to understand or feel what another person is experiencing—rank her higher than a Guardian? "You're the best and Lily needs you." Her face mottled more shades of scarlet than a blood bank.

"No, I don't need him." Lily scratched her head, hoping to scrub off the lunacy claiming her day. *Make the world stop revolving so I can dive into my vodka.*

"Honey, I feel your mixed emotions. With everything that's going on around you, inside you, you need a clear head—and a backup. You'll accept Jake's protection." Elizabeth drew her hand down Lily's damp hair with motherly affection. "And you, Jake McAllister, will handle this assignment as efficiently as your others, no matter what the Guild does or doesn't tell you. Michael kept the truth from you both to protect you."

Silent and mashing his lips together, Jake began pacing the room with short, rigid steps.

Lily knew more than she cared to know about the Psychic Guild and the men hired to protect Guild psychics. Jake folded his muscular arms over his chest, covering the New Orleans Saints logo on his T-shirt stretched tight, accentuating every hard plane of his chest and abdomen.

She licked her lips, casting her idiot hormones off the beyond-sexy arms arresting her attention. "Guard me from what? The person who pushed me in the car?" Lily couldn't deny that Jake was so damn fine from his beard stubble, his six-pack abs, his to-die-for muscular arms, and the way his low-slung jeans fit his fine ass. A distraction she didn't need in her life.

A mad muscle throbbed in Jake's jaw. "For how long?"

Stalling, Elizabeth patted down her short bob haircut. "Indefinitely. Since her identity may have been revealed...after centuries—"

Bodyguard? Indefinitely? In what universe? "I've had enough of today." Lily fled the room, slammed the door behind her, and sprinted upstairs to her bedroom, her only haven from Hobbit land craziness.

She'd always sensed she was missing something in her life since her mother and brother had died when she was eighteen. More than memories and more than the fact that her mother was gone, the feelings crushed her at times. It was as though she was meant to be someone other than a lawyer, or that she possessed psychic abilities for a specific reason, not that she remembered being clairvoyant. Part of her lived in a secret hidden world to which she had no access. Now she needed those haunting memories returned to her, no matter the cost.

∝₰

Lily's tight butt swayed side to side as she rushed away. Her face burned in Jake's memory, pale, ethereal, captivating, shooting lust to the bull's-eye. *Damn it.* He didn't need this diversion from his duties. He popped a couple of cinnamon mints to slake his thirst...for her. He chomped down the useless mints.

He understood he had to guard her due to threats to Guild members and her father's death, but no one had connected her as a descendant of the Kings of Tara. As far as he knew, the Tara line had died centuries ago. Most everyone in the ancient art world knew the artifacts had floated from one collector to another individually and at times, together. All a lie? Everything had changed. Not only did collectors seek the jewels, they sought any descendants of the Legacy, especially a direct descendant. He should feel more ire than awe at his unwitting trip down the green mile.

Air in short supply, Jake stomped toward the door. He couldn't boot from his mind the image of Lily's shapely breasts and the taut legs he wanted wrapped around his waist. *Damn, dude.*

"Let her go. She's had a tough blow."

"Why did Michael keep this secret so long?"

"To protect Lily. To maintain the ruse her mother's family set in motion. There's evil afoot." Elizabeth nodded at Jake. "You noticed a change six months ago when the Cabal began recruiting or killing Guild psychics. The Guild's certain it's a front to kidnap or trap Lily. Others are literally dying for those artifacts. The Guild doesn't know the identity of these people."

"Did Michael know?"

Elizabeth rummaged in her bulging handbag for a tissue. "For two weeks, Michael had been acting strange, refused to tell me anything. He died before—" She blew her nose, dabbed at her red-rimmed eyes.

The words stung Jake's heart. "Juliana Westwood's prescient vision of his car going off the cliff and the man standing above the road was right on the money."

"The Guild believes Lily's identity was exposed, and the Cabal killed Michael to pave an easier path to her."

Rising from her chair, she hefted her handbag over a slim shoulder. "Guard her with your life. She's too important to lose. Soon her mind will crumble and let loose a suppressed torrent of repressed psychic energy."

Weariness sluiced over him, leaving his limbs listless. "I know what my duties are."

Without facing him, she stopped in the doorway. "Do you really know? Do you also understand that she'll resist you at every step?"

Knowing the truth of her words, he glowered at her slender backside. "I'll do whatever it takes to keep her safe. I've never failed. I don't intend to now."

"If you fail and she dies, you won't live to see another day." With that, she disappeared through the doorway.

Jake sank into the swivel chair behind the desk. He

knew too well his fate if he was responsible for the death of the Tara descendant. Maybe he ought to just kill himself and save everyone the trouble. Or prove to all that he was a force of McAllister nature.

He'd keep Lily safe if he had to die in the process, whether she wanted it or not, with *everything* in his arsenal—legal or illegal.

CHAPTER FOUR

The aroma of garlic-laden Italian food tantalized Lily's empty stomach. Little doubt remained as to the chef of the deliciousness permeating her house. She was hungry enough to forego her confusion about Jake McAllister intruding upon her home...and her life. The crick in her neck had worsened, and she kinked her neck side to side as she headed to the kitchen.

She opened the swing door and stopped, spellbound. A leather band held Jake's long, thick hair in a ponytail. Slim-fitting sweatpants and a sweatshirt with its sleeves hacked off at the shoulder encased his muscular body, somehow making him appear dangerous, but in an exciting kind of way. The ripped arms with oven mitts to his wrists lifting steaming lasagna from the oven curled her toes. He had muscles, looks, and danger prowling about him. She'd rather have Jake McAllister for dinner. *Damn, I'm either suffering from starvation or I've lost brain cells down my river of tears.*

The subject of her lust spun around, bestowing a beguiling smile. "No scissors?" The intensity of his eyes gutted layers to reach her desolate soul.

"Do I need scissors?" She crossed her arms over her breasts, hiding her body's hard, pebbled reaction to his über charms.

"All you need is a fork." He set the baking dish on a trivet centered on the table. "For eating." He winked. The casserole steamed in the middle of the intimate table for two. "Sit. I'll dish it up." He slipped off the oven mitts, revealing his strong hands and long fingers. "Garlic bread and salad?"

She quirked an eyebrow. *What material is Jake McAllister made from?* "Everything, please." Her stomach growled in preparation for the first real meal she'd eaten since before she departed San Diego.

He pulled a chair out and she sat, taking the napkin he'd unfolded. Moving about the kitchen, his broad shoulders strained against his T-shirt, spearing another spike of heat to her dormant girlie parts.

"Wine?" He held an uncorked bottle of her father's favorite white Hungarian.

"Yes, please." A folded contract lay off to the side of the table—the lease agreement, now the least of her worries—and she wished she'd not been so hasty in making her implicit threat.

As if born a chef, Jake served their meals, appearing both wickedly rugged and cultured. They ate in companionable silence, and Lily demolished half her lasagna before catching his amused gaze on her.

"You like?"

"My compliments to the chef." She drained her wine glass, and he refilled it to the rim, already catering to her silent pleas to dive into a sinkhole to escape her scattered emotions. She should probably drink herself to oblivion to cease her seesaw of emotions.

The warmth enveloping her didn't arise solely from the wine. She felt as if they'd known each other all their lives. It scared her to death. She never trusted anyone right off the bat. "Why are you being so nice and gentlemanly since I've been a raving lunatic to you?" Inhaling the aroma of marinara sauce, a steaming pocket of melted cheese grabbed her attention.

"To impress you." He charmed her with a crooked, mischievous grin. For the first time since they'd met, she noticed the dimples on each side of his mouth, slightly discernible through his three-day beard scruff. His smile, along with the sparkle in his eyes, the dimples, the face framed by the dark hair, stole her breath. And his body...to die for.

Blinking up a storm, she swigged half a glass of wine.

He sat back and winked. "Have I succeeded?" he asked.

She frowned. "In what?"

"Impressing you."

"Maybe." Studying her plate, she crammed richly buttered garlic bread in her mouth before idiotic platitudes dripped from her tongue, which had begun exercising its right to freedom in the wake of her starvation and excellent *vino*. Stuffed, she leaned back, hands on her belly. "I can't believe I ate so much."

"When did you eat last?"

"Yesterday, I suppose." Lifting her wine glass, she drained it, wanting to lick the bottom to get the last drop.

Reality screamed back with a vengeance, and her nerves once again tilted on a jagged edge despite the wine sending her to LaLa-land. She hesitated a moment, but the need to slake her curiosity urged her on. "How did you meet my father? Did he place an ad to rent the loft?"

Jake sobered and crossed his arms behind his head "He hired me to do PI work for him in February. I needed a place to live while I saved money to buy a house. He was lonely living in this big place, and we stumbled upon the idea. It suited us."

"I see." Dad *had* complained about his loneliness, and

she'd suggested he join a dating site...and not a dating site for lonely PIs. Had he ever joined one? She couldn't remember—so wrapped up in her own breakup mayhem. "So *he* didn't hire you as my bodyguard or Guardian?"

He leaned forward and rested his chin in his hands. If she let herself, she'd drown in the unsettling blue pools of his eyes and never breach the surface again.

"No," he replied. "Michael told me you'd lost your psychic abilities as a child and wasn't involved with the Guild."

"My father wanted squat to do with the Psychic Guild after my mother died. He wasn't psychic, so why was he involved?" Now that life had bit her on the butt, she hated burying her head in the sand as she'd so ardently accomplished over the last few years. Sand sucked one down into a rat's nest of epic bewilderment.

"You should probably ask Elizabeth."

"I'm asking you. You ingratiated yourself into his life." *My life.* "I can't live with more secrets."

His gaze bore into her as if he recognized the anguish ripping her soul apart. "As far as I know, Michael wasn't involved in the Guild. Our working relationship didn't involve them."

"Did he know you were a Guardian? Did he have ulterior motives in hiring you?"

Jake rubbed the stubble on his right cheek, pinched his ear lobe in a gesture Lily noticed he repeated when stumped. "Honestly, I thought I knew Michael pretty well. After today, not so sure." His hand engulfed the stem of his wine glass, and he gulped the golden liquid down in one swallow. He emptied the bottle into their glasses. "My status among the Guild isn't a secret, but Michael and I never discussed it. Elizabeth referred me to him. You know she's an empath and a Guild healer, dabbling in herbal remedies. We've known each other for years."

Healer? She knew Elizabeth liked her herbs, but she didn't think anyone else was smoking in her pharmacy. The wooden chair seat suddenly felt like a cement slab, and Lily squirmed to stop her rear from going numb along with bits of her brain. "Are you psychic?" She held her breath, dreading the answer, afraid to own up to her own abilities...or lack thereof.

"Telepath, mind reader."

Immediately, Lily erected the holey walls in her mind. Had he read her thoughts?

The wine warmed the empty pit of her chest and lethargy swept over her. Not wanting to further curb her mood, which couldn't take another ding, she changed the subject. "What did he do with the furniture and my mom's things in the loft?"

Jake set his empty glass down, a light clink of normalcy. "Some furnishings are still there. The rest he gave away or boxed up in the garage attic for you. The paintings are there, except a few Michael took to the office."

"Oh." Lily toyed with her fork, doodling a stargazer lily in her marina sauce.

"You're welcome to come up anytime."

"Thanks." Rising, she picked up her plate, but Jake shot up from his chair and grabbed it from her.

"I'll clean up." He placed a gentle hand on her shoulder and forced her down onto the chair. "Sit, relax."

The crimp in her neck twinged, and she rubbed the sore spot.

"Did you pull a muscle in the car?" Six feet of smoldering sin hovered over her.

"Slept bad last night." Lily stretched her neck muscles.

"Let me."

Before she had a chance to protest, his strong fingers

began massaging her shoulders and neck. While he worked miracles, she leaned into his touch, and when he demolished another knot, an ecstatic moan slipped out. A slow spark ignited in her toes, and by the time it worked its way to her head, it zapped her big time.

She bolted up, her head colliding with his hands. "I'm sorry. I need to handle some paperwork. Thanks for dinner. I owe you one," she tossed back as the door swung shut behind her. *And thanks for the near orgasm.*

She raced into the den and sank onto the couch, begging for bleach to scrub her hormones. She couldn't pin it on the gorgeous, charismatic man in her kitchen. Nope. Nor the ex-boyfriend who'd slithered back to his ex-wife six months ago and her lack of sex since. It was the alcohol. Alcohol and tweaked nerves. Reeling in her wandering brain cells, she contemplated what to do to take her mind off Jake, the Guild, Jake, her father and legacy. *Jake.*

Neat stacks of legal files and papers sat on Dad's otherwise clear desk. Family photos adorned the walls, rather than taking up valuable desk real estate. She turned on two Tiffany lamps and sat in his comfortable chair, feeling an instant connection to him. The glow of light through the lampshades colored the room in soothing jewel tones.

A niggling idea flowered. She fingered the brass knob on the top left drawer and pulled the drawer out. The "tissue drawer," she'd dubbed it when she was six. The squat tissue box was unopened, and she set it on the desk. More memories flooded back, and she slid the drawer all the way out. In the rear, a false panel hid a second fake panel. She'd discovered the hiding spot when she was seven. Her father used to leave notes, trinkets, candy, and money for her, until the time she moved out a year after graduating from Stanford Law School.

Lifting out the sleek panel of wood, she checked both sides and set it on the desk, then pressed the hidden button that dropped the second panel forward. She rummaged around, hoping to find any little memento. Her hand grazed a smooth spot on the upper panel. Duct tape. After several yanks, the layers peeled away, revealing a key. An odd sensation accelerated her pulse and she pried the key off the tape. A safety deposit box key with no identifying marks other than a number.

After racking her brain for a clue, to no avail, she set the key on the center of the desk and picked up a stack of case files off the credenza behind her. Litigation discovery, copies of receipts, photos, old documents. Many of her father's high profile clients were ancient artifact collectors. He also arranged for high tech security services and handled all aspects of their legal and protection needs. Most files had client names on the labels, but one label intrigued her. *Twilight Origin.* The file was empty, as if someone had filched the contents. Another one was labeled simply *Rental.* Intrigued, Lily peered inside. Another layer of surprise topped the others burgeoning inside her. After all these years, she thought her father had sold their Tahoe cabin. Instead, he'd established a dummy corporation, which rented the cabin out to vacationers. Why had he kept it? And kept it secret?

She shoved the folders aside, hiding the cabin file in the locked bottom drawer, and opened the pencil drawer. Dead center surrounded by pens, mints, sticky notepads, and other office supplies nestled a nine-millimeter gun. Shock waves washed over her. Had the world gone mad and taken her father, a token member of the anti-NRA movement, with it? Not only must she come to terms with the fact that she owned missing secret treasures of ancient Ireland, but she also had to accept her father's involvement in secret nefarious activities. Deadly activities.

Dad didn't accidentally run over two nails, which drove his car in a tailspin and over a cliff. Someone had murdered him. Did everyone else know? Is that why Jack McAllister was guarding her? Was she bumbling around in the center of a category five tornado?

Every post-death word from the prescient vision psychic Juliana Westwood had repeated to her at her father's funeral rose: *Twilight's yours. Don't let them steal your Twilight, flower child. I love you Lily with all my heart. I'm sorry I've kept all this from you.* She'd had a difficult time focusing on the mysterious message at the funeral. Juliana's psychic calling came in the form of visions of crimes either having happened or soon to happen.

"Dad, why risk your life over a bunch of jewels, no matter how old and priceless?" Lily slammed her fist on the desk. She dug Juliana's business card from her purse. Her father had hired Juliana as his financial planner last week, hence the reason Juliana had psychically connected to him as he was dying. She traced the three-inch pewter sword pendant hanging on a long chain beneath her blouse. The pendant used to hang off the rearview mirror of her father's car, the conduit relaying his last message to her through Juliana's touch telepathy. Lily barely remembered the funeral and wake or her subconscience didn't want to remember. She needed to speak to Juliana, to refresh her memory, even if it haunted her forever.

Lily had first met Juliana briefly when both their fathers had shipped them off to the Paranormal Institute of New York at the age of eighteen. They'd used pseudonyms to protect their identities as required by the Institute. In Juliana's case, she went kicking and screaming to gain control of her escalating psychic abilities. In Lily's case, she'd gone willingly to recover her memories and the psychic gift she'd possessed before her mother had died.

To this day, she still had only a minute clairvoyant ability to sense people around her, a random snippet of an image or an impression, or a slight mental intrusion. According to her father, Lily had once possessed a strong clairvoyant ability to gain information about an object, person, location, or physical event through means other than the known senses, via the imprints people left behind.

At the funeral, Juliana and Lily had reconnected, learning their real identities and forging an instant bond.

Lily tapped in the digits on her phone and began doodling on a manila file folder, deep strokes of her pen, until Juliana picked up.

"Juliana, Lily Falbrooke. I'm sorry to bother you...I didn't realize it was so late."

"It's not that late. I told you to call any time. What's up?"

"You had more than one revelation about my dad's accident, didn't you? Everyone's gone selectively mute, only feeding me half a story."

"Did you ask Jake?"

Lily wanted to slap herself silly. "No, but he had every opportunity to tell me today. I know it wasn't an accident. I know Guild members are being threatened. The Twilight legacy's involved. It's all so surreal." She slipped the key in her pants pocket. "I need a break from him. This whole Guardian situation freaks me out. I need to absorb what I've learned today."

"You know the Guild assigned him to guard you, right?"

"No kidding. I'm not exactly throwing a party about them taking such steps without my permission."

"Seriously? Do you know he spent his entire time

during the funeral hiding behind a tree to watch out for you, never taking his sight off you?"

Lily's blood pressure shot to stroke zone. "So he *is* stalking me?" she half-teased. "Do you know he's been *living* in my father's house? In *my* house?"

"Are you kidding me? I'm coming over."

❦

Avoiding Jake until she had more facts to provide her own *quid pro quo*, Lily snuck Juliana through the French doors into the family room, and they rushed to her father's office.

Lily locked the door. "Alex didn't mind you coming over?" she asked of Juliana's delicious detective fiancé whom she'd met at the funeral.

"He's out on a case." Juliana hugged her purse to her middle, the thin strap wrapped around her fingers like a lifeline. The two women sat on the earthtone sofa facing her father's desk. "I thought Jake or Niles Nevin, the Guild Protectorate Director, would've brought you up to speed on my visions. Maybe they have a reason for waiting." Juliana picked at her braid.

"I want to be fully armed before I discuss further with *any* Guild member. I don't like that they know more than I do. Please, Juliana, tell me what you know."

"Or you'll fire me as your financial planner?" Juliana bumped her knee against Lily's to lighten the mood.

"Yes." She winked. "Now spill before I go batshit cuckoo."

"First, tell me how in the world Jake McAllister ended up living here."

"Apparently, he invaded my father's entire life." *Napoleon, much?* "Guess Dad fell in love with his PI services and threw the man a bone by leasing him my mother's loft for a pittance. Once I kick him out, I can breathe again."

"But..." Juliana scratched her head, plucking wisps of hair out of her tidy French braid. "Not if the Guild hired him to guard you."

"The Guild can take a flying leap off Mt. Hamilton. They're not the master of me." She groaned. "Can we not talk about McAllister? I desperately need to know if you saw Dad's accident and not just the aftermath." *Not just him dying.* Lily curled her fists in her lap, worrying her world may collapse around her again upon hearing the truth.

Juliana gloved Lily's hand, offering her comfort and sorely needed friendship. "That's how I first got involved the morning of his accident."

"You mean murder?" Lily allowed a detached aloofness to slide through the visit without opening the dam to another river of sorrow.

"Yes. The police ruled it an accident, however, Alex is holding the case on ice since my visions are seldom wrong. He agreed to work with Jake and the Guild to investigate."

"Didn't the police accept what you saw? They trust you now that you've proven yourself?"

"It took a little convincing for Alex at first." Juliana laughed. "Unfortunately, the evidence the police found refuted my kind of evidence. They found two blown tires caused by embedded nails, which triggered your dad to lose control and skid over the cliff. No evidence of criminal activity. When Jake saw my vision, both he and Alex agreed to let the police rule it an accident because of the threats from the Cabal to Guild members."

Lily hopped off the sofa and towered over Juliana as if to press her words into the psychic's head. "What do you mean Jake saw it?"

"Let me start from the beginning." Juliana patted the seat next to her and waited for Lily to sit. Blonde eyebrows drawing in, Juliana recited the vision.

Gunfire pinged like a firecracker in water, barely discernible.

Mouth gaping, Michael ogled the silhouette of a man standing under a tree on the right side of the road ahead. The right front tire blew out, the wheel thumping as steel hit the tarmac, and he swerved to avoid a head-on with a thicket of trees to his right. Another tire blew and the car swung out of control. Tires screeched and metal crashed into steel, scraping and tumbling down a hillside.

Michael's head slammed the car's roof, his wrecked cries wafting on the wind. The car rolled over and over until it landed on all four wheels. Slashes of moonlight illuminated the black vehicle through tree branches, dappled light reflecting off the shattered windshield. A splintered rearview mirror caught the ghostly image of a tall, muscular man watching from the cliffside above, an odd shaped gun in his large hand, his long dark hair streaming in the breeze.

The man on the roadside scampered toward a dark SUV parked near the Mercedes's final tumble. Michael's last vision in the mirror before his eyes closed forever was the nail gun the man threw into a navy athletic bag, harboring an indistinct circle logo on the front.

"Twilight's yours. Don't let them steal your Twilight, flower child," his ragged voice intoned. "I love you, Lily, with all my heart. I'm sorry I've kept all this from you. Keep her safe, Jake. Keep her safe."

Death claimed his last breath.

Speechless, the dam burst and tears glided unchecked down Lily's cheeks.

"I had the vision the morning of his accident and again a couple days later when Jake snuck me into the impound lot and I touched the steering wheel. During both visions, I felt a presence in my head as if someone else watched the vision. Jake. We'd forged a telepathic connection, something that occurs randomly to strong telepathy transmitters."

"That's freaky." Lily shuddered. "How do you stand never knowing if your thoughts are yours or not?"

"After a ton of practice, I learned to block most minds. When I experience visions, I can't stop them. Jake's a strong telepath and I easily connected with him. He said it had never happened to him. Freaked him out."

"Everything keeps rolling back to Jake." Lily plucked at her shamrock pendant, feeling the useless weight of it on her neck. "Will I be able to trust him the way my father did?" She rubbed her temples, wishing to rub out her disorder. "I'm a freaking lawyer, not a homicide detective."

"Now you know how I feel every time a vision hits." Juliana flipped her messy braid over her shoulder before she unraveled it. "Let Alex, Jake, and the Guild handle the case. Stay safe."

She gave her friend a level stare. "Let me decide. You had more than those two visions, didn't you?" Letting go of her shamrock, she laid her hand over the sword beneath her T-shirt. "When did you find the sword?"

"Are you sure you aren't a telepath?"

"It's written all over your face."

Stalling for a few seconds, Juliana twirled her fingers through her purse strap, her fingers never stopping. "After the accident, I returned to the crash site to search for anything that might invoke another vision through touch telepathy. I found your father's sword. The second I touched it, an image slammed me." Juliana closed her eyes and recited the vision.

"Planning on stabbing me with that toothpick?" a

vaguely familiar man said, a smooth chuckle following his deep baritone tease. An indiscernible accent laced his voice.

"Maybe you, if you don't park that beast where it belongs for once in your life," Falbrooke said. "My daughter gave me this sword, our Scottish clan design."

"Noticed. Kinda matches the sword dangling from my neck, old man."

"What can I say? You and my daughter have great taste. Similar tastes."

"Speaking of great taste." The strange man's voice sobered. He lifted a tumbler of amber liquid to his lips and tossed back the contents. "You know the Guild wants what's best for her. For all."

"Not at the expense of her heritage," Falbrooke growled out, knocking back his own drink. "I'm not rejoining their ranks. Been there, done that, it's over for me." He ran his fingers up and down the tiny blade.

"You know it'll never be over. You need their protection, especially now. Don't let Rose and Ethan's deaths have been in vain."

"In view of threats to the Guild, everyone's suspect, including you." He stabbed the sword in the leather desk pad and left it sticking in the air.

"I'm on your side."

"Are you? I heard last night from the round table that you want to bag Twilight as much as anyone who knows of its existence."

"That's fucked up." The younger stranger vaulted out of his seat and arched over the desk menacingly. Long dark hair came unraveled from the band tying it at the nape of his neck. "Who bent your ear?"

"See what I mean? Everyone's suspect." The older man shrugged. "Too many people want it. Twilight will appear above ground, and everything I've worked for to protect

what's left of my family will be for shit."

"Then let me deal with it," the stranger said, avarice flashing in the black holes of his eyes.

"Over my dead body." Falbrooke topped off their glasses with a top-label Scotch.

"May come sooner than you think."

Lily jumped up again, hands balled at her sides. "That's a blatant threat! Are you sure it wasn't Jake on the road?"

Juliana halted Lily from storming out the door to confront the murder suspect and all around hot as sin enigma infiltrating her life. "He doesn't know I had that vision, but we're both clear there was a shooter. When I asked Jake pointblank, he said he wanted to take care of the Twilight legacy to protect you and Michael, to keep the perps from going after you both."

Lily paced around the room, thinking, planning, absorbing.

"Lily, what the heck is the Twilight legacy?"

Surprised, Lily rounded on Juliana. "I thought I was the only one who didn't know. It's a set of ancient jewels everyone and their dogs and cats want to get their sleazy paws on." She explained what she'd learned about the artifacts.

"Where are they now?"

"The gazillion dollar question of the century. No one but my father knew. For all I know, the man who killed my father took them." Or not. She felt for the key in her pocket. "Guess I'm the heir apparent."

"Not the heir apparent to murder." Juliana gave her a conciliatory smile. "You're not going to let Jake and Alex handle this, are you?"

"Would you?"

Juliana's nervous silence was answer enough.

CHAPTER FIVE

At midnight, Jake rechecked the house alarm. Without giving himself away, he'd watched Juliana Westwood leave a while ago. He knocked on the den's closed door, the room where he and Michael had spent many nights enjoying legal debates and muscle car discussions over tumblers of smooth Irish whiskey. "Lily?"

The silence from within beckoned. He found her sitting behind the large mahogany desk, her skin pale, eyes devoid of her defiant sparkle.

"Jake?" Startled, she banged her elbow against the chair arm. "Damn it. Ow."

"I want you to sleep with me upstairs."

Contempt poured out of her eyes, reinvigorating the sparkle he'd come to admire. "Excuse me?"

He smiled wickedly. "You can have the bed, I'll take the couch."

"No thanks. I'll sleep in my room."

"Then I'll sleep in the guest room." He had his work cut out for him. The single women he typically guarded had no problem taking his lead, especially when it included a comfortable bed.

Lily rolled the chair against the credenza and stood. "I'll set the alarm system. No one's tried to break in, right?" She skimmed her fingertips over Michael's desk, a gesture Jake found incredibly erotic, fantasizing those soft tiny fingertips dancing over his bare skin.

"Already set. Humor me. Let me do my job."

"Whatever. I'll be working for a while." She waved him off.

Reluctantly, Jake limped into the living room, the den's door visible from the large cozy room jammed with overstuffed furniture. Plopping down on the couch, he punched redial on his phone.

"Yo, Jakeman," Ric answered.

Jake propped his foot on the coffee table. "Anything in Michael's car or accident report?"

"No sign or mention of any jewels, a key, or any clue."

Jake scrubbed his scalp to stimulate his taxed brain cells. "Michael has them stashed. We need to find them before *they* involve Lily or jeopardize her further."

Ric whistled in the background, and the muffled barking of his black Labrador retriever grew louder. "Man, you've been handed a wouser assignment." Ric chuckled, and Barney barked in agreement. "You need a second? I can yank some cords with Niles."

Jake swung his legs onto the couch, stretching out for the long haul. "No. It's my gig."

"At least she's a looker."

"Aren't they all?"

"You dog. You get all the luck."

"You kidding me? I can't tap her with a hundred-foot pole. She's not in our realm of possibilities, so keep your pants zipped." Despite the connection he'd felt since the cemetery, a rich and powerful woman was the last thing he needed in his single, carefree life.

A defiant spear of lust shot downward and he adjusted the crotch of his pants. *Damn it.* The woman had oozed into his soul already. Shock reverberated through his ribcage, smashing his lust into dust, toting his sanity along for the ride.

Barney was barking up a storm, and Jake missed Ric's last words before he clicked off.

He gave Lily a few hours alone in Michael's office before he dragged his tired body off the couch. It was too static behind the door. He knocked softly on the raised panel and cracked open the door. Lily lay on the couch, angel face serene, at peace for the first time since he'd met her. Her feet peeked out from the afghan, one clad in a green sock, the other in a purple one.

"Lily?" he whispered.

Tears wet her cheek and his heart flinched. He gently thumbed the wetness away, her skin silky soft and so very alive. All he wanted was to pick her up and take her far away from all this turmoil. Instead, he tucked the afghan around her, wishing it was his body wrapped around her.

Another round of shockwaves rolled through his oblivious mind and hyperaware body.

⊂⟡⊃

Lily awoke Sunday morning, the crick in her neck blooming into an epic charley horse. Groaning, she massaged her shoulder and neck. Despite the pain, no nightmares or bogeymen had appeared during the night. Not that she'd expected bogeyman, but she'd expected murderous jewel thieves shooting nail guns to leap from dark corners.

She thrust aside the afghan she didn't recall draping over herself and sat up, tipping her head from side-to-side to loosen her stiff joints. The key rolled off the couch, and Lily studied the dull brass against the sage rug.

After Juliana had left, Lily practiced the memory

techniques Juliana had taught her, visualizing each nook and cranny of the house one spot at a time. She'd started with their Lake Tahoe cabin, the last place she'd seen her mother and Kevin alive. Nothing seemed to help. Did she seriously want to recall the hidden events of her life? Could she ever move on without knowing her past now that it threatened to rear its ugly head?

Since that fateful summer, she'd had the oddest sensation her life was not her own to chart and travel, as though her soul belonged to another and she was borrowing the body. She'd experienced random flashes of events with no meaning. The feelings progressively worsened throughout the years, as if she'd chosen the wrong path and didn't know how to land on the correct lane to Lily McKenna Falbrooke's life.

She'd obeyed her head rather than her heart and lived the life she believed she was meant to live. Shadowing her father, she'd graduated law school. Against his better judgment, she'd chased her ex-asshole boyfriend Daniel to San Diego and landed a corporate job at a high-tech company, the perfect job negotiating intellectual property contracts, her specialty. She'd befriended Marisa Meadows, the Psychic Guild's West Coast lawyer, and they'd been best friends ever since, her only link to the Guild...or so she'd believed.

A sharp rap rattled the door. She stuffed the key in her pocket, hid the sword pendant under her rumpled sweater.

"Yeah." Rising off the couch, she combed a hand through the snarls in her hair, realizing she probably looked like death warmed over.

Jake entered carrying two steaming mugs of coffee, a distinctive swagger to his shoulders. He handed one cup to her and she mumbled her thanks.

After a couple sips of the killer brew, the man who'd

sauntered out of a GQ magazine in his impeccable low riding jeans, sweatshirt, and bare feet absorbed every iota of her awareness. "Can I ask you a question?"

"Fire away. I'm at your disposal."

She arched a brow. "Disposal, huh? I can arrange that."

She received a wicked grin in response.

Before his hypnotic *everything* sucked her in deep, she dumped her attention on the files on the desk. "Can I choose my Guardian?"

"Ready to replace me so soon?"

"You're just a gift that keeps on giving."

He laughed, a rich baritone that captured a tiny piece of her heart. He stood so close, the warmth of his well-toned body through his long-sleeved sweatshirt seeped into her. "You're like a level ten assignment limited to First Guardian. I'm the best there is. Unfortunately, I'm the one and only First Guardian in the Western Guild at the moment."

"Arrogant, much?" Lily sipped her hazelnut ambrosia.

"The Guild will refuse your request in a way you won't know they did it. They'll assure you that you're in the most capable hands they have to offer." He stepped closer and electricity zinged between them.

His fingers brushed over the top of her rat's nest. "I take my assignments seriously. I'll lay down my life for you."

He touched her cheek, sending jolts of that electricity coursing through her. Rooted to the spot, she couldn't tear her sight off his face.

"The Guild is persuasive. Remember, everyone has psychic powers." He grinned his swoony grin again, sprouting a new round of excited flutters in her chest. "They'll convince you that you need me at your side 24/7. Do you want to embarrass yourself and diss me by refusing my assignment?"

Lily gulped, totally lost in his hypnotic eyes.

"Do you accept me as your Guardian until such time as you no longer need me?"

Barely skimming over her skin, his fingers traversed the circumference of her face. His eyes lightened, then deep swirls of sapphire held her spellbound.

"Yes," she whispered, finally breaking the grip of his mesmerism. Grimacing at a fern frond holding her feet hostage on the botanical-patterned rug, she stepped back, gripping the mug so hard, she was surprised she didn't shatter it. *Yes. Hell to the yes.*

"I loved Michael like a father, Lily. I know he'd want me here for you." He swished his arm to encompass the room. "He accepted me in his life and his home for a reason."

For the last six months, Dad had withdrawn from her, and she'd truly believed he'd taken her advice, signed up on a dating site, and gotten romantically involved with someone. *Clueless, much?*

Jake's cell chirped. Despite his black warning, she mouthed, "Going to clean up." Nonchalantly, she walked to the desk, stealthily stuck her father's gun in her purse, and exited stage left. She quickly cleaned up in the downstairs bathroom, then darted out the front door before he caught her tailwind.

Answers were too elusive. Jake was too...too much of everything. She needed to escape and think alone. Plus, she wanted to drive by the crash site. Her intuition told her she needed to view it. Not for closure, but for clues. Her gut also told her Jake had nothing to do with the accident even if Juliana's vision hinted at some sort of collusion. She needed to see for herself, alone and on her own terms.

CHAPTER SIX

Lily merged off the highway onto the main road up the mountain. The observatory sat on top of Mt. Hamilton, the hill range overlooking San Jose. As she ascended the winding road, the Lick Observatory's three domes popped in and out of view. She knew the road well enough. After her mom and brother had died, her father used to drive up to hike and chill, get away from daily life and the reminders in town. He'd brought her with him a few times the summer after her first year of college, but she suspected he hadn't driven up the mountain in years...until the morning he'd driven his car off a cliff.

Fluffy white clouds scuttled about patches of blue sky. Great day to hike the mountain trails and hang out at the observatory, if not for her task reminding her that the mountain was equally deadly.

From the news reports and Juliana's rendering of the accident, she pictured exactly where her father's car had landed. She passed the fateful spot and drove up to the point where his car swerved out of control. A handmade wooden cross, wilted flowers, and burnt candles marked the car's landing, a reminder of the accident.

Traffic was light, only one car passed in the opposite direction. Hands clammy on the steering wheel, she parked on the shoulder of the road. Wind picked up at the higher altitude, the trees swaying in a gentle dance. Lily buttoned up her jacket and tied her hair in a loose ponytail. She didn't have to view the crash-site photos on her cell, since she'd already imprinted the images on her brain. Sunlight twinkled off a new section of shiny guardrail, absent in the photos.

Lily gripped the door handle, a new twist of sorrow winding in her middle. She stepped out into the gusty wind. Nervous flutters invaded her, and she stamped her feet to stop them, no longer able to afford the destructive anxiety and anguish. She'd kill for an off switch to her emotions. With ginger fingers, she snagged the gun out of her purse and stuck it in the back waistband of her jeans the way she'd seen a million times on TV. The cold metal gave her a huge amount of confidence and security. *Pathetic psychic powers aren't defensive enough for nail-gun toting killers and psycho, threatening Italians.*

Agony attempted to thaw the ice inside her, but she froze it again. Near the new guardrail, she sank down on her hands and knees and scrounged on the ground to imprint the scene on her mind.

"Come on, crappy psychic powers. I had you once. It's time to come home to roost." Her brain had buried them so deep she'd need an oil drill to draw them to the surface. "Damn it." Her voice floated away on the breeze stirring the lonely scent of pine. An eagle flew overhead and soared toward the domes, carefree and innocent. Maybe a witness?

From above the crash site, she could barely see the precise point where the car had met its final rest. An access path led down the hill, but not close to where the car had landed, and she didn't want to chance a face-plant into a boulder.

After fruitlessly scouring the road and shoulder, she

drove down the road and parked in the narrow shoulder near the landing spot. A car crawled by. Ignoring the prying driver, she dove back into the blustering wind. She righted a plastic vase of stargazer lilies stuck in a hole, wishing she'd brought a bottle of water. Faking a nonchalant stride, she tromped through the dry grass, and clambered onto the boulder to scan the vicinity. Not one clue flung itself at her, not even a hint. Exasperated, Lily scrambled off the boulder. As she jumped onto the ground, she experienced the weird sensation of someone watching her.

Only clouds sailed overhead, randomly blotting the sun. A shadow loomed over a flicker of light in a crevice of boulders to her left. She stooped down to investigate, and the flapping of birds' wings filled the air directly in front of her. Startled, she lost her balance, stumbled against a thigh-high rock, and banged her elbow into the granite.

"Son of a boulder." Righting herself, she rubbed her dinged elbow. She patted the boulder, seeking the imprint or a shadow left behind. Zip. Zilch.

When her father had taken her to the institute in New York, he'd explained that she once had clairvoyant abilities to rival her mother's psychic gifts. The extrasensory perception to see what others couldn't by the imprints people left behind. No amount of training, hypnotism, or therapy helped her regain those senses. Over the ensuing years, she'd experienced minute sensations in the shadows or from touching tangible objects, which evoked images of people, snippets of their lives, their excitement, rage, evil and so much more.

The squawking of another blasted raven on the guardrail above echoed in her ears. A gold ring dangled from its beak, light glittering off a single emerald embedded in the wide gold band.

Her father's wedding ring.

"What the what?" She blinked rapidly to dispel the freaky revelation.

The raven soared into the air, stealing the ring and taking the shadows with it. Brilliant sunlight bathed the morning, burning away the leftover wisps of shadows, burning the strange vision into ashes. Movement on the road a hundred feet away yanked her attention toward it. The silhouette of a tall, muscular man turned, dark hair flowing behind him. Jake?

"Hey!" she yelled. "McAllister?" Had he tailed her? GPS'd her car? Elbow throbbing, she rushed to the center of the road, tripped in a pothole, and fell to her knees, catching herself from bashing her face against the pavement. Pain radiated up her thighs and stung her hands. "Crap. Crap. Crap!"

The man rushed behind her and clamped his hand over her mouth. Strong arms elevated her off the ground and carried her kicking and struggling to the roadside. Muffled screams died against the man's dry palm. She bit his salty flesh, the coppery tang of blood coating her tongue. He wore unfamiliar fruity cologne, and in that instant she knew it wasn't Jake.

A car whizzed around a hairpin turn well over the speed limit. It would've flattened her into a tortilla if her rescuer hadn't rushed her out of harm's way. *Holy smashed roadkill.*

"You never saw me. Keep it to yourself. Hear me?" the man said, his voice gruff, lower pitched than Jake's voice, and not the Italian man either. "It's not time for you to die. Not by a long shot. Keep safe. We'll meet again." Something about him rang a bell in the brightening fringes of her black hole memory. Did she know him?

Before she could blink, he'd released her and zoomed off around the bend in the road, leaving her trembling, heart beating a million miles a minute. A hallucination of the man morphing into a raven rattled her, until she realized he'd tampered with her thoughts, left the imprint on her mind to psych her out. A psychic, maybe a telepath. Or she'd lost her marbles.

Legs turning liquid, she visualized her roadkill body filling the pothole and leveling the surface of the road. Was he a guardian angel, or her father's killer in disguise?

CHAPTER SEVEN

Monday dawned fair, the rising sun's rays streaking coral, pink, and lilac through the morning sky. Lily readjusted the seat in her rented Mustang, which Jake had taken the liberty of parking in her father's garage spot. She searched the car a second time, hoping to glean new clues from the car pushing incident, only scoring a lost mint from under the seat.

Despite the two weird incidents hanging over her head—one threatening, the other not—she'd not told Jake about them. Her forty-seven hour call from the Italian never materialized, and the man on Mt. Hamilton seemed to want her alive. He'd had every chance to snag her. Her life had become too bizarre for words—a far cry from her mundane life as a corporate attorney, a job and life she missed with a quiet desperation.

She studied the late model black Corvette in the third stall. Jake's car, she assumed, not afraid to make an *ass* out of him or herself. The second garage stall was home to his motorcycle. A hot coil doubled its efforts to boil in her middle. "Why, Dad? Why did you allow this man to take over our family home, your life? Why didn't you ever tell me about him?"

Her indignation took on a bitter cast as she recalled

again how evasive and secretive her father had been over the last half year. There was a time he kept her in the loop on everything.

Punching the garage door remote, she slammed the car into gear and escaped the confines of her Guardian. Again. A wooden chuckle slipped out. "Bodyguard, my ass." Being around him tortured her senses to hell and back. She had no clarity where he was concerned. She texted him and told him she'd gone to her office and would check in with him the moment she hit her desk and on the hour, every hour. Seriously, he wasn't supposed to guard her around the clock, right?

Lily arrived at the firm's downtown offices thirty minutes later, one of many gleaming towers spiraling toward a train of puffy clouds in the sky. Realizing she hadn't visited the firm in over a year, Lily scanned the reception room, taking in the familiar surroundings. Nothing had changed. The suite consisted of a reception area, two conference rooms, war room/library, break room, and eight offices of varying sizes with scattered secretarial cubicles. The oversized corner office, of course, belonged to her father. Now it all belonged to her.

After she'd graduated from law school, he'd begged her to join him. Oddly, her father had accepted her decision to move more readily than she'd anticipated. A strange *déjà vu* settled over Lily. Had he wanted her out of harm's way even at that time?

"Hey, Elizabeth," she greeted her surrogate mother slash part-time office manager approaching from the kitchenette, carrying a cream cheese slathered bagel.

"Honey, you're early. Where's Jake?" Elizabeth searched past Lily's shoulder.

"He's not my keeper. I wanted to get a jumpstart on Dad's files." For the first time since the funeral, her voice didn't crack at the mention of her father.

"Lily," Elizabeth admonished.

"If he calls, tell him I'm fine. I won't leave the suite."

Elizabeth sniffed and her brows furrowed.

"What now?" Lily threw up her hands, so tired of the secrets piling up like legalese in a contract. "If you're worried about my safety, I have Dad's gun on me."

"I'm shocked Jake didn't tell you." Elizabeth planted her right hand on her hip. "Jake's a full partner. He and Michael formalized it—"

"Are you kidding me?" Lily blinked rapidly. "He's not even a lawyer." She held up a hand to forestall answers she wanted to hear directly from the usurper's mouth. "Then please tell my *partner* to get his butt in my office the minute he lands on this freakshow island."

Elizabeth deftly changed the subject before they both landed on the clueless train. "I've sorted through Michael's files and labeled them according to priority. I've reassigned most cases to the associate lawyers and the securities files to Jake. Files are on your desk."

Her desk. *Will I ever get used to it?*

Windows on two sides of the large corner office overlooked the city from her perch on the fourteenth floor. Mt. Hamilton, the mountain of death, soared into view through the western window and she closed the blinds.

Lily spent the next half hour skimming files, taking notes on items to research later and marking items in her personal calendar.

The key from her father's desk and the sword pendant hanging on a long silver chain tugged on her neck beneath her blouse, reminding her she needed to comb his office. She'd spent time over the weekend searching the house for clues to the questions peppering her from all angles. Nothing of significance popped up, and she assumed Jake's thieving paws had already preceded hers.

The intercom buzzed, and she sent her pen spinning across the desk along with her thoughts. "Hello, Lily, this is Dawn. Jake just arrived."

Dawn had been her father's administrative assistant for five years after he promoted Elizabeth to office manager. "Thank you, Dawn." She disengaged the speaker.

Clad in a black suit, black dress shirt, and dove gray tie, dark hair tied back, Jake McAllister filled the doorway...and her heart stuttered. Dressed in a well-tailored suit booted him into godlike territory. Heat arrowed down to her southern hemisphere, and she squirmed on the chair. She fought the urge to tug down her knee-grazing skirt as if to hide her reaction.

Eyebrows quirked leisurely and a slow, sinful smile broadened his mouth, creating those dimples she wanted to dip her tongue into. He tsked-tsked, and ire scorched her chest, smacking down her mystified hormones.

"You left without me." In a lethal cat-like prowl, he approached the desk.

If she raced her car off the cliff behind her father, would Jake follow? Lily rounded up her straggling thoughts. Time to lay all the cards on the table. Who the hell was Jake McAllister and why had he ingratiated himself so neatly into her father's life?

"Start talking or start walking. You told me you were a PI, not my father's partner."

"I *am* a private investigator."

Impatience shredded her fury, both persistent nuisances refusing to abate since she'd met the man. "Explain the partnership. My father's not in the PI business." But he had expanded into the security arena for his clients. *Ostrich. Sand. Priceless.*

"Lily." Jake breathed out her name so erotically she almost caved to the subhuman lust simmering below her skin. "You were more disconnected from your father than he led me or you to believe. A pity." He shrugged his wide and deceptively elegant shoulders, and sat in one of the client chairs.

"I don't have time for this." She drummed her fingertips on her laptop, wishing to drum answers out of his thick skull.

He hesitated, seeming to weigh his words. "I'm also a securities expert. Michael partnered with me to run the securities aspect of the firm."

The blood drained from her face. She pressed the intercom. "Dawn, please send Elizabeth in ASAP."

"You want to do this now?" Jake's sultry drawl raked down her back and tingled up her breasts.

Shaken and stir-fried, she waved stone-faced Elizabeth to a cushiony client chair. "Oh, we're doing this now."

In front of her sat the two people who knew more about her father's shenanigans than she did. She loathed it and the grey edges of darkness rolling in for the kill. "Let's start with you, Jake." Lily poised a pen over a legal pad, started doodling square boxes, no entry, no exit. "From the first day you met my father."

"Do you mind if I stand?" Jake pinched his right earlobe.

"If it'll help you spew the truth," Lily snapped.

He stood and straightened his impeccable blazer. "Michael first contacted me in February about performing investigative work, referred by another colleague. I'd never met your father before February, although I'd heard of him around the Guild." He paused and asked with a hint of condescension, "Sufficient detail?"

"I'm listening." Lily nodded, dying to wring the information out of his hide, another annoyance on her growing list. On the flipside, she loved feasting her eyes on his arrogant, handsome face and loved hearing the sexy southern voice that skimmed up her back like a lover's hands. The longer she looked at him, the more her jets cooled.

"Michael was pleased with my results and hired me for other jobs." Jake strolled to the wall of windows, leaned his shoulder against a beam separating two panes. "I wanted a job change. Michael was interested in hiring someone to take his growing securities business off his plate to concentrate on lawyering. He knew about my...other duties. He offered. I accepted. Win-win."

Lily twisted the pen up and down. "Partnership is more than a job." She caught the telltale flush creeping up Elizabeth's neck.

Jake flicked an invisible speck from his pristine black sleeve. "Although I don't practice law, I did obtain my law degree, Santa Clara University."

She waved him off with a swish of her hand. "Since you were appointed my *Guardian* after my father died, he knew squat about it, right?" Jake nodded and before she could halt the avalanche of words, she said, "What I see before me is an opportunist who's wheedled himself into my father's life for a big fat payoff." *Please, please tell me I'm over-reacting or that Dad wasn't in his right mind...and that Jake's everything he says he is. Or just kill me now.*

"Lily!" Elizabeth bolted upright. "That's uncalled for. Jake's telling the truth. Your father respected him. The firm is growing exponentially, and Michael needed an associate. Jake brought a lot of business to the firm, hence the reason he made Jake a partner."

"When?"

"Michael made me partner two weeks before the accident," Jake replied softly.

Well, knock me over with a feather. A tear welled in

the corner of her left eye, and she pretended to scratch her face before it crumbled her stony façade to gravel. *Any more freaking waterworks and I'll shrivel into a prune.*

"Thank you for your time, Jake. I want to speak to Elizabeth. Alone." Jake strolled to the door, and Lily said without much energy, "I want your resume, your PI license number, and the partnership agreement on my desk by end of day."

Jake's back tensed, and he spun around, cockiness leaking from his expression. "As long as you reciprocate with your resume and copy of your law degree. I'd like to see who *I'm* partnered with." He slipped out, and the soft click of the doorjamb left Lily in stunned silence.

"What's the real skinny, Elizabeth? You need to tell me before I trip into hillbilly apeshit territory."

Elizabeth fidgeted in her chair, pulled her black cardigan around her petite frame like a shield. "You've seen the staff we've added to the firm, and you'll see it in the receivables."

"Why didn't Dad ever tell me about Jake working here or living in Mom's studio, let alone making Jake a partner?" Lily absently combed her hair back to sidetrack her frustration on her overly wavy locks rather than dig holes in her father's supple leather chair. "He never asked me for my help."

"Honey—" The intercom buzz cut Elizabeth off.

"Ms. Falbrooke," Dawn's chirpiness carried over the airwaves, "Philip Sheehan's on line one. He insists on speaking with you immediately."

Face ashen, Elizabeth gasped. "Let Jake handle the call."

"Who is he?"

"It's about a case Michael and Jake were working on. He's also a Guild council member, minor telepath, former Guardian."

Dawn's voice cut in, and Lily realized she hadn't released the speakerphone button. "He insists on speaking to you and no one else."

"Give me a few." She liberated the button before she pressed it through the phone base. "Where's the file?"

"Jake has it." Elizabeth twisted the string of cultured pearls around her neck as if they were choking her. "He'll take the call."

A sense of foreboding slithered in Lily's gut, another motley piece to the puzzle. She seized the receiver off the phone. "Mr. Sheehan, how may I help you?"

Elizabeth fled the room in stiff jerky movements, banging the door shut behind her.

The view of the golden eastern foothills calmed her while she waited for a response.

"Ms. Falbrooke, I'm very sorry for your loss." A cultured baritone met her ear. "Please accept my condolences."

"Thank you." Every condolence reminded her of the bone-deep sorrow and loneliness she didn't think she'd ever shake.

"I hate to bother you at a time like this, but as you know, certain legal matters cannot rest."

The velvet tone soothed, and a streambed of tension flowed down her arms.

"I understand." An airplane ascended skyward, bound for destinations unknown, and she wished she were on the plane heading away from the Silicon Valley of death. "I'll take it under advisement while I ramp up on my father's cases."

"I'm the Curator at the Museum of Ancient Cultures and History," he replied. "I have an offer to reiterate in the theft case involving the Museum versus Randall Campbell. An offer your father was strongly considering—"

The door flung open and Jake barged into the room,

nostrils flaring.

Grabbing the phone away from her, he barked, "Sheehan, you know the score. Don't try this again." He slammed the receiver down on the base.

Lily jumped up and pressed her palms flat on the desk. "You may be a partner, but you sure as hell aren't the puppet master of me."

"Sheehan's trying to manipulate you." Despite a mad tick in Jake's jaw, his voice leveled out, lethal and barely contained. "I've warned him not to speak to anyone except me about this matter."

"Does the matter belong to the firm?"

"You don't need to get involved."

"Get over yourself and answer my question." She clenched her arms over her breasts to keep from scratching the truth out of him with her short acrylic claws.

"Yes. He's a master manipulator even your father had a difficult time handling. It's a delicate case. Let me handle this for your protection."

Lily needed answers fast before she nosedived into a white padded cell. Regardless of all that had occurred since last week, she believed Jake. And if she wanted to pry the truth out of his tone and tan body, she had little choice but to play him like a priceless fiddle.

Jake waited for her to speak, move, or respond somehow. His perfect lips spread into a delish smile, bracketed by those beyond sexy dimples hidden in his beard scruff. That smile haunted her, stirred unidentified feelings deep within her. The warmth of his smile gave her the fuel to give in and trust him.

She licked her dry lips. "Did Philip's call relate to my father's *murder*?"

CHAPTER EIGHT

Jake extended a hand toward Lily. How did he ever think he could hide murder from her?

"Who murdered my father?"

He wanted to weave her into his arms and protect her from the world. The itch to touch her was so strong it astounded him. And the urge to have Lily as his own frightened him more than anything in his life. Feelings he'd never experienced for another woman bombarded him, and dead center in that crazy-ass mix taunted a forever-together future.

"Pony up," Lily demanded.

Jake stepped back to escape her exotic floral perfume arousing him in ways he'd best hide before she unleashed her inner tigress. "The police report indicated your father swerved after two tires blew out caused by nails in the road." Pride kept her chin up, and her fury turned her mouth into a slash. He wanted her mouth pressed against his until her plump, rosy lips parted and she twined her tongue around his.

The corners of her mouth twitched out of that slash triumphantly. "Accident, my ass." She fisted her small hands on her desk. "I spoke to Juliana Westwood."

A painful tightening in his groin dropkicked his mind

to the present. He buttoned his suit blazer to hide the telltale bulge. He didn't just yearn for Lily as his next sexual conquest. His desire flipped into something deeper, an impossible sensation escaping logic. Guarding her wasn't enough. *I'm losing my damn mind.*

"Jake, you listening?"

He leaned against the marble-topped credenza near the door, her scent torturing him into oblivion.

"I'm listening," he choked out. "The police report is uncontroverted."

"Then I'll controvert it." Lily strode to the other side of the desk and slung her purse strap over her shoulder.

Jake moved with lethal speed, stopping shy of tackling her to the floor. "Don't get involved. Detective MacKenzie has it under control. I'm working with him."

A smug smile curved her enticing mouth as she tossed her purse on the desk. "Sit." She flicked her hand at a client chair and sat behind the desk, Michael's black leather chair dwarfing her petite frame.

Good going, McAllister. You just tripped into an idiot's trap because you let your dick steer your mind. He'd lost this skirmish, but he refused to lose the war.

She flung back her head, her lustrous auburn hair blanketing her slender shoulders. "Can we quit the cat and mouse and agree my father was murdered?" She tapped her foot against the desk leg.

The time for evasiveness ended, and he replied in a gentle timbre, "Yes, your father was murdered. As for who killed him…either has to do with the Cabal targeting Guild psychics, the Twilight legacy, or both."

"Dad wasn't in the Guild."

"Once Guild, always Guild. He made a good show of his independence after your mother died, but he handled Guild legal matters within his field. He stayed connected to keep *you* safe."

Her face crumpled, as if the simmering fire within her winked out. In three steps, he crouched behind the desk. Tears glistened in her eyes and her utter despair strummed so hard at his heart he thought it would shatter his ribcage.

"I'm sorry. I tried to protect you and Michael from all this. I had no idea the cost would be so steep." A dangerous fuse of longing and uncertainty shifted in her expression. He tried to glimpse past her shoulder to prevent the inevitable, but her magnetism seized him. Leaning toward him, she touched her hand to his jaw, the beginning of his undoing. Her lips met his, unraveling him.

His mouth opened and claimed her lips. In a crazy mixture of reticence and longing, she slipped her tongue between his lips, quickly withdrew, then gave into passion, filling his mouth with the warmth of her. He stroked her tongue until she responded in kind and linked her arms around his neck. Rising to his feet, he lifted her out of the chair and molded her soft curves tight against his taut body, his rock-hard erection pressed against her softness.

Jake lost all thought, all reason. Every pore absorbed her tropical scent, tantalized his senses. The feel of her small, lithe body against his wasn't enough. He wanted to feel her inside and around him, to bury himself in her, to drown in the melting pool they'd become. He wanted to continue his slow, seductive exploration of her mouth, her velvety tongue, and her exotic taste forever.

Lily's hands tangled in his hair. Their mouths battled, one fighting for dominance, until the hungry kiss turned leisurely, mutually possessing their entire beings.

When the phone rang, reality broadsided them. Lily jerked away and he set her on her feet, holding onto her hips to steady her legs. Panting to catch her breath, she grasped his forearms. Jake rested his chin on top of her head. The call rolled to voicemail. Long silent moments crept by as they clung to one another. He didn't want to break the spell, didn't want to think, hear, or speak while he held Lily in his arms.

She breathed deeply several times, exhaled loudly. "What just happened?"

"Wish I knew," he replied in a gravely tone. He kissed her forehead, and she tipped her head back until his mouth touched hers again. Her lips were hot and plump, and when he opened his mouth to taste deeply of her again, she resisted and drew away.

Fingers pressed to her mouth, she sank into the chair. "I'm sorry, that...that wasn't me." As if depleted of energy, her hands drooped to her lap.

"You're a beautiful single woman, I'm a single guy. We're attracted to each other. Happens all the time." The lie didn't even convince him.

"No." Her head whiplashed side to side. "It doesn't happen to me."

Raking a hand through his hair, his fingers caught in the leather thong that'd loosened in their frenzy. He freed his hair already half-pulled from his band, freeing his demented head and forcing clarity back to the crazy farm.

"Can we get back to Philip Sheehan?" she asked, wrenching her blazer over her breasts as if afraid his gaze planned to plunder them, the way his mouth just plundered hers.

The topic was infinitely more palpable than the awestruck kiss, and equally perilous. The expansive desk between them helped return them to positions of control. He'd move to the far side of the moon to contain the hunger rising from the sight, sound, and smell of her. Now that he'd tasted her, he knew without a doubt he'd not stop at a nibble.

A dense silence loomed, creating a thin fog of mistrust. Lily seemed to grapple inwardly. Finally, she combed her fingers through her hair, straightening the silky auburn locks he wanted wrapped around his fingers.

"Will you split a vein or two?" she asked. "I know you and Elizabeth only gave me half the story."

"You gonna bleed me dry?"

"If I have to." Her tartness sliced through him. "I deserve to know the complete story of why my father died." She spread her fingers on the desk. "What does Sheehan know about the Twilight legacy, and why is it all bound together?"

He wasn't surprised she'd jumped to those conclusions. He'd fire himself as a dumbass PI for all the clues he'd dropped into her lap. "You do deserve to know. You also deserve to live past tomorrow."

CASEO

Jake insisted they continue their conversation in private at home and left her sitting in a tangle of tattered emotions. He needed to handle a couple clients her father's death had delayed from last week and asked her to stay put until he returned. Court cases waited for no man.

Home. Lily shrank into the large swivel chair behind her father's desk, as Jake and his wide-shouldered backside departed the office. The thought of sharing a home with him both unsettled and beguiled her.

An ocean of worry, rage, and perplexity swirled inside her. It had become evident the chapters she'd lost due to her mother's death had led her to her current time and place in her book of life. The purpose remained a mystery, a dark, scary part of herself she feared uncovering.

To bounce her mind off her new reality, she left to

hunt down Elizabeth. She'd already skimmed the case files, and it was time to pore over the firm's financials. With the increase in staff, she had no doubts the financials were in top shape. Who knew? Everything else she'd believed in had turned to dust.

Unable to locate Elizabeth, Lily ventured into the reception area. "Do you know where Elizabeth is?"

Dawn peered up from her monitor and smiled. Her short blonde layers flattered her pixie look. "She's running errands."

"Thanks." Lily turned to leave, stopped. "How can I access the financial data on the network?"

"Sorry, only Elizabeth and Jake have access."

Color me surprised. Not.

Later, when Lily returned to the office, Jake's long-legged stride paced her corner office like a father panther shadowing its wayward kits. Relief streaked over his sculpted face.

"Did nothing you've learned the last few days sink in? You can't keep disappearing on me."

Fingers stiff and begging to gouge his eyes out, Lily swept her hair back, let it fall in a blanket down her back. "Don't get your briefs in a wad, legal or otherwise. I went to the reception room and ran down to check out the gym. I didn't leave the building, and *you* left me unguarded."

"You're not to take off on your own." He stalked the perimeter of the room.

"I'm a big girl of twenty-eight. I can handle my own protection in my own office." *Over-bearing caveman!*

"Your father was a smart man of fifty-three and look where that got him?"

"You insensitive bastard." She tried to thrust past him, but he grabbed her arms.

"Until this morning, Philip Sheehan wasn't interested in you. You want it to stay that way." His fingers fell away. "Let's go home. I'll explain everything as I promised."

The conversation landed Lily in Jake's Corvette—for safety's sake and a temporary truce to get answers to all the questions torching her brain.

Trying to focus on inanities, Lily said, "Nice car. New?" The open windows couldn't disguise the new car smell and the scent of untapped leather.

"Yes."

"Must've cost you a pretty penny," she mused. A sudden thought slammed her. "Wait. You said you were saving to buy a house?" Mouth gnashed, she glared at his profile.

"True." Jake coughed.

"Don't tell me the firm paid for this extension of your manhood?" Her hands clenched on her lap to stop herself from escaping the tiny confines of the sports car. The man turned her into a mental case.

"Does that surprise you?" He shrugged, the leather seat squeaking. "Michael was a generous man."

"Don't freaking tell me how generous my father was. What else did he *give* you?"

They approached the sprawling house in San Jose's western foothills. Jake punched the built-in remote and drove the sports car into the garage. The smooth roar of the engine deadened the confined space.

"I suppose you own half this house, too. What about the Harley? Did he hand it to you with the rest of the silver platters?" Jake turned to her, grim amusement on his face, which only served to ratchet up her pounding fury.

"What about me? Did he give me to you?" Cupping her mouth, she punched the door button. An aura about him created feelings in her she'd rarely experienced. Jealousy and lust topped the über ridiculous list. Her emotions might as well belong to the neighbor's cat for all the control she exerted over it.

As she opened the door, his captivating voice scraped down her spine. "Only the car, Lily. Nothing more. A partnership bonus. He bought his new Mercedes at the same time."

"Does the car belong to the partnership?"

"No. My father bought his first Corvette at my age. He always promised he'd help me rebuild one. Michael knew the story."

Leave it to the generosity of her father to boost Jake's ego...and mollify his wounds. *Damn it, Dad.* She swallowed her irritation and jealousy. "Whatever." She crawled out of the suffocating car.

"Hold up. Let me check security first."

The compelling tint of indigo in his weird color-shifting eyes mesmerized her. He clamped onto her upper arms. Despite her irritation, she would let him lay his hands anywhere he wanted. He broke the eye-lock and forced her to look anywhere but at him. *Whose body am I renting? Do I need to return my brain to the rental office?* She'd never experienced such a strong mixed reaction to any man.

"I never came between your father and his love for you. You're his flesh and blood, and you meant more than the world to him. I loved him for that most of all." His Adam's apple bobbed. "I would give up this car, my partnership, my life for him to come back to you."

Lily blinked rapidly, diffusing her grief. Pain etched gullies on his forehead. He released her and reached for his gun harness inside his blazer.

"Who are you, Jake McAllister?" she murmured, breaking her grudging stance and grazing her fingertips over his cheek.

He bent his cheek into her palm. "A simple Guardian

trying to do his job."

"There's nothing simple about you." She uttered a short, tight laugh. There were layers to Jake McAllister she hadn't begun to peel away. Did she even want to? Did she have a choice?

He gave her a slow smile, impossibly sexy enough to boot any distrust to the wayside and plunge a searing trail down her torso. Abruptly, he left her to check exterior security before they entered the house. Once satisfied, he retrieved their briefcases from the trunk. Lily unlocked the two locks on the interior door. Despite the day's events, home was her heaven, the house where happy memories of a loving family remained strong in her heart. She punched the code on the alarm pad and entered the short hallway leading to the kitchen. She yelped and jumped back against Jake. A tornado zone had decimated the tidy kitchen she'd left behind that morning. Items from every drawer, cupboard, and cubbyhole littered every square inch of floor.

Their briefcases thumped to the floor. Gun in hand, Jake sprang in front of her, he-man on steroids. "Stay here while I scope out the rest of the house."

No one had to tell her twice. Several moments later, he returned to the kitchen, gave her a quick once over, and headed up the stairs to the loft. Lily chewed on a fingernail and spun around at a soft click in the garage. She mentally rolled her eyes at the sound of the automatic garage light winking out.

Jake descended the stairs. "All clear."

Lily heaved out a breath of relief. She locked the door and waded through the food, broken dishes, and pans littering the floor. "Is the whole house ransacked?"

"Not this bad." Jake re-holstered his gun. "Whoever did it was cognizant of the artwork and expensive furnishings. Things are shoved and tossed around but not damaged."

"How did they skip past the alarm and reset it?" Shivers took up residence in Lily's body.

"I don't know. I'll change the code, add a couple cameras." Back rigid, he scanned the backyard through the wall of windows in the dining nook.

"I'm calling the police."

"No. I'll call the Protectorate."

"No one tosses my home and gets away with it. The Protectorate hasn't done shit for me. I want the bastards to pay for this." She slammed her purse on the counter, knocking an open box of cereal over. Granola joined the feast of crap on the floor.

Jake blocked the phone from her access. "This mess is a small price to pay for what they've already done and what's still on their agenda. Once you involve the police in Guild or Cabal affairs or even the hunt for Twilight, all hell will break loose. We've been keeping it all on the downlow to get a handle on everything before the world at large catches wind."

A tremble worked its way up Lily's spine. She plunked down onto a dinette chair. Counting to ten, breathing her yoga breaths, a restorative calm welled up inside. She tipped her head back and tumbled into Jake's eyes caressing a secret place in her core, so much life and meaning, so much positive energy, trust, and security. They radiated a strange tangle of awe and lust...and something far greater. At least one of her new multiple personalities refused to budge from the Jake train.

CHAPTER NINE

A light drizzle dragged the night down as dark as Lily's mood. After changing out of their work clothes, Jake and Lily straightened the lower level of the house and the bedrooms upstairs. The kitchen received the worst of the mess with cereal, flour, and more dry food dumped onto the floors. The perps had tossed and scattered belongings in the other rooms. Although intact, pictures on the walls hung crooked. White cushion stuffing littered the floors. Lily took an inventory and found nothing missing. The methodical searching and straightening left a nauseating ruin in her gut.

Lily and Jake kept their conversation to a minimum. She was too muddled to talk about the insane attraction between them, and she wanted no distractions when Jake told her about her father's troubles. She tossed out the last bag of trash along with her residual fright to make room for her anger at the threats, secrets, and lies stacking up.

"Let's straighten the loft." Lily plumped the stuffing in a sofa pillow.

"No need."

"You helped me down here, and I want to help clean your place."

"The loft's intact." He scraped a hand over his beard. "We must've scared them off before they hit it."

Scathing words balanced on the tip of her tongue. Stalling, she bit down, reconsidered. She needed information only he seemed to have and playing nice in the sandbox topped her new agenda. His intact apartment explained much, and nothing, except he'd had plenty of opportunity to comb the house, considering his attachment to it like gum on the bottom of her shoe.

He reset the alarm. "Think what you want. But I didn't do this."

"Fine. I'm taking a shower, then we'll talk."

As Lily set her right foot on the first step of the front staircase, a foreboding bombarded her like a grenade primed to destroy the last dregs of her life. Cleaning the bedrooms was one thing. Standing butt-naked in a shower another.

"Jake." She swallowed hard.

His hand landed on the bannister, his pinky nudging hers. "You okay?"

"I can't go up alone." *Hello to my new delayed reaction gene.*

"Then come to the loft. There's only one way in," he said softly, taking her hand. He fingered a loose tendril of hair behind her ear, his thumb caressing her cheek.

"Will you snag my bags?" She hated the childish quiver hijacking her voice.

"Stay here." His long legs took the stairs two at a time and he was back in a tick.

"I'm not usually so paranoid." Lily twisted her grimy hands in her pants pockets.

"You have every reason." His free hand landed on her lower back, safe and comforting.

She walked toward the back staircase leading to her mother's beloved loft, the one place on earth she'd always felt safe. "Sorry if I killed your plans tonight."

"I had nothing else on my agenda."

Lily snickered, unable to constrain herself. "What, no date? No girlfriend?"

"Sorry to disappoint. Guardians have to be careful about encumbrances while on assignment. It's been known to cause," he cleared his throat, "problems."

No girlfriend? As a gorgeous, charming, and enigmatic man, he appeared the type to have a harem of beautiful women on speed dial.

His footsteps thumped on the stairs behind her, the sixth step emitting a familiar creak. Only her father's weight had ever made the step creak. Disconcerted, she waited for him on the landing. The loft was no longer her domain. The small landing appeared the same—painted in sage green with cream baseboards and crown moldings. A new deadbolt secured the door.

"It's open." Jake ascended the final step, shouldering her cases.

She wanted to drown in his welcoming smile. The urge to kiss his dimples grew irresistible and she inched closer. *What sorry soul has possessed you to latch on to the first gorgeous man to enter your life since you kicked Daniel to the curb?* Dipping her flushed face, she stepped past him into the studio apartment. Jake had thawed the part of her common sense keeping her centered and sane. It frightened her that she'd easily succumbed to his charisma.

Except for a new leather sofa and Jake's personal belongings, the loft had changed little. With a delighted cry, she pivoted around the room and lovingly studied each of her mother's paintings on the sage walls. Ten oil paintings of landscapes, painted to transform the unique scenery into part of a dark and mysterious fantasy world connecting all the paintings together.

She tapped the carved walnut frame of an Irish castle on a cliff overlooking a moonlit seascape. A lighthouse shined its beacon in the distance, a swath of glittering light across the turbulent white-capped sea. "My absolute favorite."

"Take it. Hang it where you can see it every day." Lily heard Jake's smile in his husky drawl. "Your father saved them for you. I'll miss them." He paused as if considering his next words. "Your mother had extraordinary talent. I lose myself in the scenery—they're magical."

Lily spun around, clutching her shamrock pin. "What did you say?"

"Which part?" He'd dumped her bags at his feet and crossed his arms over his sleeveless T-shirt.

She salivated over his thick-corded forearms. Drooling was imminent. "You lose yourself in them." Jake nodded. "Until you feel like you're part of the picture. Everything around you is beautiful. It's euphoric."

He whistled a long, low sound. "Now you're scaring me. I thought you weren't telepathic." He perched on the arm of the black leather couch and scratched his cheek, his fingers rasping through his scruff. "Which one's my fave, Miz Mind-Reader?"

Without hesitation, she pointed to a large painting framed in carved mahogany. The same ancient castle sat on a cliff with a backdrop of rolling verdant hills on one side and the emerald sea on the other in a daytime setting.

Lily sat on the arm of the recliner, a square coffee table between them. More than enough distance. "I feel like plain Jane visiting fantasy land. A murder to solve and an unnatural fatal attraction to a man I barely know. To round it all off, I just discovered I'm a descendant of the Kings of Tara. Did the world twist off its axis when I winked?"

"You're absolutely exquisite. Don't ever call yourself plain."

"Out of my whole tirade, that's all you honed in on?"

"Sure, that and the fatal attraction bit." He winked.

A hot flush scalded her neck. "I do have a sense of humor." Needing to distract herself before she said or did something more idiotic—such as kiss him again—she picked up her cosmetic case.

He laughed his incredible rich and deep laugh. Jake's larger than life presence engulfed her, seeming to absorb the air to make room for him. Life had become beyond complicated, total Winchester Mystery House baffling. She shuffled her feet, trying to disperse the molasses-thick tension, halting her hands from dipping into his long, thick hair. She'd never been into guys with long hair, but it suited Jake to a T and seemed to hit all her lust buttons.

Ugh. Time to drown my mind's eye. "I'm off to shower." *Under a glacier waterfall.*

"Need help?" he teased, scattering the tense atmosphere again.

"You wish." She laughed over her shoulder, a cold blast shooting down the tiny thrills blitzing her chest. Too fast, too soon.

CRINE

Jake strode to the large bay window overlooking the city. The purple haze of dusk greeted him, and lights began sprinkling the valley. He placed an order for Chinese food delivery since his fridge looked like it had been looted.

Normally, he loved the view of the city from the foothills on a clear night, but that night his appreciation lost precedence to the woman who'd imprinted herself on his mind and on his lips...on every sense in his body, even ones he didn't know existed.

The bathroom door opened, and steam billowed out along with a boner-inducing cloud of Lily's floral scent. Her clean, glowing face held an air of mystery. What riveted him the most was the multi-colored, mismatched silk pajamas she wore and her wet auburn hair framing her exquisite face, pure and sexy as hell.

"Hello, anybody home in there?" Lily swished her hand in front of him.

"Sorry." Jake furtively adjusted the crotch of his sweatpants. She smiled so enchantingly, he battled the urge to kill the few steps between them and mold his mouth and body to hers once again...and never let her go.

"I said I hope you don't mind I put my PJ's on to get comfortable."

"It'll be easier to entice you into my bed."

Lily squinted until she realized he kidded. "The couch will do, if you don't mind."

"Actually, I do."

Her mouth gaped open.

He raised a forestalling hand. "Hey, I have a sense of humor too." He waggled an eyebrow. "I'll take the couch. You take the bed. I changed the sheets earlier."

"What a gentleman."

"I know how you women are."

"I'll bet you do."

"What's with the green top, purple shorts and pink robe?" He pinched the satiny smoothness of the short robe, his attention on her shapely legs he wanted wrapped around his waist.

"I like color. Sue me."

"It works on you." *And off.*

⊂⊃

While Jake showered, Lily snuggled into a corner of the couch and made herself at home in the one place in the world she loved best. Oddly, Jake's stamp on the small apartment made it seem better. The attraction between them was stronger than any she'd experienced even though she balanced on an emotional tightrope. Clearly, her besotted hormones stemmed from more than six months of healing and abstinence. *Am I ready for a relationship even if Jake wanted one? Will my hidden past destroy my future? Color me mystified.*

A guy like Jake—smart, protective, telepathic without abusing his power, and devastatingly handsome—could easily break her heart. Maybe an ex-wife would show up on the doorstep with his bun in the oven and end her insane hormonal act. *No freaking way. Not twice in a lifetime.* She'd rather die alone and celibate than experience that pain again.

"Hey, you awake over there?" Too caught up in her thoughts, she hadn't heard the subject of her deranged lust exit the bathroom.

The fragrances of his spicy soap and cologne slapped her senses, an unnerving essence threatening to consume her. It took a moment for his question to wind its way through the maze. "Thinking."

"About?"

"The meaning of life." *The meaning of you in my life.*

The doorbell buzzed. *Saved by the bell of reality.* Jake sprinted out of the room and returned with sacks of food in his arms. The delicious aromas of chow mein, broccoli beef, egg rolls and more preceded him. They heaped plates and sat at opposite ends of the couch to enjoy the late dinner.

Jake wiped his mouth and demolished their blissful hush. "Ready? Open mind?"

"For you to tell me things I should know? Dying

here." She speared a broccoli flower and nodded at him to continue.

"Weeks before I met your father, Randy Campbell, a Celtic artifacts collector, retained Michael to fight a potential ownership claim regarding a chalice once belonging to the Twilight collection.

"The chalice is worth a mint. Artifact collectors believe it and the collection together are triple the value of the Twilight jewels alone. Others say the wine cup is a throwaway. According to cryptic messages in history books, those who possess the chalice can call forth the rest of the collection by psychic means." Jake took a heaping bite of rice, swallowed. "Philip Sheehan, who happens to be a Guild member *and* the curator of San Francisco's Museum of Ancient Cultures and History, contacted Randy. Philip claimed the museum owned the chalice and demanded Randy fork it over."

"How did Philip know Randy had possession?" Lily clinked her plate on the table and grabbed her glass of soda.

"The museum hired Randy to locate the chalice, stolen a century ago from an Ireland Museum. I don't know what Philip holds to prove his ownership." He took a slug of cola, swallowing down his grimace. "Meanwhile, Randy signed a contract with the museum to loan them Celtic artifacts for a traveling display opening up on December 1, which included the chalice, which alerted Philip to it in Randy's possession. Philip's not exactly a reliable witness."

Battling her silence, Lily white-knuckled her glass.

"Randy insisted his chalice is a fake. Philip doesn't believe him and is demanding its return for verification."

Lily stretched out her fingers before they locked in place. "Why did Randy go to my father to secure and authenticate it if he alleges it's fake?"

"Your father told me you were smart." Lily tossed her crumpled napkin at him. "Don't mar that beautiful face with such looks." He set his plate on the coffee table.

Lily's neck roasted. Flattery may land him somewhere in her mind-boggled territory.

"Sheehan's tag-teaming with someone other than Randy to obtain the chalice. It's why I believe the group targeting Guild members over the last six months is seeking the Twilight collection. Not that they aren't also benefiting from using Guild members for their illegal purposes."

"Illegal such as using their psychic powers for spying, trading on Wall Street, reading people's minds during deal negotiations, gambling. A conflict of interest for the Guild." She fluffed her damp hair around her temples. "Why don't they kick Philip out?"

"The Guild humors him since his wife's a powerful empath, and she's aiding us in our fight against the Cabal. We're keeping him on our good side, hoping he leads us to clues. But he couldn't find his own ass with eyes in the back of his skull and an arrow pointing to it. It's all a big mess, and your father was hired to straighten out ownership and authenticity."

A quake rent the length of her as if a ghost rolled up from her toes. Jake strolled to the closet and carried back a plaid throw. To her amazement, he unfolded it over her, his fingers lingering on her arm a few seconds longer than necessary. His touch was electrifying, working another tremble over her.

He padded across the room and leaned against the dinette table. "For more fun and games, Randy gave another chalice to Sheehan to shut him up. Of course, Sheehan ruled it a fake."

"Talk about Confusing Fake City. I'd love to read all these contracts and buy a way out."

"No kidding." Jake picked a piece of rice off his shirt and slung it in the sink. "Philip went on a very vocal assault and impugned Randy in the artifacts world about passing off fakes. Then Randy accused Philip of creating the fake in order to steal the real deal Randy insisted he still possessed, even while he called it a fake." Jake twirled his index finger by his ear.

Lily's jaw hung open. "So where's the real deal?"

"Funny you ask." He smiled wryly. "Randy gave your father photos, documents, and sworn statements proving that Randy did indeed own the original. Michael hadn't verified them before..."

Lily massaged her head. She began picking up the leftover food containers. "Where do matters stand now? Can we talk to Randy?" How did any of this contribute to her father's murder?

Jake lowered his pitch to a stage-whisper, "Randy's gone silent. Vanished two weeks ago."

CHAPTER TEN

Lily's mouth hung open like a flytrap. The nuthouse was looking like a safe haven. She wandered to the picture window. The twinkling city lights below helped alleviate her chaos. Jake's reflection on the glass scrutinized her from his perch on the table.

"Coincidental to my father's death? Did the Cabal snag him?"

"Randy took his sailboat out two weeks ago from Monterey and didn't return. A fishing crew found his boat floating in the harbor the following day." Jake cleared his throat, as if the memory upset him. "He was…is an expert sailor."

Lily spun on her heels. Jake's back was to her, wound tighter than an eight-day clock, hands fisted on the table. She snuck up behind him and rested her hand on his back, not missing his flinch of surprise. "Is he a friend?"

"Yes, to my entire family." When he turned around, his nostrils flared. "I'll die before any harm comes to you." He tucked a lock of hair behind her ear, his fingers lingering warm against her skin. "When Randy retained Michael, he gave him the chalice, proof of ownership, and authenticity. Your father locked the chalice away. Only God knows where."

God and possibly Lily Falbrooke. If she ever found the lock the key fit. She fisted the key in her robe pocket and plopped down on a wooden ladderback chair, needing space from Jake's heat crawling all over her.

"Randy told Michael he had a ruthless collector hot on his heels to get his hands on the chalice at any price."

"You think Randy was also murdered?"

"It's not out of the realm of possibilities. He knows those waters better than anyone. He built the boat from the ground up and was more familiar with it than his girlfriend's body."

Lily tapped her fingernails on the chair rail along the dining nook wall, noticing for the first time her chipped purple and blue polish needed a major overhaul. "Someone killed my father to obtain the chalice and not as a Cabal target."

"That's my belief."

"Because it would lead them to the Twilight collection," she mused aloud. Jake's silence provided his assent. "It doesn't freaking make sense." Lily picked at the purple polish on her right flipping-the-bird finger. "Why wouldn't my father give it up if he thought his life was in jeopardy? Who owns the chalice if Randy doesn't come forward and his proof is validated?"

"He has no family." His butt hit the leather recliner by the front window. "No one's outright connected his disappearance to your father's death." He gave her a long assessing look.

Lily waggled her fingers for him to continue. Eventually, he'd get to the questions bouncing around her brain. For now, she was content to hear Jake's voice slide like satin across her skin.

"All that leaves me with is an unknown murderer—who'll target you. The sudden appearance of the fake chalices set the game in play to locate the Twilight collection."

"Which so far has flown under the radar. Wonderful." Confusion licked a path up Lily's spine, dampening the velvet touch of his voice. She contemplated tossing the mysterious key into the fray. But Jake had begun tugging on his ear, his gaze veering off into the corners of the room. She wasn't quite ready to join the Psychic Friend Network yet. "Either Philip or some other collector executed the murders to snare the chalice, hence get to Twilight," she mused aloud.

He broke open a scab on his foot and winced. Blood welled and he watched the red bead as if mesmerized. "Before Randy went off the grid and your dad died, they'd each met with Philip."

"For the love of God." Lily tossed up her hands.

"Show and tell meetings. Michael took copies of the ownership papers. Philip said he had proof of ownership. I never saw Michael alive after that meeting. I have no clue if anyone knows your true lineage. But we have to assume everyone knows now."

"Again, who legally owns the chalice?" Tension so dense it practically hung in the air greeted the silence. "Cough it up."

His eyes locked onto hers for the first time since she forced herself not to look into them after their sizzling kiss. His gaze no less compelling, she wanted to lose herself in the ever-changing depths that rivaled a storm-tossed sea.

"*You* own it," he whispered. "Even if Randy's alive."

Welcome to my clusterfuck celebration. Her life had flipped from boring and ordinary to dangerous and surreal. In a blur, Jake kneeled before her, his arms braced on the chair seat, encircling her but not touching.

"What a nightmare."

"You've been dealt a rough hand."

"What? You're not used to murder and mayhem every day?" she asked. A slow sensuous smile stretched his mouth, a very kissable mouth mere inches from hers. She tried to scoot back, but if she moved farther away, she'd fall off the chair and mimic an idiot losing the last fragments of her mind.

"Do I make you nervous?"

The fresh, alluring fragrance of his soap cried out for her attention. She held her breath to ignore the scent infusing her insides. "Yes."

"Why?" Instead of taking the hint to back off, he squeezed his arms closer.

"You just do." Her lips compressed. "Can we finish so I can get to sleep and gain clarity to make sense of this tomorrow?" *Please, please back off before my body flakes on my brain.* Oh, no she didn't need the complication of Jake McAllister as icing on her clusterfuck cake.

Jake lifted his arms without touching her and returned to balance his hip on the couch arm. The few feet between them weren't enough to cool her amped-up hormones.

"Why do I own the chalice if it was sold off from the collection? Where did you enter the picture?"

Crossing his arms over his chest, he flexed and his muscles bulged out. Lily licked her lips, tamped down her desire staging a roaring comeback. *Come on rebel brain, where's the love?*

"Randy assigned ownership to your father. That's when I joined the party."

Had Randy set up her father to take the fall? "Why did Dad agree to play in this playhouse of viperous artifacts collectors?"

"Michael had me follow leads as to the authenticity of the piece." Jake's countenance softened, but the harsh edge remained in his voice. "I never found evidence to disprove Randy's case or prove Philip right." He propped his left ankle on his knee. Lily had the insane urge to caress it and work her way up his body.

She pulled her knees to her chin and wrapped her arms around them to hide the evidence of her untimely desire. "Why did Randy bequeath it to my father? Was he altruistic enough to want the collection whole once again? If he even believed Dad had the collection."

"No idea. Michael received the assignment papers after Randy vanished. By then, it was too late." He continued despite emotion roughing his voice, "Randy trusted Michael to keep it out of the wrong hands. No one wanted it to end up with Philip or the million other collectors. We weren't sure whose drum Randy was marching to—the Cabal, another collector, his own."

"Is the Museum suing for contract compliance?"

"No. They want to keep it out of the press. Any lawsuit will take the case well beyond the time the pieces are scheduled for display."

"It must be Philip's pet project then. Why is the Guild involved? Did anyone else know the chalice had resurfaced?"

"The Guild protects their own. Unfortunately, the high-ups don't share their intent with Guardian peons. But I've heard from the trenches that sapphires bestow a shit-ton of psychic powers on the beholder. The Twilight sapphires are the rarest and strongest, according to legend." Jake leaned forward, elbows on his knees. "You know it all now."

"With one major missing ingredient." Lily weaved her fingers in her hair to keep them from exercising their desire to shove the key in Jake's face. "Where's the chalice?"

"I don't know."

Instincts forced Lily to believe him. Relief loosened

the perpetual knots in her shoulder. "Do you think they found it when the house was ransacked?"

"Doubt it."

"You already searched?"

"Haven't had time since you've been here."

"What about the offices?"

"Scoured top to bottom."

"How much does Elizabeth know?"

"The same."

"If you know so much about this, why didn't my father trust you enough to tell you where he hid it?"

"For the same reason he kept you in the dark." His unnerving eyes pierced hers. In a nanosecond, they transitioned from aquamarine to the deepest sapphire. "He wanted to handle it on his own, not get anyone else killed," he finished softly. "I begged him to let me deal with the mess, to take the entire collection off his plate to protect him and you. But he took his obligation to Randy seriously—too seriously. And he didn't want me next in line with a bullet in my head."

Was that what Jake had referred to in the vision Juliana relayed to her? Taking the collection from Michael for protection rather than for his own greed? She considered both angles for a moment, but her head and intuition synced up without another epic battle. Everything Jake said about her father hit her positive trust meters. The whirlwind friendship and partnership they'd fostered still festered, though. Her father trusted deeply, but he wasn't stupid. Once one earned his trust, he'd go to the ends of the earth for that trust. What had Jake done to earn that faith and love so quickly? Because Jake was a Guild Guardian who could protect her?

Lily stifled a yawn. A six-panel *shoji* screen separated the living area from the alcove where Jake's bed sat. The alcove her mother used as a play area for Lily and her brother when they were toddlers as she painted. Her mother had hand-painted the six-foot high screen with versions of the castle, its lush emerald grounds, and cliffs with the expansive sea at its door.

"What's next on our agenda?" She turned toward him again.

"You'll do nothing. I'll handle Philip."

Oh, Jake McAllister didn't know her too well. Mr. Debbie Downer towered above her as if to intimidate her. *Fat chance.* "How can you handle squat if you don't possess the chalice, or the Twilight collection?"

"I'll find them." Jake's confident arrogance promised results, and a challenge.

"Then?"

"You leave the rest to me." He took her measure. "Until then, I'll be sticking to you like a fungus."

"Bring it."

He advanced toward her until his toes butted against the chair legs. "I plan to."

"A fungus peels off easily." Smirking, she escaped around the black-framed screen. She tossed the extra blanket and pillow nestled on top of the queen-sized bed to Jake.

❦

Jake stretched out on the couch, the events of the night twisting him in the wind. The red glowing clock on the microwave read two fifteen. Idleness boiled in his gut, igniting his endorphins. Hell, he'd survived on an hour's sleep too many times to count. Didn't bother him in the slightest.

Stealthily, Jake padded barefoot to the bed. Lily had trouble written all over her. The conflicting parties inside him fought ferociously for control. His fists curled and unclenched at his sides. With her angel's face, her rich auburn hair fanned out over his pillow, her petite body was hardly a wrinkle in the bed. *His bed.* Right where he'd wanted her, beside him, gloved all around him. Her too familiar floral scent shot straight to the mark. He resisted the urge to brush his mouth over hers, and over every exposed cell of her soft, silky flesh. He uttered a string of curses under his breath.

In the throes of a nightmare, Lily tossed and moaned. Evil vibes surged out of her mind and into his, frightening him. How could he protect her from the ravages of a mind she had yet to unravel on her own?

Slowly, his fingers fluttered across her smooth forehead of their own volition, landing on her petal soft skin. His heart thundered against his ribs, and his breathing grew shallow. Unspoken words pushed to the forefront of his consciousness. He whispered them, stroking Lily's velvety skin, her still damp hair. A contented sigh captured her soft cry. He extended his telepathic receptors, seeking to demolish the nightmare plaguing her sleep.

Brain wave energy gushed in his mind as if whipped by a snapping power line. The impact threw him back, and he jerked his hand to his side as if he'd tapped a live wire. Energy competed and allied with his, her mind connecting to his, binding his thoughts, creaking open the long-closed gates to her mind, and inviting him in. Shock shut down his telepathic receptors before she latched onto them, simultaneously maddening and euphoric. He swayed on his feet, and a painful erection pitched a tent in his sweatpants.

"What the hell? This can't be happening." Shaking his groggy head, he marched to the kitchenette, flung open a small cabinet, and grabbed the bottle of Irish whiskey. Pouring a double in a tumbler, he knocked it back neat, straight down the gullet, no stopping at GO. The whiskey hit his stomach full barrel and draped a prickly blanket over his soul. It did nothing to eighty-six his insane need to have Lily.

One last heart-slam, and wrung out, he headed to the stairs, locking the door behind him. He'd kick off his search in the den. One way or another he'd find the collection before Lily did and end the multi-faceted torment layering his soul.

CHAPTER ELEVEN

New seams had split open in Lily's brain, leaving her achy and on edge, on the verge of an eruption. Even though the strange flapping of moth wings swarmed her skull, no memories popped through the seams.

"Home to the criminally cuckoo," she muttered. Was her psychic suppression finally busting loose? Fisting her eyes, she took a second to recall whose bed she lay in before the foggy outlines of a fitful dream crashed down upon her.

Her head hit the fluffy pillow and the images reemerged. The first, Jake had leaned over her, touched her and whispered soft words in her ear. Second, a darker presence with connotations of both evil and passion, darkly erotic and demanding replaced the calming presence. A faceless man had skimmed his tongue down her neck, dipped into the neckline of her nightshirt, leaving her in a breathless mixture of panic and anticipation. Had Jake used his telepathy to intrude upon her mind? Lily shivered and hopped out of the cold and unwelcome bed.

The sense of violation from the house break-in had abated, and she snatched her bags and hightailed it to her own bedroom, not a McAllister in sight. It seemed too easy to avoid Jake while getting ready for work, but not so easy to avoid him in his car, and she wished she hadn't left her rental at the office.

The minute his wheels hit the road, Mr. Sex-on-a-Stick said, "Don't go anywhere without me today."

Ire plowed through her. She refused to sit idle while her father's murder went stale. A high-pitched horn blared to her right, startling her contemplation of the commuter train crossing they approached. She wished she sat in the cattle car rather than in the hot seat of Jake's signing-bonus-ego-extension hotrod.

"Do you have a death wish?" Jake asked as if reading her mind.

"Far as anyone knows, I'm not involved in the chalice case," she retorted. He white-knuckled the steering wheel. She admired the way he filled out his custom-tailored suit, so sinfully gorgeous and devastating. "Do you always wear black?"

"Don't change the subject," he ordered.

"I'll think about it." Office buildings crawled by, her mood as gray as the overcast obscuring the rising sun.

"Open the glove box."

People rushed past on the downtown streets, dressed in light layers to balance the last days of an Indian summer hinting the gloom of early fall.

"Lily, did you hear me?" Jake's demanding tone sliced and diced her meandering thoughts.

Yes, Puppet Master. She popped open the glove box. "What—"

He threw her a hesitant glance before it slid back to the crush of traffic snarling their route to the business district.

"I don't need—"

"I don't care what you think you need." A cyclist cut them off and asserted his rights to the road. Jake slammed his foot on the brake pedal, locking Lily's seatbelt between her breasts. "Stick it in your purse. Safety's on; it's loaded."

Gingerly, she picked up the gun by the handle. The small weapon fit comfortably on her palm. She'd already hidden her father's larger gun in her briefcase, too big to tote in her purse. "I have my dad's gun. He taught me how to use them at our cabin before he signed off the NRA." Lily didn't know why she felt compelled to tell him.

"I know, he told me."

Pins and needles chased down her arms. "He did?" How much did Jake know about her? Why had her father placed so much effort into discussing her with a virtual stranger? Had her privacy gone the way of Bounty Hunters 'R Us?

"Keep both guns with you 24/7." He swung the ground-hugging sports car into the garage attached to their office building, the parking spots already filling with busy workday traffic.

The delicious scent of him chased away the pins and needles as his sexy voice melted a tiny piece of her heart. "Oh, so you were kidding about shadowing me?" Lily stuck the gun in her purse, hiding it out of sight, out of mind.

Jake maneuvered the car into a reserved spot on the first level and punched the ignition off. "No, I wasn't kidding."

Tell me what you really think, Jack Bauer. Lily snatched up her bulging purse. She reaped a hint of security knowing it and her briefcase contained a gun...especially since her gut instincts warred with her head and heart when around Jake.

"I want you to search your father's office for a key when you have time today."

Lily blinked rapidly. Did he know about the

mysterious key? "I thought you searched it already?"

"You might find clues I missed." Jake opened the door and with catlike grace peeled his toned body out of the cozy vehicle. The sports car fit him to a T.

Lily remained seated, wondering if she should tell him about the key. She touched the sword pendant hanging on a chain now attached to her purse. Biting her lower lip, she didn't notice the passenger door opening until Jake extended his hand, long strong fingers hinting at a working man by the feel of his slightly rough skin against hers. She allowed him to tow her out of her seat and nearly into his arms.

Jake smiled down at her, his mouth wide, creating those delish dimples she loved. *Institute for the Criminally Horny, here I come.*

"Has anyone ever told you how exquisite you are?"

New swarms of butterflies hatched in her stomach. No one had ever called her exquisite. The men she'd known or dated didn't possess the word in their mental dictionaries. She smoothed her hands over her black silk dress and fitted matching duster—the same outfit she'd worn to the funeral. As a nothing special kinda of gal, exquisite didn't apply, especially wearing a running-on-empty wardrobe.

Lips kicking up, she eased her hand out of his. "I bet you drop that line on all the women you meet."

"Only one." His silky words dissolved her into a puddle.

CRBO

After halfway threatening to fire Elizabeth if she didn't give her access to the financial records, Lily sat at her father's desk. Elizabeth had the gall to tell Lily she'd have to confer with Jake before doing so—until Lily subtly reminded Elizabeth who co-signed her paycheck. Progressively uneasy with Elizabeth's odd behavior, she wasn't sure if she fully trusted her father's most loyal employee and family friend of over twenty years. The jagged pieces didn't fit the puzzle quite yet. Maybe she was overthinking, overreacting.

Sighing, she booted up her notebook. At least her wardens didn't have access to her personal email account and the emails forwarded to it from her father's personal and business accounts. After scrolling through routine business messages, she came to an email delivered at midnight from Philip Sheehan.

"Bingo." She clicked on the email, and perspiration peppered the nape of her neck.

Dear Ms. Falbrooke,

I'm disappointed our conversation terminated so brusquely. It would be in our mutual best interests to discuss the issue I referred to yesterday on a face-to-face basis. There are loose ends your father and I were tying up, and McAllister is thwarting those efforts. He may not have had Michael or your best interests on his agenda.

I would be honored to meet you for lunch today if convenient for you. I hope to make it worth your while to resolve these final issues to our mutual satisfaction. It would behoove you to keep this to yourself, as it was a private matter between Michael and myself.

If you are unable to attend, please reply. Otherwise, I'll meet you at Adamo's Seafood in San Francisco at 1:00.

Respectfully yours,
Philip Sheehan.

"Well, well, well. The canary sings for his next meal." Lily steepled her fingers under her chin. The meeting might satisfy her curiosity and initiate a lovely start to drop-kicking her father's killer into a six-foot hole. Not used to people handling things for her and tired of obtaining secondhand information, she wanted to assess Sheehan on her own without Jake's interference. Too much about him confused her, and she wanted a clear head in the meeting, especially if Sheehan believed Jake may be playing his own ball game. Not that she wouldn't keep an open mind in that regard.

Too jazzed to give her inbox more than a cursory overview, she decided to deal with the emails from her San Diego office later. Soon she'd have to tender her resignation since she intended to remain in San Jose. She refused to let her father down by not doing her best to take his place at the law firm's helm.

Gathering up the envelopes her father's probate attorney had delivered earlier, she crammed them with case files and financial files from Juliana Westwood into her briefcase. Enough room remained to shove her laptop in the case, but she managed to break a fingernail in the process.

"Damn it." She sucked on her fingertip as blood welled beneath the nail bed, showing through the chipped purple polish. "Three time's a bloody charm," she muttered as she picked at the other two nails she'd mutilated in the last week.

She cracked open the door and peeked out, met empty hallways in both directions. She tiptoed to Jake's partially open door. Indecision engulfed her, and she teetered on telling him her plans versus escaping her luxurious imprisonment.

Burying her head in the sand had surpassed all her other faults for the last year. *Once bitten, twice shy, three times and I may as well die.* Jake's phone ringing gave her butt a callous kick. She whizzed past the door, through the empty lunchroom, and out the fire route to the stairway in the rear of the tower. Running down fourteen flights of stairs was far better than confronting Jake's fury.

One part of her wanted to trust Jake with her entire freaking life. The other part exuded basic caution concerning any business or personal relationship...with any man. At the rate she traveled, she'd have to flip a coin to determine if Jake sat on her side or balanced on the devil's right hand. Fog stuffed her head, and she blasted it away with steely resolve. Too many variables stacked up against him ever keeping her fully in the loop. And she needed to be in the loop or she'd wither up and join the rest of her dead family. *Control-freak lawyer, much?*

Heaven help the part of her drowning in a sea of bliss every time she smelled, saw, or heard Jake McAllister.

CHAPTER TWELVE

Deserting her rental car for the second day in a row, Lily hailed a cab outside her office tower.

An hour later after a couple stops, she hit the road in the driver's seat of a black SUV rental and a new prepaid cell phone. On the way off the grid, she stopped at home to grab her still unpacked suitcases and snagged the Tahoe cabin key off a key rack in the kitchen. Leaden on her palm, she stared at the key she hadn't touched since the summer of the accident—the last time she'd been to the cabin, before her father supposedly had sold it.

The drive up the highway to San Francisco didn't shine any light on the secrets, lies, and mysteries surrounding her like a blanket of knives. Trepidation hit her full force. After all this time, could she return to the family's happy, loving vacation home and confront the past?

Lily flung off her nostalgia and entered the congested traffic leading to San Francisco's famous waterfront. The restaurant on Fisherman's Wharf offered a sparkling view of the white-capped bay and the Golden Gate Bridge, keeping the place rocking at all hours. Why had Philip Sheehan chosen this spot for a business lunch rather than cater to her location? *Whatever.* The über public destination hit her safety buttons. Even so, fear tangoed in her gut, and she double-checked the gun in her purse.

Her pulse accelerated as she entered the crowded restaurant. She kept her eyes peeled and checked the location of the exits, glad she wore low-heeled pumps in case she had to make a swift getaway. Philip Sheehan waited in a corner booth at the back of the dining room. The unfamiliar man stood, offering his hand and a charming smile. Apparently, he hadn't attended her father's funeral or she might've remembered his full head of salt and pepper hair. Distinguished, in his fifties, tall and lanky, he wore his stylishly cut rack suit well.

Lily shook his manicured hand. "Hello, Mr. Sheehan."

"Ms. Falbrooke." He beamed bright, the corners of his lips curling to the exact point on each side, exhibiting a perfect row of dazzling white teeth. *Time to hit the kill switch on the tooth whitening sessions.* "I'm honored to meet Michael's lovely daughter. May I call you Lily?"

"If you feel it necessary." She hid a smile and sat on the cushioned bench, grateful for the high backrest shielding them from potentially prying eyes if their conversation exploded.

His body stiffened a fraction at her comment, then a rich laugh followed. "Ah, I see humor as well as beauty wasn't wasted on you."

"Among other traits." She set her purse on the bench next to her and unfolded the linen napkin on her lap. As expected, the linen instantly left white fuzz on her black dress.

Philip returned to his seat across the intimate table. "You and I will get along quite well." His long elegant hand covered hers on the tabletop in a too familiar gesture.

Avarice crawled across his face. He obviously wanted more from her than an ancient artifact or a map to a cache of priceless gems. Suppressing a flinch at the idea he may have offed her father, she freed her hand and wiped if off on her napkin.

His smoldering violet-gray eyes tracked her movements. The unique eye color set off an alarm, red flags hidden in her aimless memories. He eyeballed her as if she were the only item of seafood on a steak menu. She fidgeted on the padded seat. *Damn, he's selling me a hefty load of charm.*

The barest presence feathered her brain and she erected her shutters. Unconsciously blocking telepathic intrusions was a talent she'd relearned over the last decade, but for some weird reason since she'd awoken that morning, the task had become near impossible.

"The *ciopinno's* magnificent," he interrupted her mental side trip.

"Tried and true?" She closed the menu and regarded him with open frankness.

"Can't go wrong, unless you'd prefer the clam chowder."

The waiter took their orders, and they waited for him to depart before traveling down the bumpy road to truth and lies.

"Are we done with the niceties?" Lily's gaze penetrated the depths of his darkening disdain, searching for any clue.

Philip's wide sensuous lips spread in a quick smile. "Very well. Shall I give you background on the pending lawsuit?"

"What lawsuit?" She shrugged, focused on blocking out the noisy cacophony surrounding them. "From what I understand, you don't have a bridge in which to cross the bay." She grew uneasy under his placid demeanor and the mental glimmers he kept shooting at her. *Bastard.* She knew from hanging with a few Guild psychics in San

Diego that Guild bylaws forbade members to delve into each other's mind without permission. *Oh, wait I've been flying solo. Am I a member or not? And since when did murderers obey rules and regulations of stupid clubs and cults?*

"Then you've been misled," he replied. "I gather Jake McAllister has stuffed your head with unsupported facts."

Pelicans dove in and out of the water, watching, waiting for any tasty morsel to satisfy their non-discriminating pallets. They afforded her a needed diversion to form her response.

"I've familiarized myself with the case." She picked out a piece of warm sourdough, a San Francisco staple. "Tell me what you want and what evidence you possess to corroborate it." She tore the bread into pieces on her plate.

"I respect directness in an adversary." He loosened his tie, dipped into a briefcase on the floor, and set a slim black folder on the table.

"I'm an adversary now?" She failed to hide her sarcasm.

The waiter returned with their order. The aroma of Philip's fish stew nauseated her. She took a sip of her diet cola to quell her queasiness and dug into her chicken Caesar salad.

Philip ate a few bites of his *ciopinno*, smacking his lips in delight. "The last discussion I had with your father..." He tilted his head, exhibiting a pathetic attempt at compassion.

Lily waved her fork. "Let's leave propriety behind us."

"By all means." He opened the file. "The main issue remains as to who legally owns the real chalice of Tara. I'm sure you're aware the chalice was sold off from the Twilight collection centuries ago." He paused, and she nodded. "The original chalice was located and purchased on my behalf, and then absconded by my buyer and replaced with a fake before I gained physical possession. The museum is alleging lesser issues of fraud, slander, and whatnot."

"According to my father's files, Randy Campbell is the legal owner of the *real* chalice. I agree on various issues of fraud and harassment on either side, and agree fakes are possibly floating about." She allowed a benevolent smile.

"Lily." Philip set his bowl to the side. "Randy played your father for a fool, and I'd rather not see the same happen to you." He raised his hand as if to deflect the harpoons shooting from her eyes. "I'll not disparage the dead—"

She nudged her half-eaten salad aside. "You're not going to win this war no matter how much honey you ooze over me."

He flicked the folder. "Read the contents."

Curiosity overruled. She flipped the file open, sifted through the pages one by one. By the time she closed the file, fury primed to light her up like a fireworks display over the Pacific. Someone was definitely playing her for an idiot—someone by the name of Jake McAllister.

Schooling her agitation, she asked, "May I keep this? I'd like to verify the contents."

"By all means."

"Did you show the contents to my father at your last meeting?"

"Yes. I offered not to sue him if he handed over the chalice within forty-eight hours." He drained the last of his wine. "You know what happened next."

Lily regarded him remotely. "Do I?" An implied threat seemed to dangle her words in the air.

He sputtered, recovered with a quick slug of water. Red-faced, he said, "You're a smart woman. I'll let you figure that out on your own."

"Believe me, I will." She spun her spoon on the scarred wood table. Silence ensued while the waiter cleared off the table and presented the check to Philip.

"If you're implying foul play on my part, I can assure you, you're needling the wrong man." He perused the bill, set it aside. "You may want to dig in your own backyard for answers."

A sudden aloofness hit her core, separating her budding feelings for Jake and the chalice case. "I beg your pardon."

"Do you know Ric McAllister?"

Lily shook her head. Jake's brother, she presumed. Her stomach heaved leafy greens side to side in preparation for his bombshell.

"A brilliant, charismatic young man. An overachiever who gets what he wants, whether deserved or not." Philip drummed the table, his tight smile fleeing. "Ric's a broker and finder of ancient antiquities, among his other talents." His glance joined hers alighting upon a fishing boat sliding into a slip a few piers down, the men hard at work cleaning the day's catch. "He was a good friend of Campbell's. With Campbell's disappearance, there's little standing in Ric's way to sell the chalice to the highest bidder and pocket the cash. Possession is nine tenths of the law. Many bidders are waiting on the sidelines for the catch of a lifetime."

Whoa, drop an anchor on that boatful of smelly fish. "And you're telling me this why?"

"I want you to know everyone is dispensable in one way or another. All it takes is a bad decision, a wrong choice."

"What bad choice did you make?" *Besides kissing my ass.*

"Hiring Ric McAllister."

Her heart banged her chest like a fish trying to

escape its net. "Excuse me?"

"McAllister persuaded Campbell to make *his* bad choices and McAllister conducted the bait and switch."

"So Ric gets what he wants?"

Philip's smile turned smarmy and deceitful. "It's that McAllister charm. I'm sure you ladies concur for other...more personal reasons." He paused for obvious affect. "Did you know Jake McAllister is Ric's older brother, and they own a business *together*? What do you suppose that business is?"

Hints of McAllister collusion spurred her onward. She picked up her purse and the folder. "Would you sell your soul to get the real chalice in your hands?"

A muscle twitched in his temple.

Answer enough. She shoved back her chair. "Thank you for lunch. It was most...enlightening." *No model-behavior star for you today.*

He remained seated. "I'll hand you the same offer I handed your father. Due to the circumstances, I'll give you until Monday to respond."

"You'll have it, one way or another." Before he could respond, she exited stage left and rushed out of the restaurant. Hand gripped on the gun inside her purse, she was so intent on peeking over her shoulder to see if he followed that she barreled into a man waiting outside the doors.

"Oh!" She caught her balance, her hand landing on a hard pectoral muscle. "I'm so—" The most intense charcoal eyes she'd ever seen met her stunned gaze. His gaze consumed her, leaving her insides boiling. She had the strangest sense of *déjà vu*. Had she previously met the most unforgettable godlike man? *No way.* She would've remembered him even if she hadn't lost half a lifetime.

Steadying her, he rested his hands on her shoulders and beamed a radiant grin. "My fault for blocking the entrance."

His face riveted her before her gaze skimmed the length of his muscular body shrouded in a charcoal gray suit to match his eyes. Ebony hair combed back off his forehead and grazed his broad shoulders—hair darker than Jake's hair. Not that Jake was a slouch in the GQ looks department, this heavenly hunk was even better looking, and something about his aura drew her to him like a moth to a flame, both exciting and ominous. It rattled her how her father's death had hurled her senses into a never-ending tornado.

Recognizing her rude behavior, she harvested her wits. "I'm sorry. I wasn't paying attention." That intrusive tingle made another impromptu appearance, and she had to lock her arms to her sides to keep from scratching her head.

The man released her, one hand slipping down over her purse. "My pleasure. It's not every day a goddess steals my heart—twice to be exact." He set sizzling fingertips on top of her hand resting over his heart.

CHAPTER THIRTEEN

Jake's cell buzzed a text message. He abandoned the case file he was studying and flicked on the screen, not recognizing the number.

> *Lily and I missed you at lunch today.*
> *Say hello to the Flower of Tara for me.*
> *~Philip Sheehan.*

He leaped up and pounded down the hall. He slammed open the door to Lily's office, and it banged with a loud thud off the wall. Empty. Her laptop and briefcase were gone. Her smartphone sat on the center of the desktop, a sticky note tacked on it. "Nice try, Jake."

"Ah, hell no." He spun around to find Elizabeth and Dawn in the doorway. "Where is she?"

"I haven't seen her since this morning." Elizabeth sniffed with annoyance. "Not in a good mood either."

"What was on her schedule?"

"Gregory Sutra dropped off Michael's probate documents," Dawn replied. "You asked me to keep her calendar clear for two weeks."

Jake growled low in his throat. "Did you see her leave?"

"No." Dawn stepped backward into the hallway as if afraid he'd go loco on her.

At the moment, he wanted to kick himself into next week. He drew Elizabeth into the office and shut Dawn out.

Elizabeth laid a hand on his arm. "What's wrong?"

He showed her the text from Sheehan and the note Lily left. "She's begging for trouble." He prowled the room, stopping in front of the windows. Mt. Hamilton rose in the western hills, both a beacon and harbinger of death.

"Damn it, Jake, you're her Guardian. You should've been with her."

"She's not exactly stoked about the situation. I gave her space and warned her." Jake dragged his hand through his hair, tugging on a snarl, sucking up the pain. "She has a gun. I thought she understood the stakes."

"Does she know about Randy and Sheehan's situation?"

"When she saw the house ransacked, she demanded answers."

"Oh, my." She wrung her hands. "And you left her alone after telling her how much danger she's in?"

"I didn't exactly leave her alone," Jake shouted. "I stuck a tracking device on her cell, in her car. I instructed her not to leave the office. I made sure she has a gun. I had Dawn watching the front door while I took care of a few firm matters. Apparently, she skipped out the fire escape." The disgust on her face ripped the remainder of his intestines to shreds. "Apparently, she has a death wish."

A dawning horror paled Elizabeth's disgust. "What else did you do? A gun and tracking device aren't enough and you know it."

Jake picked up Lily's phone, rallying his thoughts as he looked at her innocent text messages. Finally, he whispered, "I flayed her mind open like a tuna last night. I think I may have broken through her repression. Apparently, she's susceptible to mind control." A psychic phenomenon that existed in few people with any type of extrasensory ability. No wonder she'd repressed her memories and abilities—to keep herself safe from someone like him with the ability to coerce others with his telepathy. His confession increased the guilt burrowing holes in his gut.

Elizabeth jack-knifed into a rigid stance. "She agreed to it, right?"

Very few telepaths had the ability Jake possessed. If the Guild got wind... He couldn't hide the remorse from his expression.

"Jake, how could you?"

"She was having a nightmare. I wanted to ease it so she could get a good night's sleep. But once I telepathically reached out to her, something in her head hooked me. I immediately wanted to ooze past her block, help her regain her psychic ability. It snowballed." He gripped her shoulders, seeking forgiveness and guidance. "I don't know what happened."

"You had no right." A tear dripped down Elizabeth's stricken face.

He dipped his head to block out the guilt mirrored in Elizabeth's eyes. "Evil lurks around her, in her. I felt it last night. Plus, she's keeping info from me. Opening her up like that forged a deep and lasting psychic connection unlike any I've ever experienced. I actually felt *her* in my head. I knew she'd left the house this morning, and I was able to track her here. Another reason why I felt confident leaving her alone in the office for a short time. I was just down the damn hall." Elizabeth winced under his grip, he released her and wheeled around, his arm muscles tight with strain.

"You've signed your death warrant in the Guild." Elizabeth's shock filtered into his suffocating guilt.

"What if I helped her?" he argued lamely.

"Doesn't matter! It's against Guild laws, punishable by stripping your seat in the Guild, your identity, fines, and even criminal penalties. Thirteen years up in smoke."

Despite his illegal and suspect compulsion, he believed he'd taken the right steps. Or had he? How could he let this slip of a girl demolish his entire life? "Damn it. I know. I know."

A coffin-like silence weighed down the prickly air. Elizabeth rested a hand on his shoulder. "Honey, are you falling for her?"

Warring factions tangled Jake's mind. As much as he wanted to deny, deny, deny, Elizabeth knew him too well. The moment he'd cast his sight on Lily at the cemetery, he'd known she was special, a powerful psychic, far more powerful than himself or even Juliana Westwood, one of the most skilled telepaths he'd ever met. Untapped power surrounded Lily, and she was destined for a greater life...separate and apart from him. Worst of all, falling for her wasn't in his life's playbook...*play* being the operative word. Falling in love wreaked havoc on his Guild duties. What ten-pound pack of stupidity had docked on his shoulders?

"Jake?"

"I don't know." He collapsed onto a client chair. "I did the right thing. It may save her life."

"It won't mean a snowball's chance on Mars if the Guild gets wind. You'll have nothing left. You might as well be dead. Then where will Lily stand?" she said without an ounce of accusation.

"Will you tell them?" Jake gripped the chair arms so tight, his knuckles popped.

Elizabeth took a contemplative moment before she

said, "No and neither will you. Our first priority is keeping her safe. You're First Guardian, and if you can't keep her safe, no one can." She took a long moment to think, and heaved out a heavy sigh. "You'll have to help her break down her barriers. You started it. Finish it."

A muscle flicked in Jake's neck. "Agreed." He let up on the chair arms before his fingers froze into place. "We have another problem. She left the building without the barest shadow in my mind. She somehow figured out how to block me."

"Why didn't you check on her if you didn't feel her? Jake, what's wrong with you?"

"Fuck. I don't know what's wrong with me. She's killing me." With Lily's smartphone in his hand, he paced to the window and scowled at the Lick Observatory high on Mt. Hamilton in the distance. The sun twinkled off the top of the domes, taunting him to return to Michael's crash site. "I've never mind-connected with anyone, other than last week when Juliana sucked me into her vision of Michael's death. Last night the merging was intense. Shouldn't I sense her more with or without her blocking me?"

"Her psychic ability's not a hundred percent free. You just cracked her foundation so to speak." Elizabeth pinned a sympathetic look on him. "You set the wheels in motion, now finish it."

The phone cracked in his grip and he flung it across the room.

⟐

Lily escaped the restaurant without a tail. "The luck of the Irish," she murmured, pressing on the precious key hanging around her neck. She'd take the smallest bit of luck she could afford.

She'd solicited the assistance of the gorgeous man—Connor—outside the restaurant to detain Philip Sheehan while she escaped in her SUV rental. He'd asked no questions and delighted in aiding a damsel in distress. Of course, he'd exacted equal consideration in the form of a dinner date. Playing along, she gave him her San Diego business card and told him to call her. Hell, when Jake completed his assignment and nothing panned out between them, she might take Connor up on his enticing offer.

The Italian man's threat to call her in forty-seven hours had turned to dust. He must've pranked her. Or had the Guild or Jake apprehended him in secret? Regardless, she kept her eyes peeled as she drove out of San Francisco. She glanced in the rearview mirror for the hundredth time since leaving the city, spying no distinct car tailing her for any length of time.

The four-hour drive to Tahoe gave her plenty of down time to think about her life from the moment she'd received the devastating call about her father's accident while eating lunch with Marisa in San Diego through her meeting with Sheehan. Most of all, she couldn't shift her snarled thoughts off Jake. If Philip had truly given her the goods on Jake and his brother Ric, on what side of the fence did Jake play? Did they plan to sell the chalice and pocket the money? Were they trying to obtain the entire collection? Had Jake finagled his way into her father's life to obtain her mysterious inheritance, ostensibly to protect her? Or had Philip conned her? Questions begging for answers twisted and turned in her ravaged mind.

She mumbled a string of cringe-worthy curses. Just when she'd started to trust Jake, he planted a GPS on her phone and probably one on her car, the newest mangled piece of the never-ending puzzle.

"He must think I'm an idiot. I may have lost my mind

temporarily, but it's back home and raring to solve these mysteries once and for all." She tapped her fingernails on the steering wheel, setting the wheels in motion in her head. "I have no intentions of whoring myself out to the highest bounty hunter bidder."

The Sierras were ruggedly beautiful, albeit stark where forest fires and mudslides had claimed the evergreens, leaving behind charred stick trees begging for a drop of liquid hope. She hadn't traveled Highway 50 in so long. The trip up memory lane sank her jubilant mood with every mile traveled, and not even her favorite Celtic rock music helped lighten her burdens.

One stop for gas and groceries later and she drove up the driveway to the cabin. The large two-story structure set among the pines and evergreens of the Tahoe hills on the south shore. The nearest neighboring cabins were within view if one searched hard enough for them through the forest, a few miles from downtown Tahoe, the perfect location for wintertime skiing, summertime boating, and anytime gambling. It was a place to regroup absent murderers, chalices, and Guardians, especially when that nefarious world believed Dad had sold the property.

The cabin sat on a low hill above the expansive lake. The spectacular wedge of aquamarine caused her senses to bloom, her pulse to leap in recognition. She stepped out of the SUV and inhaled the brisk air. The invigorating scent of pines cleared the last vestiges of Bay Area grunge out of her system. Always a family refuge from the drudgery of daily life, work, and school, the cabin served as a sanctuary to reconcile her past with her present. After ten years, she needed to know the details of the tragedy haunting her before moving on to wherever life led her next.

Through the trees to the right, she spied a neighboring house built of castle stone with a turret in the front facing the lake. Something about the turret tugged on her insides. That frisson of awareness invaded her again, and the shadows arose in her mind, like tiny nuggets people had left behind for her to find. The sensation had grown stronger since she'd departed San Francisco. Shaking her head to dispel the vagueness, she dug the house key out of her purse, and the ring caught on the borrowed gun.

"Better safe than stupid." She hauled out the gun and crept to the rear of the house, scrutinizing every window and door for signs of forced entry. All secure. She punched in the alarm code and unlocked the back door, scanning the dark corners, ears picking up silence from the interior. Entering the cabin wasn't as tough as she'd anticipated with the past pushed into her mind's attic.

Hunting lodge décor overpowered the former homey rooms in her father's attempt at booting the past behind him. He'd left her mother's paintings scattered on the walls. Several new animal prints complimented the dark leather furniture and a musty scent of neglect. "*Eau de man cave.*" At least he'd refrained from hanging stuffed deer heads and scattering bear rugs on the hardwood floor. Regardless, she'd brighten it up again if she decided to hang onto it. Now that she'd returned, the cabin represented so much to her. It was like exiting a stifling crowded elevator onto a deserted island, both scary and liberating at once. "Time to confront your demons, Lily McKenna Falbrooke."

CHAPTER FOURTEEN

Jake's mad race home forced several pedestrians to flip him a well-deserved bird. As he squeezed out of his car in the empty garage, he surreptitiously checked out the dark-haired man sitting in the solar energy van across the street. Before Jake got a good look, the suspicious man swung around to peer into the bowels of the van, shielding his face.

Unease skittered under Jake's skin. After Lily had gone to bed last night, he'd swept the house for surveillance equipment but hadn't found any bugs. The damn devices were so small you needed special equipment to find them. Ric had the equipment and time for a thorough sweep.

He disengaged the alarm and rushed through the kitchen. Lily's floral perfume clung to the air, creating a persistent stirring within him. He took the stairs to her bedroom two at a time. Empty, suitcases gone.

"Darlin', where are you?" Steel claws gouged his soul in fear of losing her, or living without her in his life.

Kids whooping in the neighbor's backyard prompted him to move. He rushed down to the kitchen, the jangle of the wall phone halting him in his tracks.

"Lily?" he barked into the handset. A derisive laugh

met his ears. Philip Sheehan. "You son of a bitch." Jake punched the counter. "I told you to keep her out of this."

"Considering the fact that I don't take orders from you, it's none of your business."

"Where is she?" Jake snagged a bottle of water out of the fridge. "Where'd she go after your lunch?"

A chuckle chased Philip's words. "I was calling her, compelled to add a tidbit to our lunchtime conversation."

Jake gulped down half the bottle, the cold water sating the angry fire in his throat. "Look, asshole, stay away from her. Anything to do with the chalice goes through me."

"Not after today." Another chuckle. "Ms. Falbrooke's quite the beautiful and appealing adversary a man could sink his—"

Jake bristled at the idea of Philip sinking *anything* into Lily. He pounded the off button and slammed the phone on the counter. Philip was a cylinder short of an eight-banger, and Jake had to bide his time while he hunted for evidence to tender the man up as someone's prison bitch. And to obtain the chalice and the entire Twilight collection. And keep Lily alive and safe. *Ten tons of problems.*

The last rays of sunlight lit spikes on the stone floor. Darkening clouds gathered, preparing to crush the light. Just what he needed, another early fall rainstorm to impede his search. When he returned the cordless to the base, he spied an empty key hook sticking out from the corkboard next to the phone. The key ring with the white miniature skis was missing. He'd replaced the key on the hook during their cleanup after the break-in. Fear slunk deeper, a blistering vine coiling in his torso, its tentacles reaching for his heart. Guild Guardian rule number one: don't get romantically involved with your charges. *Too damn late.*

Scrambling like a rabid dog, he called Ric from the backyard to avoid possible audio bugs in the house. A half-hour later, he was packed and Ric had emptied out his SUV in the closed garage. His brother finished a sweep of the house and found five audio bugs, including one in his loft apartment. Ric disarmed all but the one in the kitchen. Jake didn't want to play his card too soon, so they remained in the kitchen and jabbered about muscle cars and football for the benefit of their spy.

Ric chugged down his beer. "I need to get going, bro." He winked at Jake, setting in motion Operation Bait and Switch. "Got me a date with a sweet little babe I met last night." Ric's New Orleans accent was barely discernible after the years he'd grown up in California. Of the three McAllister brothers, only Jake as the oldest had retained a skosh of his southern drawl.

Ric shared his same build and height, same color hair. He could pass off as Jake's twin except for Jake's longer hair and stubble. Jake stuck Ric's baseball cap on and tucked his hair under the cap, then slipped on Ric's New Orleans Saints windbreaker. His brother agreed to stay in his apartment and watch over the house. Of course, he also had to concede use of his car *and* motorcycle to Ric's eager lead foot.

"Man, I'm out of here." Ric clinked a beer bottle on the counter. "Can't keep the wench waiting."

"Catch you later, little bro." Jake tied the top of the stuffed grocery bag he'd raided from the pantry and shouldered his overnight bag. "Don't do anything I wouldn't." He gave his brother a dark warning look and settled the cap low on his forehead to obscure his face. "*I owe you*," he mouthed.

The van still sat across the street, the driver no longer visible. Clouds stretched across the afternoon sky like a spreading bruise, appearing more like dusk. The blackening sky didn't bode well for an easy trip once he hit the Sierras, and time wasn't on his side.

⊗⊗

The phone and electricity were in working order since the dummy corp that owned the cabin kept the utilities on for renters. Lily unloaded her dinner and laptop, and locked the SUV in the garage. If necessary, she'd snag a hotel room and get out of danger's way just in case someone knew about the cabin. Ash gray clouds obliterated the blue sky, and the inclement weather dropped the temperature fast. A storm crept into the area...wind and thunderstorms according to the weather forecast. She decided to light a fire rather than turn the heater on and heat the whole house. The idea of a cheery fire answered the call to more than her comfort, and she hoped it burned away her dreaded sorrow.

Earthtone rocks extended up the walls to the ceiling and out two feet to form a hearth and bench along the wall to the windows on each side of the fireplace. Soon Lily settled on the hearth in front of a roaring fire. With the gun on the coffee table, the security alarm set, she finally relaxed.

Longing for Jake pinged her, and she wished he sat next to her enjoying the cozy and romantic setting. How had she let the man seep under her skin so fast, especially after the travesty of Daniel? Whatever mistrust she harbored toward him, she had a difficult time fighting the overriding security his presence afforded her and his damnable charisma. Was it natural? Or had he exerted some weird telepathic trick on her?

"Argh." She rubbed the goosebumps popping on her arms. "I can't think about him in that way. Not until I figure out on what side of the fence he played." Denial was her new best friend.

A shower of sparks shot up into the fireplace, fracturing her musings and sending her gaze around the large open room. One familiar spot to another brought back so many memories of joy. Regardless of the last family vacation before the accident, she sensed a peacefulness she hadn't experienced in years. Although tragedy had shattered their lives that summer, too many happy memories of her intact family kept her from dwelling on that horrid time. Was it a harbinger best left buried for another decade?

"Damn it, Denial. I'll never move on if I keep burying my head in the sand. It'll keep me from having a life...from having Jake." She sucked in a breath. "Holy crap, Jake?" Tapping her shamrock pin, she laughed at the incongruity of her life, while also hoping for a little more four-leaf clover luck to smack her on the forehead.

Her stomach gurgled, begging for the sandwich and soup she'd picked up in town. Settling in for dinner, she poured a glass of fortifying Zinfandel wine and prepared to review the boring probate and financial documents. Eye gouging might commence in the near future.

With laptop and meal, she settled at the table and opened the stack of probate papers. The sweet fruity blend of wine seeped delicious cheerfulness in her middle and lessened her surprise at her father's healthy net worth. A few bites of her turkey pesto sandwich and the minestrone soup pacified her belly threatening to solicit a new host.

Stunned, she reread the papers and matched them to the financial reports. Her father had amassed millions, leaving his entire estate to her. At least she now understood Jake hadn't finagled himself more into her father's life than what he'd confessed. His partnership in the law firm wasn't a full equal share, relieving her mistrust of him several more notches.

The Guardian in question was probably swearing up a storm knowing she'd escaped his so-called expert protection. She snickered, wiped crumbs off her keyboard. Red-flagged messages from Elizabeth and Dawn earned her immediate attention. She emailed Elizabeth and told her she needed time to clear her head. Monday was soon enough to resurrect her life in San Jose and take up her position as majority owner of the law firm.

Reluctantly, she emailed Marisa and informed her she needed to stay in San Jose indefinitely to run her father's law firm. *"You can always drive my clothes up and take a perch with me,"* she hinted, tapping *"xoxo"*.

Next up, she emailed her resignation to her boss. Truth of the matter, for the past six months, she'd thought long and hard about returning to San Jose. Her father's death had become her catalyst. During the years she'd resided in San Diego, she'd always felt the pull of home in every email and phone call from her father, Elizabeth, or her old friends.

Logs in the fireplace popped and sizzled, competing with the increasing roar of the wind outside. Lily toted her tray to the kitchen. Rain pelted the roof and gusts of wind whipped the trees in a fury. By the time she wiped down the granite counters, sheets of rain slashed the house. Wind whistled through the windows, a forlorn melody expressing the isolation inside her.

In case the storm grounded her, she checked emergency supplies. Plenty of candles, matches, batteries, flashlights and a portable radio rounded out the bare necessities. Canned goods and bottled water stocked the locked pantry, and she'd already spied the generator, fuel, and kerosene heater in the garage. Windstorms occasionally knocked power out and Dad had always kept the house stocked, especially for winter trips.

The wind rattled across the roof, and she snuggled onto the couch. Entranced, she watched the flames pulse up and down in the fireplace, the crimson and ginger embers gnawing the wood. A log fell and splintered apart, splintering something inside her. She used to love sitting beside her mother on the hearth after a wintry day playing in the snow, the heat seeping into their frigid bodies. Her mother had regaled her with stories of ancient fantasy worlds in such detail Lily swore the lands in her paintings existed.

Throughout the years, when she'd ranted about her lost memories to her father, he comforted her, told her, *"Things in your life will pop up on their own when you're ready to receive them. Like tomorrow, you'll wake up and step into the day. Sometimes it'll be an easy day. Other days will be challenging and hateful and all you'll want to do is crawl back under the covers. Either way, you'll be ready for whatever life throws at you. All you can do is buckle in and ride the ebbs and flows from one day to the next."*

A loud gust knocked a branch against the side of the house, clawing its way into the cabin and under her skin. Lily drew the afghan to her chin, debated leaving for the hotel. "Don't freak out while you're in a cabin in the woods by yourself," she berated herself. "Or call now for a white jacket and padded cell."

A red ember shot out of the narrow opening in the fire screen onto the hearth, balancing on the edge. She leaped up and brushed the ember back with the fireplace shovel before it fell onto the floor, and she banked the fire in preparation to leave. As she returned the small shovel to the tool stand, the memory of her mother showing her a secret hiding place in the wall snapped a bolt of illumination in her head.

Her heartbeat quickened, and she scrutinized the

rocks behind the wood box. Surely, her father had found it. Or had he even known the cubby existed? Lily pushed the box aside and studied the stones. Rocks in various shades of cream, beige, and taupe appeared solid within the grout lines. She pried and pulled at them. Zilch to the nth degree. Flushed, she rolled up the sleeves of her sweater and studied the right side of the fireplace.

"Bingo. The wood box used to sit on the other side."

It didn't take long to locate the loose rock from the picture emerging in her brain. She yanked, and the stone grated along the side rocks and slid forward. A satchel nestled in the hollow, and she drew the bundle out. Reverently, Lily stared at the smooth leather pack, defying it to be a figment of her imagination or delusions of cheap wine.

Lightning danced in the sky and thunder rocked the house. Branches batted the porch cover. The sharp bang of an object blown onto the deck unglued her, sending her jumping up. She double-checked the windows and doors, then returned to the false security of her afghan.

A leather tie wrapped around a wooden bead secured the flap of the worn leather envelope. A leather-bound book filled the pouch. She drew it out and traced the tooled Celtic knots banding both sides. Embossed in gold on the center of the front cover read, "The McKenna Legacy, by Roselyn McKenna Falbrooke."

She set the empty pouch on the burl-wood coffee table and read the inscription on the inside flap: *To my flower child, Lily. This is your heritage as well as mine. I love you with all my heart, Mom.*

Fresh tears cascaded. After an epic cryfest, she drowned her sorrow with the Zinfandel. Drinking herself into oblivion wasn't such a bad idea, but she'd never get on the road if she drank one more drop.

Her mother's familiar neat handwriting crammed the

journal from first page to last. Turning to the beginning, she began to read.

The storm windows rattled alarmingly, but her mind refused to allow it to disturb the score of a lifetime. The words she read hovered in the air, engrossing, unnerving. The lights flickered, a snap like a bullwhip crackled, and the cabin plummeted into darkness as the power blew out.

Excitement fluttering in her heart, she snagged the flashlight she'd found in the pantry and lit the journal. She didn't know how long she sat reading before reality knocked her back to the present. Misty eyes cleared as she bound the book in its leather casing. By the dwindling light of the fireplace, she returned the journal to its nest.

She sat back and absorbed what she'd read. The journal contained so much information about her mother and the McKenna family of psychics, and her own clairvoyant abilities from before the accident. All the history about the Twilight collection and its power and worth to their family dating back centuries. How to use the collection, especially why she should be wearing the ring to protect herself from those who could stake a claim to her mind. The fact that her mind was an open sieve and that any psychic worth his or her salt could latch onto her if she didn't maintain her walls. She snickered. As far as she was concerned, her walls were pretty permanent with her forced suppression. Maybe her suppression wasn't such a bad thing if any old psychic had the ability to control her. Her snicker evolved into a shudder. The journal contained so many missing chapters to the book of her life.

Branches scraped along the side of the house more insistently. A dull thud hit the back porch, and her heart lurched. Faint scrabbling noises on the front porch ceased any attempts at calm. No trees grew close to the front, nor was there anything on the porch at the mercy of the storm. Flashlight in hand, she snuck to the door and peered through the slats of the wooden blinds. The sheeting rain and darkness obscured her view a few feet beyond the covered porch.

Paranoia bested her, and she stuck her gun into the waistband of her pants, the steel cold against her spine. The measure of safety evaporated after another insistent rustling at the mudroom door. The doorknob rattled and something scratched the doorframe. She waited for a knock or someone to call her name. Nothing.

Lily vaulted up the stairs to the open loft, gun in one hand, flashlight in the other. The back porch door was visible from the farthest of the four upstairs bedrooms— her brother Kevin's old room. She turned the flashlight off and ran to the window in his room. For several moments, she focused on the downstairs door, gaining her night vision. Fierce streaks of light splintered the sky, illuminating a man on the porch. She clapped a hand over her mouth and choked down a strangled scream.

CHAPTER FIFTEEN

A shadowy figure peeked through the blind slats of the window beside the back door, too short to be Jake. Had a bounty hunter followed her from San Francisco? Was someone watching the cabin? Who else had a burning urge to venture out in a storm? Had she reset the house alarm? *No, no, no!* No electricity. No protection other than the cold, hard weapon in her grip. Screw Denial. The gun was her new best friend.

Glass shattered and tinkled onto the tile of the mudroom floor. The wood blinds rattled and clanged. Adrenaline popped in her veins, sending her pulse racing. She refused to wait and let the cretins who'd killed her father destroy her. She refused to grant them one more point on their score sheet. *Hell to the no.*

Lily felt for the key in her pocket, scoured her mind for passages from her mother's journal. There was a reason the collection remained hidden. A reason why her father died to keep it buried. Absent her parents' guidance, she owed it to them and their heritage to do the right thing. Plan solidified, she crept down the dark as death hallway to the stairs, her socks soundless on the hardwood.

The smoldering fire hissed and popped, offering proof

to her presence on a silver platter. Weighty footsteps wafted up from the great room. Through the spindles of the wrought-iron banister, she spied an average-height, stocky man garbed in black from his leather boots to his dark beanie. His left hand engulfed an ominous gun.

"I know you're here, Lily Falbrooke," the familiar hoarse Italian voice greeted. *Well, hello not-so-gentle-man who'd pushed me into my car and threatened to turn my ass into grass.* "Cozy setup you got going in the old family home. Show yourself and let's have ourselves a little chit chat." Footsteps clomped toward the stairway.

She jerked back and a floorboard squeaked beneath her feet. Wincing, she bit her bottom lip, tasting the metallic tang of copper.

"Where ya gonna go from upstairs, girl?" His voice glided closer. "Planning on jumping out a second story window?" He sniggered like a Chihuahua sneezing. "I just want to talk. No harm, no foul."

Lily took the bait to lure him closer. "I've called the sheriff."

"Doubt that," he paused, sniggered again. "Your phone's on the table next to your laptop. Try again."

"I have a satellite phone. Who doesn't up here?" The sneer in her voice rolled out strong despite the desperate lie pinning her to the hallway wall above the great room.

"Then we don't have much time to lose, do we? Give me what I want and I'll be on my way. Simple as that."

How simple? How much of the Twilight lore did he know? Did he know the purported psychic uses of the sapphires were next to useless without a true-blooded descendant of the Kings of Tara? Did he want them simply for their priceless value?

"You didn't call on the forty-seventh hour. I thought you gave up."

"You didn't heed my advice and stay away from the

Guild. McAllister got in my way. Shit changed. No rules now. Time's up."

His footsteps thumped on the stairs, the persistent knock on the third step giving way under his weight. Lily scooched along the wall closer to the stairs, aimed the gun down the stairwell, and fired blind near the man's thighs.

A roar charged the air, a whoosh of motion, and a snarling heft threw her backward. Her backside slammed the hardwood, nearly knocking the wind out of her sails. He followed her downward spiral and nailed her to the floor. She lost her gun and it skidded under the loft coffee table. A beefy hand snarled in her hair and banged her skull against the floor. Pain lanced her head and stars winked in her murky vision. The man's cigar-breath itched her nose, and she sneezed in his face, giving her a second to grope for her gun while he wiped his arm across his face.

"Fucking bitch." He grappled her as she writhed to escape his oppressive body.

Blood seeped out of his left thigh, dampening her jeans. Touching him left an imprint of evil on her mind, an igniting ember. She experienced a sudden helplessness beneath him. Hands encircled her neck, and she concentrated on that tiny flame, digging deeper, at the same time trying to roll them closer to her gun. His dead weight mashed her down, and as he pressed on her windpipe, her air supply diminished. One more suffocating roll to the left and her hand butted against the gun. Flirting in and out of coma territory, she managed to press the end of the gun barrel against his temple.

His hands flopped off her neck and she gulped in air. They stilled, his body imprisoning her. The mournful wind outside eclipsed the sounds of their ragged panting. A double blaze of lightning lit the tableau for a second, the precipitating boom of thunder drowning out the thundering of her heart in her ears.

"Do it, bitch. But it won't help you, 'cause you'll never live to keep your hands on Twilight."

"What's the collection worth to you? Who do you work for?"

He snorted and his skin grew ashen. "Everyone in the biz wants to steal Twilight. As long as the collection's in play, it'll be at risk. *You'll* be at risk. Give me the chalice...we'll call it a day. You keep the collection...until someone else claims it. I walk. You live. For now."

"You work for the Cabal? The Guild? Philip Sheehan? Randy Campbell." Jake and Ric's names were on the tip of her tongue, and she paused, not ready to place her bet, not ready to hear his answer. "Did you kill my father?"

"Doesn't matter."

"Matters to me," she said through gnashed lips, fighting the numbing pain of him flattening her torso into a pancake.

"I didn't kill your old man." Blood soaked her pants, the metallic scent churning her stomach. Had she hit his femoral artery? Lily gathered her inner strength and heaved upward, dislodging him enough to scurry out from under his body. Eyes closed, he rolled onto his back and stiffened. She knew next to nothing about first aid, other than to tie a rope around his thigh above the wound to slow the blood loss.

"Dude?"

No reply.

She prodded her toe into his shoulder. No movement.

Gun to his temple, she checked his carotid pulse. Nothing. Tears streamed down her cheeks, and she checked again. Dead.

She sagged to her hands and knees, her palms landing in the pool of blood dribbling onto the hardwood. A sharp pain slashed her skull, and his evil intent broke down a mental barrier. Philip Sheehan's visage materialized, and she saw the two men arguing on a pier in San Francisco. Sheehan handed the man a thick envelope. The man rifled through a stack of bills, satisfied with the payout. The image of the chalice flashed through her mind even though she'd never laid eyes on it—a large pewter receptacle. Celtic knots and an ancient script engraved it, and round sapphires studded the stem. Mystical, mysterious, luring and lost. The sensations floated in Lily's consciousness, diving into a black hollow when the howling wind whipped a fresh splat of rain against the landing window and drove her out of her clairvoyant trance. Cringing, she sat back on her knees, frantically wiping her bloodied hands on her pants, wanting the blood off her skin so bad, she'd soak them in bleach to rid her of the man's imprint.

"What the what?" she choked out the words. Was that what her mother meant by Lily reading the imprints people left behind? Different from the vague random impressions that typically surprised her.

Over the last decade, she'd experienced distant memories from her lost time, like an underground flow of lava that never ceased moving. It reached the air at times in tiny puffs of smoke, gone in an instant. The tidbit turned molten, sweeping her along into those strange foggy cogs on the wheel of her own private hell. She never comprehended if the images or sensations were memories or prescient visions of her life or belonging to another entirely.

Lily took deep breaths to re-center her mind and body the way she'd learned in yoga class. She gathered her wandering emotions and dragged the man into the first bedroom, a former guest room.

Oh my God. I killed a man. Her knees gelled. The price of admission into her shitstorm just quadrupled.

In the upstairs hall bathroom, she scoured her hands raw, sinking farther into a dark hole bursting with the remnants of her old life and her new nightmare.

CHAPTER SIXTEEN

A severe thunderstorm had knocked out power in parts of the region, and a sense of foreboding tailgated Jake to Tahoe. Rain slashed his windshield and even with the wipers on high, he barely made out the cabin in the dark until he parked in the empty driveway. No lights, not a sign of life. What if Lily hadn't driven up to Tahoe? What if the Cabal or a bounty hunter had captured her? *No. No. Can't think like that.* All his instincts pointed to Tahoe...even the slight tug on his telepathy didn't disappoint his gut.

He parked Ric's SUV in the driveway and braved the downpour. Wind whipped his hair out of his face, and rain stung his eyes and nose. Head dipped, he slogged toward the garage and shined his flashlight through the lone window on the side. A late model SUV with a rental agency sticker was parked inside. Relief coursed through his tense body.

As he rounded the rear of the garage, a human blur rammed him into the wall and kept on running.

"Hold up!" He gained his balance and yanked his gun out of his shoulder holster. A crunch and crash sounded in the foliage leading into the park lands beyond the property. The blurry silhouette of a man raced into the forest greenbelt.

"Better run far and fast." The wind tore the words away as Jake lowered his gun. He used the porch railing to guide him along the slick path and up the steps to the back door. Wood blinds clanged against the frame of a broken window next to the door. Icicles crawled across his flesh, freezing his too brief moment of relief.

Jake dug out the spare key Michael had given him months ago when he'd told Jake about the cabin and how he'd hidden his ownership behind a rental company. Dying to see Lily alive and well, he unlocked the door and stomped into the dark, too static house. A smidgen of her fear merged in his mind, a stronger presence than any other he'd experienced since breaching her mind. Embers sizzled in the fireplace, the living room empty. "Lily? You here?" No response.

Tearing through the first floor, he flicked the flashlight in each dark corner, checked the kitchen, bathroom, laundry room and bedroom before making his way up the staircase. He passed through the loft, tripped over a lump on the floor in the first bedroom and again banged into the wall to catch his balance.

"Son of a bitch." Sweat grew in his pits. Another dose of apprehension bristled along his skin. Fearing what he stumbled over, he decided to return to check out the speed bump on the floor after investigating the other bedrooms.

He scoped out a bathroom and two other empty bedrooms, then stopped at the closed door of the fourth bedroom. He shoved the flashlight in his pocket and hefted his gun. As he nudged the door open, something hard whacked the back of his head, cold and calculating.

The blow dropped him to his knees. His grip on his gun weakened, and the weapon clanged to the floor. He fought the wave of nausea threatening to send him to oblivion. Dizziness wrecked him, and he pinched the doorframe to hold himself from face-planting onto the floor.

"Don't move. I've got a gun!" Lily's familiar voice untied the knots he didn't know had tied his intestines into a basket weave. "I'll blow another hole in your ass if you move a muscle."

"Lily, it's me," he managed to rasp out the words.

A beam lit him from behind. "Jake!" She ran a hand over his temple, into his wet hair. "Oh, no. Are you okay?" She squeezed in between him and the doorjamb and squatted in front of him.

Her silhouette was a precious sight for his blurry vision. "No. Help me up," he said tersely.

She let him put his arm around her shoulder while he attempted to stand. "I'm sorry. You scared the crap out of me."

"The bed," he snapped. He swallowed rough several times to avoid losing his drive-thru hamburger. The back of his knees bumped the bed. He leaned down slowly, his feet dangling to the floor. His head hit the pillow and lightning bolts shot through his skull. "Not...working. Help. Me. Up."

She assisted him into a sitting position, and he hung his head between his knees to stop the room from spinning. It made his head throb worse, but checked his budding queasiness.

Light bounced off the walls, illuminating Lily. She knelt in front of him, cupping his cheeks in both hands.

"Look at me," she said. Slowly, he raised his head a fraction. "How many fingers am I holding up?"

She held his chin with one hand while the other held up what he believed were two fingers, or maybe four. He took his best shot. "Two."

"Good. Can you stand?"

Uncontrollable tremors chattered his teeth. "Let

me...lay down." He listed to the side, and Lily caught him in her arms before he fell.

"You probably have a concussion. The last thing you need is sleep." The control in her lilting voice was a godsend. "I need to get you downstairs. Can you walk?"

"I think so." His head hurt like a son of a bitch.

Squatting, she swung his arm across her shoulders. "Lean on me."

They struggled down the stairs, Lily guiding him to the couch. Too spent to budge another inch, he leaned on one arm to hold himself upright. Lily peeled off his boots and jacket. She ran out of the room and returned with water, aspirin, and a plastic bag filled with ice.

"This'll hurt." She eased the ice pack against the knot above his neck. He gritted his teeth, stifling a groan. She sat next to him and held the ice pack in place.

The firelight danced across her face and he'd never seen her so lovely, so ethereal, like the angel he'd first witnessed at the cemetery. He wrapped a tendril of her fiery hair around his finger, caressed her cheek. "Thanks."

"For cold-cocking you?"

"For knowing what to do. And for being here alive and safe."

She frowned. "Were you worried?"

"Yes, and I'll deal with you later for disobeying me." The ice worked its magic and the pain began to abate.

"Disobeying?" she echoed. A tiny smile curled up his lips. She flicked his thigh. "Oh...you're joking."

"What did you hit me with?"

"Your gun."

"Damn, Lily, if you're gonna knock a man out, you need to know where to hit him." His hand covered hers and held it against the ice on the base of his neck.

"I tried." She winced. "Well, hell, I've only seen it done in the movies. Give me a contract and I can tear it apart, but guns and bounty hunters—"

Tremors took over his body, and she leaned in closer to lend him her inviting warmth. "What's with you women and your guns? Juliana practically blew off my toe last week."

"Are you kidding me? Is that why you limp?" She kinked her head to the side. "Wait a hot minute. *You* gave me the gun to protect myself."

"I kinda threatened her when we were up on Mt. Hamilton investigating before the funeral. She wanted to see if her touch telepathy might give her a clue, and I wasn't much of a gentleman at first."

Lily giggled. "I knew I liked her for a reason."

"Ha fucking ha. If you two start hanging out together, stay far away from me."

"Hold the ice pack." Lily slipped her hand out from under his and grabbed the puddled afghan off the floor. Snuggling close to his side, she wrapped the blanket around them, and her warmth penetrated his glacial flesh. "Better?"

"Infinitely." If she edged her hand any higher on his thigh, she'd be privy to the hard evidence of his desire, and he wasn't talking about the lump on his head. Jake adjusted his jeans under the blanket, easing the pressure. "What's on the floor in the first bedroom upstairs? I nearly brained myself tripping over it." Lily shuddered, and Jake hugged her closer to his side. A pleasant jolt of surprise shot into him when she allowed him to tighten his embrace.

"The man who pushed me in my car followed me here. Didn't you see the broken window in the mudroom?" Her soft body tensed against him. "I'm not so bad at self-defense, in case you were wondering."

His dismay mushroomed. "No shit. What did you do to him? Is he tied up?"

A sob jiggled Lily against him. She sniffed, opened her mouth, shut it.

"So I wasn't your first victim tonight?" He tried to lighten the tension. When she didn't speak, he said softly, "He's dead?"

After a long pause, she told him what'd happened and the threat the man had made the other day. Jake flipped the blanket off and struggled to rise.

"Where do you think you're going?" Lily's hand landed on his chest, and she tried to hold him in place.

"To board up the window. See who's upstairs. Make sure no one else is hanging outside. Someone dashed off when I arrived." Reluctantly, he shifted her hand from over his heart and set it on her thigh. "Help me. We'll make it fast. I need to unload." With Lily bracing him, he stood and his head only wobbled once while he gained a woozy balance. "Once the Guild got wind of the Italian guy, we had a target on him, but he slipped surveillance. Why didn't you tell me about the threat earlier?"

Lily bit her bottom lip, fessed up. "I was afraid he'd come after you and Elizabeth. He warned me to keep mum or else. Then he didn't call and I brushed it off."

Once outside, the wind whipped their hair around and rain soothed Jake's fevered cheeks. A clear set of boot prints and sneaker prints sank into the mud beyond the front porch. Fighting the storm and Jake's zapped energy, they cased the perimeter of the house and discovered another set of boot prints in the planters near the back porch. They followed the trail, but it veered into the federal lands behind the house.

"The other guy's long gone. I doubt he'll return since I'm here."

Silent, they carried Jake's bags and her suitcases into the house. He boarded up the window with plywood they found in the garage. They checked the man upstairs, then rolled his body in a tarp and dragged him out to the garage.

Lily opened her mouth, shut it. After a short pause, she asked, "What's next?" She fisted her shamrock pin. He loved that she placed so much faith in the luck of the Irish and hoped she always had Lady Luck in her back pocket.

Fighting to remain out of her head, he knew from her expression that she hid things from him. "Nothing. We'll deal with him in the morning."

"What if his accomplice returns?"

"Then we'll deal with it." A bone-numbing exhaustion snuck up on him, and after changing into dry clothes, he collapsed onto the couch.

"You look like crap." Lily laid the back of her hand on his forehead.

"Concussion, probably." A flush had worked up his neck, but he shivered as a chill attacked his exposed extremities. "Why did you come up here?"

Lily threw a couple logs on the fire and stoked it into a blaze. Silent, she lit candles scattered around the great room. Finally, she replied, "I needed to get away to think."

"Then you weren't *thinking* when you picked this place."

She spun around. "You don't have to be rude. I came prepared. And I wasn't planning on staying overnight. I have hotel reservations under a fake name."

Her hands rested on the waistband of her low rise sweatpants, her long-sleeved sweater pulled taut across her pert breasts. He licked his lips. The firelight lit bright sparkles of annoyance in her emerald eyes. Again, he didn't think he'd seen her so tantalizingly gorgeous.

"As far as the world knows, my dad sold this place. No one knows he owns it, except you, I guess. Seemed safer than home."

His eyes swam and his head clouded up.

Lily rushed over to him. She propped pillows up to keep the back of his head from making contact with the sofa, then draped the blanket over him. "You're cold *and* burning up. How do you feel?"

"Like I was struck by lightning."

Before he knew it, Lily crawled under the blankets and wrapped her arms around his torso. Instinctively, he snuggled her close. The warmth of her soft, supple body penetrated faster than a dozen blankets.

He smiled, inhaling her fruity shampoo. "This feels good."

"Don't get excited. This is just until you warm up. Besides, you're in my bed."

"Exactly where I want to be."

A hush settled over them as both adjusted to the presence of the other.

Lily leaned her head on his shoulder. "I experienced a weird vision upstairs, a clairvoyant thing. I think my psychic powers are breaking open my blocks."

Jake glanced his head off the couch arm. Pain shot anew through his skull. The idea that his telepathic delving precipitated her breakthrough shot a tremor of excitement into his chest. He probed her mind and met the same resistance he'd experienced all day.

"We have to talk tomorrow. Sheehan contacted me to gloat."

Lily's entire length tensed iron-hard against him. "He can wait."

"I thought finding your father's murderer was the most important thing."

"It is." She snuggled closer. "I...it's...for a long time I've felt like I didn't know who I was."

"Who better than a PI to help you figure it out?"

"Easy for you to say. Until this week, I had no clue of

my identity. Now all of a sudden—" Her lips clamped together. "Sorry, I can't talk about this right now."

They lay on their sides facing each other, a hair's breadth between their faces, Lily's head pillowed on Jake's arm. She smelled of fresh meadows in the spring sun, and Jake savored the heavenly scent. Their eyes locked and didn't waver. She caressed his arm, his shoulders. Through his fleece sweatshirt, her touch created sensations inside him he had a difficult time naming. He longed to feel her hands on his skin, but he'd come undone if she touched his bare flesh.

"Jake," she whispered, pressing her forehead to his.

His lips brushed hers once, twice, stirring the air, until he rested his mouth on hers. Their lips pressed together for several long seconds, then ever so leisurely he parted her lips between his and the kiss deepened. Their tongues entwined in a slow sensuous dance. The kiss turned passionate and took Jake to a high he worried toppling from and smashing into a million pieces.

She lay flush against him in a perfect fit. He snuck his hand beneath her blouse and stroked the silky skin of her back while she weaved his damp hair, her delicate touch shooting tingles straight to their hard-as-a-rock target. Never before had he felt such an intimacy with another woman, from a touch and a kiss, tongues exploring each other's mouth in an evocative ritual. He wanted to caress and kiss her all night, not ram himself into her to slake his perpetual hunger for her.

He plastered himself around her soft curves. He'd never been so hard before. The exquisite throbbing dulled the horrible banging in his skull. The timing was wrong, and he wanted to savor the moment he buried himself inside her, clear-headed and pain free.

Jake's mind nudged hers, trying to locate her open doors. Did she feel him? At that moment, he held no regrets for exacting the illegal and intrusive deed. Instead of butchering his career in the Guild, it may save him in ways he had yet to comprehend.

After several long moments lip-locked in the most passionate kiss he'd never forget, they broke apart, gasping for illusive air. Unrestrained desire hazed her dark eyes. He knew his own eyes mirrored her lust.

"Lily," he rasped out, brushing the tousled hair off her face with one hand, the other resting possessively on her back. "I want you."

"Really? I couldn't tell." She slipped her hand between their bodies and rested it on the stiff bulge in his sweatpants.

Jake sucked in his breath. "Be careful or you'll get more than you bargained for."

"Surely, you have more control than a teenager," she kidded.

"Not with you around." The pressure of her hand increased, moving it up and down the length of his erection. He groaned. "Stop." He halted her hand from exacting further excruciating damage. "Tomorrow, that's all yours."

Easing away, a frown replaced her regret. "I'm sorry. I don't know what sorry soul's possessed me. It's a mistake to take this any further." She lifted the covers and struggled to escape his arms.

He hauled her down and pinned her between him and the couch. Headache be damned. "You're not going anywhere."

"Let me up, Jake." Ire mashed her swollen, pouty lips.

Jake kissed her nose. "Give a dying man his last wish." Tenderly, he caressed her face, his fingers catching in her mass of deep red tresses.

"Give me a break. You're not dying." Feebly, she pushed at him, exerting no real insistence.

He trailed his lips across her neck, whispered in her ear, "I will have you. When all my senses are alive."

"You think so." A little click sounded in her throat.

"You want me." A statement rather than a question.

"Like hell. I was granting you comfort so you didn't sue me for assault."

Despite his brain revolting to escape his skull, Jake roared in laughter.

"Laugh all you want, macho man. We'll see who wins the war."

A thundering bolt of pain blasted his head, and he stifled a moan. "Screw me now." His strength flowed off his shoulders, down his arms. "If you're going, then go and let me rest in peace."

Lily struggled out from under him, propped herself up on her elbow, and felt his flushed cheek. "Are you okay?"

"No." Her fingers were torture on his skin, and the painful throbbing in his groin intensified its tempo.

"Can you be serious? What do you need?"

A few moments of silence escaped. "To touch you. To guide you out of the darkness."

To his dismay, she left the couch, and he stifled a different kind of groan. *Damn.* As she tossed a couple logs on the fire and banked it for the night, her petite curves incited feelings he wanted to deny. She left to blow out the candles. Too many minutes crawled by. Sleep bogged down his eyelids, and he was almost dead to the world when the soft sounds of clothing dropping onto the floor shook him awake.

"Jake?"

Stunned hardly described the feelings she kindled in his blood. Naked except for crimson bikini underwear, she seemed to float between him and the fireplace. Her alabaster skin glowed peachy in the firelight, her petite body perfection. Her hair cascaded around her shoulders and over her breasts, almost midnight black against her pale skin, throwing off spikes of fiery red. He held his hand out to her. Ignoring it, she rolled up his sweatshirt, exposing his abdomen, his bare chest, and he helped her raise it over his head.

They stared at each other for eons. "I want to touch you, too," she admitted shyly.

He scooted over on the couch and made room for her again. She snuggled into his open arms, at first not moving, both lost in the feel of flesh against flesh. Tentatively, he outlined her right breast, circled it, then cupped it, a perfect fit in his palm. Not too big, not too small, just the right size and weight. Flawlessness in his hand.

She stifled a cry, and his lips kicked up. Her hands explored his chest, his light smattering of chest hair, fueling the inferno building inside him. Jake molded her softness to his cold, solid angles. They twined their arms around each other, and her body heat injected the medicine he needed to placate his bone-snapping cold.

A log disintegrated and collapsed into fragments, shooting up a whirlwind of sparks that vanished quickly and vanquished his chill. Lying with Lily in his arms before the blazing fire with the storm raging outside satisfied Jake's every need to shelter her. Lily's tantalizing exploration of his bare skin petered out, and he waited for the proverbial shoe to drop.

"How'd you know about the darkness?" she asked. "Darkness has enveloped me and refuses to grant me a moment's peace. I have no one left, except for the memories in that darkness." She huffed. "And a crapload of them are stuck in the blackest void."

Unable to speak for a moment, Jake's quivering lips lingered on her hair. "I know how you feel. I miss Michael too. That bugger seeped under my skin in such a short time. You know how appealing he is...was. I miss cooking for him, spending dinners together. He actually enjoyed my half-assed cooking."

"Dad didn't discriminate when it came to food. I'm the worst cook alive and he always ate what I cooked. How do you know how I feel? You have a family."

"Both my parents are dead. We grew up with my aunt and uncle in San Jose."

"Oh. I'm sorry. I know so little about you."

"The Guild gave me and my brothers a sense of family." He snuggled her so close, she became an extension of him. "You have me, Elizabeth, the Guild. We're your family now."

She sighed. "My life has flipped into a hundred degrees of crazy. I don't feel safe or content anymore."

"You're safe with me." Jake kissed her head. "I won't ever hurt you. Your ancestors and family defended and died for Twilight. I won't let you die for it."

She kissed his chest, held him tight to her. The world disappeared except for the two of them. They fell asleep bonded to one another by their skin, their touch, and the strange magic of the multi-faceted connection that had brought them together.

CHAPTER SEVENTEEN

Steely arms embraced Lily, molding her to his hard body. The man murmured words of adoration in her ear. He caressed her back, and his hand slipped to her stomach where he skimmed his fingers over her sensitive skin, igniting her nerve endings.

"You're mine," he whispered. "Only I can protect you and give you what you need. Come to me."

"I'm here, aren't I?" She tipped her head back, expecting to gaze into Jake's aquamarine eyes and recoiled in surprise at the face of the handsome stranger from the pier restaurant. Connor something or other. She struggled in his arms, but his grip tightened.

"You're not—" She was about to say "Jake" until he cut in.

"Trust me. I won't ever hurt you, or let anyone else hurt you." Arms loosened and she tumbled into the safe haven of Jake's arms as if she'd come home after a harrowing trip to hell.

Venturing a peek upwards, she feared whose face she'd view. But Jake's face greeted her, a fierce desire bordering on love in his expression. "I knew it was you," she whispered.

The freaky dream dissipated and Lily awakened.

That blasted feather breached her mind again, its fluttering disturbing yet not unpleasant. Face buried in Jake's chest, his roped arms held her so close her breasts pressed flat against his torso. Last night, she believed she'd awaken to regret her decision to sleep in his arms, but it felt so right. Not that they'd gone beyond touching and a few kisses.

"It's an act of trust to sleep with another person. Simply sleeping in each other's arms can bring two people closer than the physical joining of bodies." Lily recalled Marisa's words. She'd never experienced such complete and absolute trust with any man. Until that moment. The intimacy of sleeping together in the near buff without taking it to the next level had been incredibly erotic, and she'd never forget the sensations, even if it may have been their equivalent of a hit and run.

She danced her fingers along Jake's arm, skipping from one little white scar to another until she counted seven. In sleep, his expression adopted a boyish charm, and his lips kicked up and deepened his dimples. She brushed her lips over his, started to dip her tongue into one of the tiny depressions, but lucidity barreled over her, startling her into action to escape his body before she sank too deep.

The fire had died, leaving ashes and a chilly Tahoe morning. The electricity was still out. She needed to rekindle the fire, or they'd never escape the warmth of their bodies. Not a bad idea. But she had things to handle—matters to discuss. A body to report to the sheriff. *Ugh.*

Remorse chased the goosebumps bursting on her arms. She'd shot a man. Dead. Even if he had broken into her house and threatened her with bodily harm. She was a lawyer for hell's sake, not a cold-blooded murderer. Criminal law theories tumbled in her brain. She'd confess the truth to the sheriff and take the hit. No ifs, ands, or buts. Self-defense, defense of property. The man broke in, aimed a gun at her, threatened body and home, threatened to steal from her. Open and shut case. Still didn't appease the guilt poking at her.

She considered waking Jake, but he needed his sleep after the blow she'd rained on him. Guilt staked another claim, and she satisfied it with a contributory negligence allegation. He shouldn't have snuck up on her and scared her halfway to the grave.

Without waking him, she eased out of his entwined limbs, quickly donned her clothes in the cool room, and then revived the fire. Once flames roared to life, she opened the blinds on the bay window. A glorious sun had burned away the clouds and chased off the thunderstorm. Leaves, fir needles, and tree branches littered the wet, sparkling yard, and she had the urge to view the placid lake up close in her slice of heaven.

Using what little warm water she managed to squeeze out of the hot water heater, she freshened up, changed her clothes, and stuck her phone and gun in her jacket pockets.

Once outside, sunlight blinded her, and she took a moment to adjust her sight. The crisp coolness refreshed the morning, and she breathed in deep to cleanse her lungs. The air smelled of a newborn forest, raw and woodsy, tinged in wood smoke. She made her way to the path leading down a slight incline to a natural ledge overlooking the lake. The year her parents had purchased the cabin, her father had installed a railing along the natural stone steps. It saved her many times from a face-plant into the boulders from the slick or icy pathway.

Sunlight shimmered off the houses edging the blue-gray lake like fairy cottages. The turreted house several hundred yards away appeared benign and lonely despite the niggling awareness in her subconscious. Lily snapped panorama shots from one side of the lake to the other, capturing the splendor to remind her of that magical morning. Her homecoming...and so much more.

"Now that's the most beautiful sight I've ever seen." Jake infiltrated the serene hush.

Pride filled her as if she'd created the lake herself. "The lake's absolutely gorgeous after a storm," she replied without turning around.

"That's not what I was referring to," he said softly behind her.

Lily blinked rapidly. "Oh," she said, afraid to confront him or lose the impact of his words.

He wrapped his arms around her waist and pulled her to his chest, clasping his hands beneath her breasts. He kissed the top of her head as she settled against him, once again feeling she'd come home, so unsettling, perplexing, and beyond delicious.

The unsullied world heightened a renewed sense of intimacy between them, as if the storm insulated them in their own tiny bubble.

"Sleep well?" she asked benignly when she wanted to ask so much more. He weaved their fingers together. "Feeling better?"

"Never better." He nuzzled her neck, his breath tickling her skin.

"I miss it here, skiing, boating, the fun times of a happy family."

"I can imagine. My family didn't do many vacations. Never enough money except an occasional trip to Disney World in Florida, local amusement parks, camping. I'd love to spend a few weeks here for some R&R." He squeezed her hand, imprinting himself on her.

They stood for several long moments, until Lily unlinked his hands and turned to face him, resisting the intense urge to maintain contact with his skin.

"How did you know I came to Tahoe?"

"I'm a PI, remember?" Smiling, he shook back his loose hair, earning her most annoyed eye roll. "I noticed the key gone."

The floodgates of reality swung open, and a mud-thick tension oozed out. "We need to talk."

"I know."

Slicing the tension, she asked, "Nice SUV. Another toy?"

"My brother's."

"Ric?" Her forehead furrowed, and she failed to hide her exasperation.

"Lily, have I given you a reason not to trust me?"

"After last night? Call me crazy." She emitted a dry laugh. "I don't think I could ever not trust you."

"Whoa, what? Who else is on that sacred list?"

"My father. Juliana. Most of all, my gut."

"You believed me when I told you Michael wanted me to watch out for you? You believe Juliana Westwood's prophecy and after-death message?"

She shrugged, hesitated, decided to test his loyalty. "My father left behind a key to a safety deposit box."

He merely smiled down at her. "You've had it all this time?"

"Since the night of the funeral." The damp cold seeped into her bones and she shivered.

Before she'd fallen asleep in his arms and after he'd made no move to take advantage of what she tentatively offered him, she'd decided she needed his help, despite what Philip Sheehan had insinuated. Not that she believed the conniving jerk after her image of Philip paying off the dead man. She glanced toward the garage, flinched. More than she cared to admit, she needed Jake's help to nail her father's murderer. Why pretend she knew how to investigate a murder? Meanwhile, she'd figure out where she fit in the bizarre world of her father and mother's creation.

"I need to ask you something that's been bugging the hell out of me." He brought her purple fingernail to his lips, and kissed it. "You know how PIs need to know everything."

"A girl's gotta have secrets, PI or not."

"You have every right not to answer." His patented grin liquefied her knees. "What's with the one purple fingernail? It's not part of your multi-color fetish."

She blinked back her surprise. He might make a great PI of the heart. In that moment, all her trust meters were spitting out welcome signs. It felt right telling him something only Marisa knew. "It reminds me of what I've lost."

He kissed her palm and tingles chased up her arm. "Darlin', your family's still in your heart. Why suffer the daily reminder?"

She laid her palm on his cheek, and he leaned into it, as if afraid to lose contact with her. "No. Not my family. It reminds me that I've lost a part of my life, my abilities, and I need to remain open for their return." Sometimes she shut down and her goal slipped into NeverNever land for a while. Even if the unknown frightened her to hell and back, she never wanted to lose sight of her goal.

Jake kissed her palm again, goose flesh chasing the tingles on her arms. "Let's go inside."

She twined her fingers in his, his firm grip comforting and said, "The power's on."

"How do you know power's on?"

"I'm psychic." Tapping her head, she suppressed a teasing smile. "The porch light's on. By the way, how's your head?"

"Not so bad. I took more aspirin. I might live to get

shot at and cold-cocked again." He rubbed the small lump on the back of his head.

Silent and thoughtful, they returned to the cabin. Lily took a long, hot sobering shower. After Jake set a steaming cup of coffee in her hands, he took her place in the downstairs bathroom.

She set the cup on the hearth, removed the rock from the wall, and dragged out the leather-encased journal. Delving deeper inside the cubby, she rummaged around until she touched the round depression she'd remembered from her myriad dreams during the night. A mix of excitement and anxiousness coursed through her. The depression popped out, revealing a tiny slide-out shelf and two keys on a key ring. She slid the shelf back and replaced the rock. The moment the rock slid into place, Lily felt the sensation of a soft and warm hand on her shoulder, sliding to her neck, and massaging out the kink that'd formed overnight.

"You always get these kinks, right here." Her mom's *empathy emerged as the memory of her fingers pressed into the aching knot. "What has caused this one, sweetheart? Did you have a bad day on the lake with your friends?"*

A dream made of sound and sensation, an impression of a forgotten past. The vision of her lost time before the accident seemed as though the reality belonged to that other person hidden within her.

Shaken and stirred, Lily shoved the journal into her briefcase, then studied the keys. One key had Bank of Tahoe stamped on it. The smaller one would fit a suitcase or small box. Scanning the large room, she wondered what the key fit. The room was devoid of anything with a lock, and the gun safe had a combination lock.

Jake strolled into the living room, toweling his hair, bare-chested in a pair of worn jeans. She loved his muscular legs in the snug jeans and forced her ogling gaze upwards. Enough of his firm chest and flat abs peeked around the towel to send Lily's heart rocketing to the moon.

She pocketed the keys before she dropped them, inwardly salivating over the man-feast before her. She wanted to touch him, but knew if she did, she'd never stop, and at the moment, she couldn't afford the distraction. Not yet. Maybe not ever.

He took four long strides toward her. "I hate this," he almost growled.

"What?" she croaked.

"This morning after awkwardness." He wrapped the towel around his neck, holding onto the ends as if he too warred to keep his hands from ravishing her. "I meant what I said last night."

"What? That you'll not hurt me?"

A dark eyebrow winged up in challenge. "I will never hurt you, nor allow anyone else to hurt you. I will never take what's yours. My sole job is to protect you. I swore an oath to the Guild, to your father, albeit a post-death oath. What I meant was, I *will* have you," he said, soft and ominous.

Another piece of her heart melted. "Why, Jake? Why do you want me?"

"You're absolutely enchanting, inside and out." He slid his hands into her hair and lowered his lips to hers, his mouth soft and sweet. Sifting her damp hair, he increased the pressure of his mouth. When she parted her lips, his tongue slipped inside the warm hollow. Swirling his tongue around hers, he tasted of minty freshness and longing. His kiss tantalized the thawing pool in her core.

The feathery strokes in her head magnified, as if Jake's mind tickled hers, mimicking the pressure of his lips. Was the intrusiveness a side effect of her awakening powers?

She didn't trust herself not to strip him bare and kept her hands fisted on her sweater when they tried bribing her head to let them exercise their right to freedom.

"Can we dispense with the BS?" His lips skimmed her cheek. "I can't stand not touching you when I want."

The naked desire in his eyes dipped to her soul, and she lost control—for a moment. She leaned forward, caressing his biceps. He smelled good enough to lick, but she did the next best thing and pressed her lips to his chin in a tender kiss, then released him. The timing was wrong for entanglements, but she couldn't deny her fierce attraction to Jake, the need pulsing in her body, filling all her senses, the desire to allow him inside her awakening mind, her most sacred place.

He groaned. "I take it that's a yes?"

"On one condition." When he tried to draw her into his arms, she resisted and he relented. "I need you to drive me to town. Then we talk before we progress." To the point of no escape, no return. "Plus we need to deal with that little problem in the garage."

"You're killing me." He mock groaned. "What's so tempting in town that'd drag you away from what I'm offering?"

"Arrogant SOB." She swatted at him. "Get dressed and let's go."

"What's in town?" He slid the towel off his neck.

"The sheriff. And the Bank of Tahoe."

"No need for the sheriff. The Guild will take care of our bundle. So you think it's the real chalice?"

"Don't ask questions."

CHAPTER EIGHTEEN

The moment Lily stepped over the threshold into the garage, prickles skated up the back of her neck. The brown tarp-wrapped bundle had vanished.

"Uh...Jake? Did the Guild already handle our problem?"

In his he-man protective role, Jake shoved in front of her, blocking her view of everything except his fine backside. "No. Shut the door and stay here."

He retreated to case the exterior. She drew her gun, snuck outside, and combed for footprints in the mud. She found Jake following a set of heavy, slogging prints leading toward the greenbelt.

Ire riding the air, Jake nailed her with a wrinkly glare. She slid her shamrock pendant back and forth on its chain, reached for her pin, realizing she hadn't worn it that day. Luck wasn't on her side. Or was it? "I checked his pulse. I thought he was dead."

He marched to the front of the garage, toed a broken stick on the ground. "Another set of prints."

"You think his allies snagged him?" Niggling doubts and the laws of self-defense left her feeling like she was crawling out of her skin. Leaves swirled around her in a sudden gust, blowing her guilt into the wind.

"Yep. Let's beat it."

Lily clambered into the sun-warmed SUV and placed her briefcase on the floor between her legs. After Jake slid into the driver's seat, she asked, "Do you think our mystery guests will try to break in while we're gone?"

"We'll know when we return." He reversed the vehicle onto the road. They'd traveled less than a mile when Jake said, "Don't look back. We're being tailed by a white pickup."

In the side mirror, she spied the truck two blocks behind them. "Fan-friggin-tastic."

"Maybe we ought to skip the bank?"

"No," she said vehemently. "I don't want to wait. We need to get out of Tahoe, and I'm not leaving without—"

"They'll know you're retrieving the chalice and jewels." Jake approached a stop sign, and the white truck slowed a few hundred yards behind them.

"Let them."

"Why gamble yourself?" He pounded his fist on the steering wheel.

"Why do you think? I need to get my hands on them. I need to understand why everyone's hunting the collection, what power it holds. It's time Twilight saw the light of dawn."

"It's too risky if it's at the bank."

"Are you afraid you can't protect me? Or the collection?" The truck behind them maintained a steady distance. She studied Jake's profile, a muscle ticking in his right jaw.

He heaved out a sigh. "You have your gun?"

She snagged the nine-millimeter out of her purse, flicked the safety off, then slid it back in. "Never party without it. Detour the bank and park at one of the big casinos." She spied the bank ahead, sitting between a towering hotel casino and a fancy strip mall. The first large casino sat a block up the street. "Park at that one." She pointed to the shimmery, glass-fronted building, the parking lot half-empty before the weekend crowd.

"You sure about this?" Jake swung to the right into the evergreen-lined parking lot behind the building, pulling into the first available spot.

"At this rate, I don't know when I'll make it up to Tahoe again. I need to see why my father died."

He gloved her hand in the warmth of his skin. "Darlin', I'm sorry. I know you do."

"You promised to protect me, no matter what?" Lily asked, hating her reliance upon a bodyguard...a man, even if he was sexy and dangerous Jake McAllister and a Guild Guardian to boot.

"No matter what." He leaned over the gap between the seats and drew Lily to him, holding her tight and brushing a reassuring kiss over her mouth before releasing her.

Jake hopped out of the SUV and searched the parking lot for the white pickup before opening her door. "He's waiting by the exit. We'll lose him in the casino."

"When I'm in the bank vault, call a cab to take us to the cabin to throw him off." She climbed down and looped the shoulder strap of her briefcase across her torso.

The bald, wiry man in the white truck sprinted after them, crouching low behind vehicles. The moment Jake and Lily entered the casino, the clinking of slot machines and piped-in music competed for attention. Jake grasped Lily's hand, and they zigzagged through slot machines and card tables, double backing now and again to lose the middle-aged man. Jake ground to a standstill behind a bank of dollar slots and she crashed against him. In one fluid move, he wheeled around and snaked his arm around her waist.

"We lost him." Grinning, she held onto his arm.

"You think this is fun?" His lips curled up. The smolder on his face made her blood sing.

"Almost as much as last night," she teased, rubbing his leather jacket sleeve.

"Why don't we check in and make use of a room while we're here?" Without waiting for a reply, he crushed his mouth to hers. The comfort of his body radiated into her, warming her too-long frozen parts. Despite their rocky beginning, he was now her island of calm in a raging storm.

She reluctantly cut the kiss short. "Let's get to the bank before we become a hitman's dream." She touched her lips to hold in his residual cinnamon taste from his incessant chomping on mints.

Grumbling, Jake led her to the side entrance, and they escaped outside without incident. They jogged to the bank, Jake glancing over his shoulders the entire block. They'd lost their tail, and grinning, Lily gave Jake a high-five.

They approached the vault counter inside the small bank. "Wait out here." She touched his cell sticking out of his front pocket, sliding her fingers across his zipper. "Call a cab. Guard my back, oh faithful Guardian."

"I'm going to spank you."

"Promises, promises."

The teller accessed the box records, and to her surprise, a close facsimile of her signature was inked on the signature card. Had she signed it before her Lost Summer? Trepidation anchored her shoulders, and with a pat on her rear from Jake, she hurried into the vault, hugging her briefcase tight to her middle.

After the teller left her with the box in a confidential alcove, she sank onto the thinly cushioned chair. Her palms dampened. The feather swished again, protecting her from her own mind's chaos. Double alarm bells rang, and her heart fluttered like a swarm of birds in her ribcage. Shaking off the odd sensations, she concentrated on opening the safety deposit box.

Will all this prove her heritage as written in her mother's journal, as Jake and Elizabeth had warned? Or was it all a sick joke in the making? She'd spent the bulk of the night reconciling the fact that she wasn't the Lily McKenna Falbrooke she'd known for twenty-eight years. Her fantasy legacy proved the restlessness of living in alien skin since her mother had passed on. Did the box hold the secrets and proof of her identity?

Mental forehead smack. "Come on, Flower of Tara, daylight's burning, bounty hunters are prowling." She peeled away the metal box lid to reveal two items: an old, worn leather jeweler's box and a large velvet pouch with a drawstring at the top. From the heft and shape of the pouch, she didn't need to peek inside to know it held a chalice. *Authentic or another lousy fake?* She resisted the strong urge to investigate the items on the spot, to lay her hands on these ancient relics denoting a scary new future. Plucking a backpack out of her briefcase, she packed the items inside and strapped it on beneath her coat.

She exited the vault and Jake's gaze devoured her, then fixated on the briefcase, a foil for the backpack. "Your friend's out front." He steered her toward the rear of the bank.

Dismay belted her. Bottom lip quivering, she stuttered to a halt.

"Don't flip out on me now. Security will let us out the employee entrance. The cab's already waiting."

"What about the guy in front?"

"Security's distracting him." His tone softened. "Don't worry. He doesn't know we're here."

"Thank you." She flashed a wan smile. "I couldn't have done this without you."

"Then do what I tell you."

The coast was clear as they left the building, slid into the cab, and drove out the back parking lot. Jake curled his arm around her shoulders and hauled her to his side, his solidness wrapping her in the haven of his body. She wanted to sink into him and test-drive him for a while without all the Twilight nonsense between them. Was she simply another Guardian assignment? Did he want her the way she wanted him, or would they just walk away when all was said and done? Or would her psychic abilities and lost memories come back to bite her big time, screwing her up for good?

Ten minutes later, they made it to the cabin without incident. "Do you think he'll show up?" Lily asked.

"I had the security goon feed him false info that he overheard us say we were heading to the airport." They crunched on wind-blown twigs and leafy debris in companionable silence to the rear door. "He may show up, but not for a while."

"You hot on the security guard or what?" She elbowed his side. "Good thinking, by the way."

"A little money goes a long way toward stroking his ego."

Lily squinted at him. "Oh. Telepathy," she said. He grinned. "So what was his habit? Poker slots, roulette?"

"A nice bottle of wine and a dozen roses to take home to his wife for their anniversary."

Melting a little more inside, she squeezed his arm. "You're just a softie."

"When it counts. Anything for you." Spoken so low, she almost missed his last three words. Reality strengthened her weak knees as he clicked the safety off his gun. "Let me go in first. Wait in the mudroom." He dropped a meaningful look on her that held an "or else" vibe.

Gun in hand, Lily disarmed the security system and unlocked the door. His footsteps faded into the living room, up the stairs and beyond. She reset the alarm and stashed her backpack and briefcase in the gun safe in the downstairs bedroom closet.

Jake returned and drew her into the bedroom. He eased her jacket off her shoulders, and it slid to the floor, his mouth creating delicious sensations on her neck, kissing, nibbling, and licking a path to her ear. He guided her hand to the front of his pants and she connected with his pulsing erection, loving the stone hardness and length of him.

"See what you've done to me." His tone acquired a frayed edge as if she'd already driven him to the brink.

"Jake." He nipped at her lobe and she whimpered. "We were going to talk." She held his arms for balance before her dissolving legs betrayed her. "It's not safe."

"Power's on. Alarm's set. We talked, we hit town." His mouth poised over hers. "Now we touch." He captured her mouth in a hungry kiss destined to unravel her. His hands slid under her blouse, his fingers cooling the boiling flesh of her stomach, slithering up toward her breasts.

When his fingers found no hindrance, he moaned against her mouth. He eased his mouth off hers, grinning wickedly.

"A B-cup doesn't always need a bra."

"I love your thinking." He cupped her right breast, his thumb erotically teasing her nipple. "When you stood naked in front of me last night, I thought I'd died and the most beautiful angel had arrived to fulfill my deepest desires."

"An angel, huh?"

"Don't mock your gifts." He crushed her mouth in a searing, mind-numbing kiss, leaving her drowning in all of him.

Lily hooked her arms around his neck, holding his head down to maintain the blissful contact of his mouth on hers. Their tongues tangoed and danced, and the kiss went from passionate to fierce to sensual until they were forced to part for air.

Both panted as if they'd skied down the tallest Tahoe peak, a gazillion bounty hunters on their tail. He leaned a hip on the dresser, his twilight eyes devouring her. He tasted of cinnamon again, and she licked her lips to savor him. He growled and fingered the loose hair off her face.

"Now what?" she squeaked out.

"I'm going to make good on the promise I made last night." He took her hand in his and angled toward the bed.

"To protect me?" She found her legs refused to work. One part of her wanted to damn the world. The cautious part warned her against any type of relationship. One loser burning her in a lifetime was enough, and she didn't do casual.

But her heart soared and the dormant embers inside her needed stoking before they burned out for good. After the tortuous peak his kiss elevated her to, she'd die if he didn't fulfill his promise. Jake held such power over her heart and body from his touch, his musky scent, his whispered words, the seductive steely evidence of his arousal. It scared her more than the thought of never regaining her memories or her identity. Flaming door number one? Or fiery door number two?

CHAPTER NINETEEN

Jake scooped her in his arms and kicked the door shut behind him. As if she were the most precious gemstone, he laid her on the bed, his large body hovering over her, his knees and arms bracketing her. His gaze mirrored her desire and touched her deep inside.

A claw played hide and seek with her heart, tempting and wary in tandem. "Jake, maybe this isn't such a good idea."

He trailed kisses across her neck, triggering waves of decadent pleasure. "I thought we had a deal?" His lips seduced from her neck to her ear, fueling the meter on her starving hormones. He nipped at her lobe, and then his tongue outlined her ear, sparking electrical pulses in her veins.

"I..." She gasped as his hands inched their way under her sweater and seared her flesh. "There's too much going on. I'm on the rebound. Not fair to you," she managed to say in a rush before his lips sacked her brain's rule.

His hand froze, and he lifted his head, his face dark and intense. "Go with your feelings." He rested on his elbow and cupped her face in his large hand. "Do you want me? If you don't, I'll take a dip in the cold, cold lake."

Lily remembered how safe and warm she'd felt in Jake's arms last night. Although she feared the outcome of making love, she ached for that feeling again. She had to see how far this attraction took them or she'd never concentrate fully on finding her father's killer and dealing with her life. They were consenting adults, no commitments, no promises. Nothing barring them from taking a hike in the end.

His eyes darkened to the color of midnight, luring her heart, body, and soul into their epicenter. Lips full and moist and parted for her, his cheeks suddenly flushed. She lost all reason and control and granted her heart the win.

"What have you done to me?" She planted a kiss beneath his chin, his beard scruff tickling her swollen lips. Lily edged out of his embrace, and with trembling fingers pulled her sweater over her head. Jake sucked in a breath. He couldn't take his sight off her nipples, exposed and ready for him. Her stomach clenched in pleasure.

"God, damn, you're beautiful," he said, arousing her last dormant hormone. He leaned forward, his mouth latched onto her right nipple, and she cried out from the fire lancing her body. He freed her nipple with a pop, the loss of his hot lips on her flesh like a piece of her soul being ripped out. "Take my shirt off. I need to feel you against my skin."

In a slow, provocative strip dance, she rolled his shirt up, and he helped her pull it off. The black T-shirt puddled on the floor on top of her green-striped sweater. In another slick move, he rolled her under him. An expectant tremor rocked her as her body flushed from his piercing gaze, solidifying her decision. She felt like she would die if he didn't touch her.

He reached down and unzipped her jeans, peeling

them off her legs inch by excruciating inch as his mouth and tongue followed the scorching trail of her pants to her ankles.

"Did the washer eat your socks?"

One orange and one red ankle sock. "A soul without color is a soul without depth. Life without color is too static, too many shades of mundane gray." Lily kicked her jeans onto the floor, and her hand alighted on his belt. "What color's teasing your soul today?"

"I'm black to the core, darlin'."

She tweaked his hair brushing against her skin as he hovered over the vee of her thighs. "That'll change the second you enter me."

"You got that right." With quaking hands, Jake helped her slip out of his jeans and black boxer briefs, and he tossed them onto the heap of clothes. His erection sprang free, hard, thick and made of perfection. "You'll change me forever."

"That's my promise to you." She wrapped her hand around his shaft, and he jerked back and groaned.

෧෫෬

Jake's heart boomed, and somewhere in the center of his black soul, he felt a soft illumination on the fringes. He'd never seen a woman as perfect as Lily, her breasts full, firm, and her pert, rosy nipples a startling contrast to her alabaster skin. *Damn, he loved her breasts.* Lifting her easily onto his lap, she straddled him, burying his throbbing erection between her legs as she pressed against him with the slightest provocative movement. He'd never been so painfully hard, nor so sensitized to a woman. Her naked breasts grazed his chest erotically, and she whimpered. He wanted her so fiercely his nerve endings ached. The scent of her perfume mixing with her own scent inundated his senses, and he wanted to drown in her soul. Her body flowed against his like bubbly liquid, inciting him before she reneged on her promise.

He claimed her mouth with a deep penetrating kiss, and his tongue met hers in an evocative duel, ending in a tie. The kiss built slow, but as Lily crushed her nipples to his chest, tantalizing his bare skin, raw need usurped his caution. She emitted a tiny groan, but he didn't let up, nor did she let him. She linked her arms around his neck and clung to him, forcing her soft perfection to mate with the hard planes of his torso. Arms holding her tight, he drew her so close their skin had surely fused together.

Without breaking the kiss, he rolled her over again onto her back, and she stretched to her full length beneath him. Their kiss grew crushing until he parted his mouth to drag in air. Lips red and swollen, she excited him, lured him for another taste, another thread of his control unraveling, another ray of light on his soul.

She stroked his flesh from his chest down between their stomachs, reaching lower. He took her hand before she reached her destination, their fingers entwined as he stretched her arm above her head. He wasn't ready to sink into her yet despite his overwhelming need. Wasn't ready for the end of his life as he knew it. First, he wanted to explore every inch of her body. Wanted to give her pleasure before he took his own. Wanted her more than anything or anyone in his life. It wrecked his mind, his heart, and plugged an emptiness he was stunned to discover existed inside him.

She took his mouth in another staggering kiss while he let go of her hand. Her body arched wildly. Dying to taste more of her, he eased out of the drugging kiss, leaving her writhing and moaning.

"Jake. Don't stop kissing me."

He buried his face between her exquisite breasts,

kissing every bit of her peachy smooth skin, nibbling and laving at one rosy nipple, creating a desperate inferno inside him. "Like this?" He traced kisses from one breast to the other and resumed tasting and teasing the other nipple.

"That works. Oh…Jake," she cried out, tugging on his hair, her body thrashing beneath his, grinding herself against his sensitive erection. Ignoring her need, he continued to suck on one pebbled nipple, then the other while she passed her hands over his shoulders, his back, her fingernails making their way down the length of him, kneading his butt.

He kneed her willing legs apart. "You're so beautiful," he said hoarsely, "so perfect. Everything about you—your heart, your mind, your luscious lips, the bridge of freckles across your nose, your fiery hair, your strong and lithe legs—makes me insane." Before she could utter a word, he set about pleasuring her with his fingers, his mouth and tongue until she lay spent, panting and begging to fulfil her promise.

She trailed her fingers down his erection, soliciting a growl. He nudged her hand away. "I'm not done with you yet." He planted kisses from her mouth to her breasts, teased and taunted her nipples to bullet hardness again.

He lost it completely. He gave her no time to recover before he quickly slid up her body and sank unhurriedly inside her. She sheathed him in electric heat, tight, wet, and wild. A heaven he never wanted to leave.

Lily gripped his muscled arms and cried out at his gentle assault. He kissed her, the contact of their lips deepening their pleasure. She bowed her hips to suck him in deeper, and he sensed the core of her soul as it met his, her color infusing and illuminating his darkness. Her mind brushed his and he felt the onset of her pleasure. He moved with a fevered rhythm, all thoughts kicked to the wayside except his need to feel her gloved around him.

CRSO

Jake's mouth devoured hers as if he'd just returned from a deserted island and she was his life's fuel, the color in his black and grey world. Lily returned his fervent kisses, wanting more, *needing* more, and drowning in sensation. She drove her hips upward and met him thrust for thrust. The friction of their bodies trembled her hunger against him.

The fluttery sensations in her head swelled and she experienced a painful pleasure. A wintry splash of shock decimated her burning need as Jake's pleasure echoed in her head. Their bodies merged deeper, tighter, and her mind opened and captured his. His mind sucked her in with each plunge, an impression of his lust etched on her brain. Jake's hardness pulsed, rolling shockwaves through her, triggering another orgasm. She cried out from the exquisite onslaught of intense pleasure. He ceased moving, cloaked in her fully. His darkened eyes held an odd mix of bewilderment, lust, and awe.

"Jake?" A gentle cloud flitted across her mind, quickly chased away as Jake dropped his mouth down on hers in a long languorous kiss.

With a slow, deep push, he was fully sheathed inside her again, danger and ecstasy in one thrust. Stunned, she gasped and tried to ignore the rumblings inside her head. But the chaos consumed her.

Perspiration popped on Jake's forehead, and he lifted his mouth from hers. For a moment she shut her eyes, savoring the sensation of him lodged within every cell of her body. Then her eyes opened and locked on his in wonder.

"Sweet hell." His look touched her core as if only he

had access to her deepest depths. Leaning down, he softly kissed her, holding his parted lips against hers, not moving, just breathing her in for a long moment before he continued loving her.

Each push inside her stoked her fire. A strong wave of Jake's pleasure caught her by surprise. His thrusts increased in tempo, and as she rose up to meet him to suck him deep, she felt pleasure surging back and forth between them. It was impossible to tell which sensations were hers and which belonged to him. With a savage cry, she thrust her hips against him harder, seeking more, crying out in pleasure as he brought her to the edge again. His answering groan was deep and husky. Her hands dug into his butt, skated over his backside, trying to trace from memory the Psychic Guild logo tattooed across his upper back, a trinity knot interwoven with a heart, a symbol of power and love.

Between gasps of air, he said, "Go over...for me. I want...to see you...come undone. For me. For you."

The building tension reached a crescendo. With a scream, she let loose, her body contracting and releasing. A tsunami of pleasure poured through her, sending him over the edge. His release bombarded her, immobilizing and overpowering. For a moment, shared sensation locked them together on a rolling wave, and she never wanted it to cease.

Sated and gasping, Jake fell on top of her, and when he tried to ease his weight off, she tugged him back down. She needed to feel every inch of him against her tingling body. Sweat slicked their bodies, a tribute to the force of their joining, molding him into that dangerous man she'd met just a few days ago. A sexy, scary, mysterious danger Lily wanted, inside and around her.

They lay in the aftermath of lovemaking, the covers twisted and hanging half off the bed, as twisted as Lily's long red hair mating with Jake's damp tresses, like a bright fire consuming the darkness.

Orgasms still jolted her system, and she couldn't make sense out of what just happened. But then she'd never made love to a psychic. *Holy orgasmic heaven.* If she'd known having sex with a telepath could be so erotic, she'd have dipped her toe in the water long ago.

"What did you do to me?" Awe laced his voice as if he'd just made love for the first time and cherished it more than anything in his life. She pressed her cheek against his chest, his galloping heartbeat exciting and pacifying at once. He cuddled her closer to his inflamed body, tightening his arms around her as if afraid to let her go.

"What did *you* do to me?" Lily kissed his chest. "Telepath sex? Is it always that intense?"

"No." He emitted a hoarse chuckle "Had to be your psychic powers enhancing it." Jake skimmed the oversensitive skin of her back, prolonging the zing of her orgasm.

The feathery sensation in her head quivered wildly, both provocative and unnerving, almost agitated. "Stop it."

"It's not me, Lily." Jake kissed her forehead. "It's you. Your untapped chaos. Your color, as you so aptly called it. Speaking of...why not just wear rainbow striped socks?" He tweaked her hair.

"You'll figure it out someday." She had no interest in giving up that secret part of herself and telling him her mix of color was her insignificant way of having disorder in her orderly life, inwardly allowing her to step out of bounds. Sometimes, a girl just had to live a little outside the boundaries of staid lawyer. She could always count on color if nothing else. "Do you feel me in your head?"

"Yes...inside me, around me. Damn. I need to taste

you again."

"Already?" She choked on a laugh.

"Not quite. Soon. Very soon."

Awe filled her but couldn't temper the fear that something unexplainable happened between them. Her body coursed with sensations and power. It frightened her, awed her...unsettled her.

Just when she was trying to figure out her own mind and soul, along came Jake McAllister rocking her tenuous foundation.

CHAPTER TWENTY

Lost in silence, they held each other close. Lily tried to make heads or tails of what just happened but it defied any definition written in the laws of nature or man. Had she read more into what he probably considered a casual hookup? And what the heck kind of psychic powers had she buried for the last ten years? Afraid to break the comfy spell between them, she plonked the memories in a protective pocket to tear apart later like a bad contract.

Teasing her fingers through the damp hair on his chest, she asked, "Do you get paid to be my Guardian?" Jake chuckled. "I mean...not like that!" *Welcome to my mortification.* He squeezed her tighter. "There's a lot I don't know about you...the Guild, the Protectorate, etc., etc." Her hand quit wandering and he covered it with his own solid hand, settling it over his heart. The scent of him breathed around her, and a warm glow carried her on euphoric waves.

"You'll learn." He pressed a kiss to her head and continued to stroke her back underneath the sheet he'd pulled over them, reawakening her longing.

"Tell me about being a Guardian."

Jake shifted upwards on the pillows, bringing her with him without breaking his hold on her. "I come from a long line of Guardians. Most every male in the McAllister family going back for centuries has been one, same as your father's family. Many McAllisters have possessed various psychic powers."

Shock suffused her and she lurched back. "My father's family? No. Wait, what?"

"Ah, darlin', so much has been withheld from you." He brushed away chaotic tendrils of hair hanging over her face. "I'm sorry for that."

"My father was a Guardian to my mother, but he wasn't psychic nor did he come from a family of psychics or Guardians."

"From what I understand, the Falbrookes have always been involved in the Guild. He was a Guardian until he married your mother. Then he guarded only your mother...and you."

Epic eye-opener. Why does everyone and their dogs know more about my family than I do? "So Guardians are allowed to marry?"

"We forfeit our duties except toward a psychic we might marry, and if we marry before our contract terminates, there're other items we forfeit."

"You're under contract?"

"I'm not at liberty to discuss that. We're forbidden by the contract and the Protectorate."

She pinched his arm playfully. "Talk about secrets and non-disclosure agreements."

His body stiffened and she planted tiny kisses on his chest until he relaxed again.

"We don't only get monetary payment. It's written in the Protectorate bylaws. Like a knighthood." His chuckle vibrated against her cheek. "We get status, other tangibles, and intangibles at certain milestones of service."

"And that's between you and the Protectorate?" She

tongued his nipple until it formed into a stiff kernel.

"You'll make a fine Guild psychic. Smarts and beauty all in one package. Anyone would be a fool not to kneel at your feet."

Her fingers inched past his navel, raising an army of goosebumps, inciting his low growl. "Surely that's not expected."

Her fingers grasped their hardening goal. He groaned and his body grew as rigid as his erection in her tightening fist. "Not exactly, but pretty damn close," he said.

She ignored that new mind-bender. Later. "You were chosen as First Guardian because you're the best or were there other reasons?" She rubbed his smooth erection, lightly pressing on the iron beneath the soft sheath.

"I *am* the best," he rasped out and sucked in his stomach.

Despite his arrogance, his hesitancy kept her attention on the question. "But there were other reasons, too?"

"I don't know. I haven't spoken to Niles yet." He stopped the slow dance of her fingers upon him. "They're avoiding my phone calls."

The tensing of his body filled her with unease. "That disturbs you?"

"Niles never avoids me."

"Do they have Guild offices where you can confront him?"

"The Guild stronghold's in the Santa Cruz hills." He beamed her a triumphant smile. "I guess I'll be the one to show you off as our newest member when the threats to Guild members have been contained."

Releasing him, Lily eased out of his arms. "I don't know if I want to join, or if I want to take an active role in the Guild. Big if."

"If Juliana Westwood joins, won't you join with her? Isn't your friend Marisa a member?"

A smile curved her lips as she leaned over and said, "Will you always be my Guardian?"

He pressed his mouth to her lips in a long, sweet kiss. "I go where I'm ordered," he breathed against her mouth, his hands creating a new inferno on her skin. "Whether *you* order me or not."

The jarring chirp of his cell in the kitchen foisted reality back into their momentary escape. Lily watched his gorgeous, naked perfection stride out of the bedroom, feasting on the Guild tattoo that covered most of his back and wide shoulders, sliding to his sublime ass. Was there another man alive as beautiful as Jake McAllister in the buff?

"Hello to you too, Elizabeth," Jake greeted.

Grimace spoiling his handsome face, he padded into the bedroom, standing tall as if born to parade around in his naked glory. Brow furrowed with tiny lines, he remained silent listening to Elizabeth, while he hitched on his pants and snatched up his T-shirt. After a few moments, he handed Lily the phone. "Talk to her while I feed the fire."

"Hey, Elizabeth." Lily slid Jake a wan smile and pulled the down comforter over her breasts.

"What fool notion did you get into your head to take off without protection?" Exasperation wearing an authoritative timbre accompanied Elizabeth's reprimand.

Lily was a grown-ass woman for cripe's sake. In fact, if she truly was the Flower of Tara Whatever the Hell, why weren't people kissing *her* ass?

"Elizabeth, I love you, but I don't have to report my whereabouts to you," she said not unkindly. "I sent you an email. I have a gun."

Elizabeth clucked like a mother hen. "Honey, you

aren't safe alone. Philip Sheehan's on the prowl and you're in greater danger."

"As in what greater danger?" Icy apprehension froze the last languid bit of strength left in her sated body. "What's got you all wound up?"

"A Guild Guardian was attacked last night. The Guild sent him to your house and the Cabal ambushed him. We didn't know you'd already left town."

She jack-knifed up, clutching the bedcovers over her breasts.

"We suspect they're trying to get to you." Elizabeth's pitch softened. "We have no proof, but Niles thinks Philip outed you to the entire Cabal, additional proof he's working for them and not on the Guild's side."

"Oh, God." Her teeth chattered.

"You need to understand the danger surrounding you. The Cabal doesn't simply want the chalice and the entire Twilight collection. They want you. There's a belief that you alone can wield whatever psychic powers drinking from the chalice enhances."

"I found my mother's journal. It's all spelled out," she whispered.

"Then you also know if the Cabal obtains the chalice and bags you, you'll be their psychic conduit for whatever evil intent they've masterminded."

Bile soared to Lily's throat and she swallowed rough. Jake took one look at her, closed the distance between them, and cloaked himself around her.

"We'll tackle this together as I promised." His whispered words settled around her shoulders like a warm blanket.

Almost dropping the phone, she forced her hand to hold it against her ear. "But my powers suck. I'm useless to them."

"Not with the chalice and the collection, especially the

ring," he replied.

A fleeting vision of an antique filigree ring with a large round sapphire seated on her mother's hand materialized from the ashes of her memories. *"Don't let them put this ring on your finger, Lily. Never put it on until you're ready."* The memory drifted in her mental haze. A horrid realization rose on the memory's tailwind, and she dug her fingernails into Jake's arm. "Did *they* kill my mother?"

Elizabeth sputtered, silenced, and Lily guessed the answer. She loosened her tight grip on the phone and it slipped on top of the comforter. Both her old and new life rear-ended her, a big fat vat of lies. No wonder she'd always felt an unspecified greater purpose was just beyond her grasp.

Dimly, she heard Jake talking to Elizabeth, barely aware he'd left her numb-from-head-to-toe body wrapped in the comforter. Eerie chills shook her, and she desperately needed a hot shower to sluice away her troubles.

Shuffling in a fog, she gathered a towel and her cosmetic case and headed for the downstairs bathroom. Calm overcame her as she dumped the towel and travel bag on the vanity. When she turned on the water, she realized she'd grabbed a hand towel instead of a bath towel. On her way back to the linen closet, she heard Jake's fierce voice escalate.

"I'm doing my best to protect her as I'm sworn by oath." After a short pause, his ire broke through, his voice ominously low. "I've cracked open her mind, we had sex...and it opened the gates farther. Michael basically paid me to be in her life, and I've been appointed First Guardian, what more—"

CHAPTER TWENTY-ONE

A fist gripped the back of Lily's throat, leaden and throttling. Jake's words of betrayal cleaved through her like a machete, infusing her with an impotent rage. Without knowing how one foot stepped in front of the other, she moved into his line of sight. The next instant, his guilt nailed her from his position in the kitchen.

He clicked off the phone and killed the distance between them in one stride. "Lily?"

"You cracked open my mind? And having sex opened it further? What the hell, Jake."

He gave her a deer in headlights look. "It's not what you think."

Hysterical laughter erupted from her, until her laughter evolved into bitter tears. She wiped her face on her sleeve. "What? I'm just a job to you? Screw my head, screw my body, screw me all ways to Sunday, right?"

"No, God, no." He scrubbed the back of his neck.

"Seriously? Did you or did you not break into my head?" Is that what her mother wrote in her journal about her being susceptible to mind control...if her mind was open? Did Jake know this? "Are you controlling my mind? Am I your personal minion? Was your sole intent to screw me to open my mind and lead you to the Twilight collection?"

"I did it to protect you."

"So you've been in my head since the night I spent in the loft?"

"Yes."

"Did you know having sex could crack me open further?"

Guilt on display, he hung his head. "I wasn't sure."

"So that's why our sex was so intense. You manipulated me, us." Listing to the side, she wanted to wither up and die.

"No, Lily. What we felt was real. You have to believe me." He stretched out a hand to her, but the daggers she shot from her eyes shot his arm down.

"But you didn't think to tell me, to ask my permission, to let me decide." She stomped her foot on the floor, wishing she was stomping his so perfect dick into the hardwood floor.

He opened his mouth, shut it, opened it again. "I...I got caught up. You're so fucking beautiful, touching you was magic. What I feel for you is more real than I've felt for or with any other woman. I couldn't spoil the moment. I lost it. I just lost it." A tiny click in his throat cracked his voice. "I'm sorry I betrayed your trust."

His raspy, desolate tone flew over her head. How dare he violate her and the psychic abilities *she* couldn't reach? "Can you read my mind?"

He quailed. "I'm a telepath."

"I'm blocking. Can. You. Read. My. Mind?" she spat the words out like tiny icicles.

He examined his feet for a too long guilty moment. Raising his head, he said, "Yes. I breached your blocks. I can read you most of the time. If I wanted to. The night in the loft, you were having a nightmare. I tried to soothe your mind...I lost control."

It explained the new presence in her head. It explained zilch. How could a telepath hold such abilities to break blocks erected in another person's head? Ones she hadn't managed to crack open in ten years. "Why can't I sense or read you?" As soon as the words spilled out, she cupped her mouth. It finally sank in. She *had* sensed him, during the most intense sex she'd ever known. "Oh no. No, no!" She cringed, banging her battered elbow against the granite counter, sucking down the pain.

"No, Lily." He stepped forward a foot, stopped. "You have to believe me. What happened between us had nothing to do with my telepathy or coercing you."

Her face scalded ten degrees of fire. "Did your telepathy shatter all my blocks?" She wanted to slip to the bottom of Lake Tahoe and disappear beneath the silt.

"I don't know." Defeated, his shoulders slumped forward. "I said I'd never lie to you."

"A lie by omission is still a lie." Drooping against the counter, she pulled her arms tighter to her middle, pressing on the rumblings of betrayal. "What did you mean by being paid to watch over me?" she demanded.

Jake jammed his knuckles against the counter edge. "That's not what I meant. Michael valued my work. We had a fair and square deal in forming the partnership."

Lily opened her mouth to blast him a new asshole, but when he held up his hand, she closed it, granting him a chance to explain, granting her time to gather her revolting wits. Not like the rat bastard deserved it.

"Your father asked me to watch over you if something happened. I thought he was being melodramatic or joking. Now I know better. After he died, I wondered if he was securing my position in your life for the purpose of protecting you. The partnership, the lease on the loft." He leaned his elbows on the counter, dropped his face in his hands. "When we get to the Guild stronghold, I'll request another Guardian assigned to you."

"Don't bother. You're fired." Despite his betrayals, desolation punched Lily in the gut. "What about this bond thing between us? Is it permanent? Can another telepath help me regain my abilities? My memories?"

"After a while with no contact or close proximity, the bond will dissipate." He stuffed his hands in his pants pocket, shuffling his feet in an uncharacteristic manner. "You'll eventually work it out as your walls tumble completely." His shoulders jerked in a stilted shrug, and all the emotion drained from his face. "Maybe Juliana can help. I'll stay out of your head...like I'm doing now. It's best I stay away from you...unless you figure out how to block me completely. This is one reason the Guild forbids certain telepaths to become involved, or one to guard another. Since you aren't a telepath, and they felt you needed a higher level of Guardian, I fit within the boundaries."

Cement encased her heart. "What will happen when they re-assign you elsewhere?"

He leaned his elbows on the counter again, as if not sure what to do with his arms and hands. "I won't be reassigned."

"Why not?"

"What I did without permission is against the Guild laws. I'll be punished."

"Punished? What, a freaking slap on the hand?"

"The Guild will strip me of my position and boot me out. They'll take away all the perks I've earned, and I'll face a cash fine. They may even slap a leash on my psychic abilities."

Were they living in Middle Earth? "Good."

He shook his head and regarded her with an aloof air. "We need to get out of here. We'll go to the stronghold—

you'll be safe there to carry on with your training, keep your treasures safe."

Lily's knees wobbled. She believed he had been protecting her—or trying to when she allowed him—but his intrusion still felt like a violation of the worst kind, especially to a psychic, even if he may have helped her after all other efforts had failed. Could she allow the violation to stand? Did he deserve punishment? Could she walk away from him in the end? Not that she wasn't ready to kick his ass to the tar pits for deceiving her and traveling to a place no person had a right to travel. The Guild and their guardians can eat shit and die for all she cared.

Numb in body and mind, she headed for the shower, snatching a towel out of the closet on her way. *Welcome to the Twilight Zone of the Twilight Zone.* Nothing made sense in her life anymore.

Later, after Jake took his turn in the bathroom, he cautiously slipped into the living room, his wet hair slicked back and hanging loose to dry. He was clad in jeans, chest bare. She had to shift away before she lost all her control and smoothed her hands over the flat planes of his abdomen and chest. Part of her needed to touch him as if he were her elixir of life. The other part wanted nothing to do with a man who'd desecrated her worse than Daniel ever had.

"Lily?"

"What?" She tossed her cosmetics loose in her suitcase.

"I'm not sorry I breached your mind. I'm sorry that I hurt you and betrayed your trust. It was for no other reason than your protection."

Tears welled and she blinked hard to stall the torrent. She hated them, hated his sincerity tricking her desolation. "I feel you in my head." She kneaded her scalp to increase her latent abilities or to gouge him out.

"Your abilities are blooming, your walls falling. Our link is stronger now."

"You said what happened...wasn't a normal sensation for two psychics. What gives?"

He hitched up his jeans and picked up a wrinkled black T-shirt off the bed. "Sometimes there can be a shared sensation, not as intense as what happened with us. The intimacy helped open your mind when I probed...with my telepathy." Crimson replaced the pink tinge on his cheeks. "I don't know what happened. Something to do with your abilities reacting to mine."

Air swept over her as Jake passed her on his way out of the cloistering bedroom. The irresistible scent of his cologne lingered. She inhaled deeply, wanting to capture it forever, wanting to spit it out and pour bleach over it.

A short while later they were packed and ready to split. Not looking forward to a tense ride home, Lily clutched the backpack containing her mother's journal and the Twilight legacy—her legacy—in her arms. She almost didn't ever want to view or inventory the jewels. She just wanted to go home and lose herself in her new life, absent the collection and the Guild and all it represented...and Jake. Another betrayal in a life of tragedies, lies, and secrets.

An idea brewed but she worried instigating another discussion that'd make her mimic a high school kid learning fourth grade science. But curiosity beat down her indecision.

Jake was cleaning hot ashes out of the fireplace when she approached him. "Does anyone else know what you did?" she asked.

He returned the wrought-iron fireplace shovel to the stand and faced her. The clang echoed up to the ceiling. "Elizabeth."

"Then we tell whoever we need to that I agreed to it. I won't be responsible for your expulsion from the Guild, as insane as the freakin' laws are," she retorted. "But I want you out of my house, out of my life."

"It's not so simple." He took the backpack out of her arms, set it on the hearth, and held her hands. Part of her cringed at his touch, the other part wanted to paste her entire body to his and never let him go. "Lily." He pulled her closer until a few inches separated them. "I need to tell you something. You won't like it."

She tugged her hands out of his loose clasp. "Now what? Why all the secrets?" She sat rigidly on the couch.

"I promise you there'll be no more secrets. No holds barred, okay?" Jake tapped her wrist gently, withdrew. "Guardians aren't allowed to tell people certain things since it affects our performance when others know our psychic powers. Some Guardians hold powers normal psychics don't, one reason why we make effective guards." He knelt in front of her. "I can compel people through my telepathy."

Holy epic breach of trust. He'd sucked her into his web, like a broken, seven-legged spider. Well, hell, that explained a lot. Why her father dove into his web of lies. Her attraction to him at a time when men were the devil in her book.

"You son of a bitch!" She leaped off the couch, kicked her suitcase. "Your betrayals just never end. You've played me and my father for stupid fools all along, haven't you?"

"The attraction I feel for you has nothing to do with any powers I possess. I didn't coerce you into falling for—"

"Get real." She scowled. "Who said anything about falling for you? I don't want to hear any more of your bullshit." Backpack and suitcase in tow, she stomped to the back door. "*Ever.*"

"I'm telling you this because the Guild won't believe you agreed to let me in your head."

Boots thumping on the hardwood floor, he rushed behind her, practically bowled her through the door.

"Then I guess you've executed your damn death sentence from the Guild," she said.

She had to wait for Jake to catch up to her to unlock the SUV. Good thing he remained silent since she refused to defend her hands their right to freedom if he provoked her further. She wasn't a slapper, but there was a first time for everything.

He stalked to her side of the SUV to unlock the door, and he suddenly stiffened. Bewildered shock opened his mouth, and a network of lines etched his forehead, bracketed his eyes. The keys dropped, jangling in the quiet winter day onto the asphalt driveway. He staggered, his jaw hanging open.

"Jake? What's wrong?"

He listed toward the SUV, and that's when Lily spied the wooden shaft of an arrow sticking out of his back. His telepathy exploded in her head, a cacophony of severed thoughts. A searing pain speared his head and echoed in *her* skull.

CHAPTER TWENTY-TWO

Lily cried out, holding her head with one hand, reaching for Jake with the other. He knocked her down to the ground and rammed her under the SUV. The acrid smell of wet asphalt wrinkled her nose. She scrambled to her side to tow Jake under, but the arrow protruding from his shoulder lodged against the vehicle. Panting, he lay on his side, his nose inches from a puddle.

She thrust away her backpack for the man and enigma that drove her crazy from lust to loathing. "How bad?" Parting his leather jacket, she revealed the arrowhead shot clean through his shoulder. "Oh, God." Blood darkened his faded black T-shirt.

Jake dangled the car keys. "*Put the ring on. It might help your psychic abilities.*"

The unspoken command freaked her out. It didn't take a rocket scientist to know she possessed the ring, but why waste her time with such drivel? Surely the ring didn't hold immense fantasyland power.

Pain contorted his face, and he craned his neck to hunt for signs of the archer. "Put. It. On."

"Fuel for them to abduct me? No freaking way."

"You're telekinetic *and* clairvoyant. The power of the sapphires, especially the ring will enhance your psychic abilities. Now that your mind's receptive—"

"Telekinetic like Stephen King's *Carrie*?" She'd never met a telekinetic. Mouth open like a hungry goldfish, she absorbed his crazy-ass proclamation. "No, I'm not. I'm only a crappy clairvoyant."

"Telekinetic. You might not trust me, but trust in yourself."

Without questioning him further, she wrenched the zipper open on the backpack, and scrabbled for the leather box. With renewed speed, she fit the tiny key from around her neck into the lock and lifted the lid. The huge sapphire on the gold filigree ring eyeballed her like a beacon among the other jewels nestled on black velvet.

The sapphire cabochon was slightly dull, the swirling colors of blue muted like an unpolished rock. She slid the ring on her naked right ring finger. It fit as if made for her. Starlight seemed to emanate from the stone, glittering like the dome of a star-studded midnight sky. As much as she wanted to pretend fantasyland had swung open the doors, the glow was now merely sunlight catching on the sapphire. Energy surged through her veins and electricity sparkled from the center of the stone. Optical illusion or delusion?

That hidden being inside her sprouted, as if rising to life in her womb. *She* felt right for the first time in her life. Sluggish mental power awakened within her psyche. The walls Lily had built on the worst day of her life shattered, freeing her mind...freeing her. The need to use the gifts she'd suppressed eclipsed her constant need to deny them. A breeze tickled her mind, intrusively and painfully, until Jake withdrew like an icepick retreating from her skull. Lily sucked up the burst of pain.

"Damn. It's true." Shock colored Jake's bloodless skin. He ogled the ring as if it were alive. "There really is power in that stone." His words were calm and reverent as he transfixed on the heavy gold ring.

"My mother didn't know I was telekinetic. How did you?" she demanded, more awed than upset.

"An eerie energy in your head, powerful, untapped. I've only felt it from one other person. My mother."

Lily ogled him. "Oh. You were in my head just now. Do you feel my psychic abilities?"

"I'm not using my telepathy, nor have I since...you know. I told you I wouldn't..." He scratched his jaw. "Never mind. You need to get us out of here. Crawl out on the driver's side and unlock the SUV."

"What about the shooter?" She cast her gaze around the SUV, meeting only innocent trees.

"He's out there. He won't harm you. Seriously, they all want you alive. This is why." He tapped the ring, then her head.

Unsettling air currents shifted, solidified almost. Jake brought her hand to his lips and kissed the ring, then kissed her palm. Despite the pain of his betrayal, desire danced across her breasts. Heart beating triple time, she touched his feverish cheek. The star in the sapphire dazzled her, propelled her into motion.

"Let's hit it before you bleed to death."

"I won't bleed until you remove the arrow."

"Now you tell me." Crouching low, she slithered over the damp driveway to the other side of the SUV, scanning the perimeter for their assailant. Not a soul in sight, not even the shooter, she climbed into the SUV and started the engine. Then she darted to the other side where Jake leaned against the doorjamb. He motioned to their bags and she stashed them in the cargo area. As she spun on her heels, a man emerged from the woods to the right of the garage, bow slung over his shoulders, a gun in his large hand, aimed pointblank at her heart.

"Going somewhere?" A chuckle chased his question.

"Not without me. Hands in the air, Lily McKenna Falbrooke. As for you McAllister, don't move a muscle."

"Lily," Jake whisper-shouted, straining in the vehicle to reach his weapon on the floorboard, where he'd discarded it when he collapsed. "Can't reach my gun. Lure him closer, then concentrate, use your telekinetic ability to force him to drop the gun, knock him out."

"How?" she whispered, holding her ground. The man approached in measured footsteps, a lascivious grin on his ruddy, whiskered face.

"Concentrate. Interrupt his bioelectricity. In your head, mimic the motions of prying his fingers off the handle one by one, swing a homerun across his knees to stop him. Use your mental resources."

Holding her hands in the air to show the man she was unarmed, she centered on the burgeoning telekinetic abilities she didn't trust, on the chaos Carrie had created in the infamous movie after a bucket of blood had doused her at a dance.

The shooter's steps crunched the gravel bordering the driveway. He stopped six feet away.

"What do you want?" she asked.

"I think you know."

"Tell me, so I get it right." She tossed out cerebral commands that floundered into the ether. Epic joke, right? She wasn't scary Carrie. These weren't the powers she'd suppressed for ten years. Her mother never wrote a word about telekinesis. Or had her powers not manifested until now? The idea gave her a boost of confidence. *I can do this! I'm scary Carrie's alter ego!*

"I'm here on behalf of the Cabal, netting the score of a millennium. Hand over the prize, and let's go, sweetheart. We'll leave your friend here to die in peace."

Die? Talk about delusional. His aim was worse than his reality. Fear forced Lily to refocus, and she tossed out another mental command aimed at the man's right hand wrapped around a nasty gun. His index finger kinked and his left eye twitched. She tried again and again until his whole hand loosened on the handle and the gun slipped from his grip.

As he leaped the distance between them, another gun fired, the shot booming like thunder, crushing the normal sounds of kids playing along the distant shoreline. Lily jumped out of the way from becoming a heavyweight champion's victim and wheeled around. Jake supported his weight against the open door of the SUV, a gun dangling from his right hand.

"Grab his gun. Let's go," he commanded.

Fighting her shock, she rolled the man into wet bushes so neighborhood kids didn't stumble upon him, and pocketed his gun.

"Get the pair of wire cutters out of the tool box." He jabbed his gun in the direction of the garage.

By the time she returned, he'd already tossed her backpack and briefcase onto the floor behind the driver's side. Her heart galloped from the flurry of activity and adrenaline spiking in her blood.

"You want me to cut it in the back?" She hazarded a guess.

"Sometimes I wonder if you're as innocent as you say you are."

"Now who's wasting time?" She analyzed the long narrow shaft protruding from his shoulder. The fletches were raven dark, as if made from Jake's hair.

"Cut it close to my jacket, but not so much that I'll push it through."

One hand holding the arrow, she encircled the shaft with the wire cutters "Here goes squat." She snipped the arrow and tossed the shaft and wire cutters into the back of the SUV. Jake lurched forward and stifled a muffled cry.

She propped him against the seat. The white of death claimed the skin of his face, ravaged deeper lines around his eyes and mouth. She wanted to smooth his skin and erase his pain. Perspiration drenched the neck of his T-shirt. Cologne emanated strongly off him as his body succumbed to the pain.

"You don't look so hot." She touched his forehead and withdrew her fiery hand. "We need to get you to the hospital."

"No hospitals. They'll call the sheriff. We need to get on the road."

"You need tending. I'm a lawyer, not a doctor...or a freaking psychic."

"Darlin', don't belittle yourself." He winced. "You did good. You diverted his attention so I got my shot in. You'll get the hang of the rest."

Who is this man who tortures my mind and body in all ways, even when wracked in pain? "The bleeding's slowed." She snagged a T-shirt out of his bag, and found a rope in the cargo hold. It took her what seemed days, but she managed to wrap the wound and tie it off without causing Jake a world of hurt. She thought he'd lost consciousness, but he lifted hooded eyelids, the fringe of dark lashes startling against his pallid flesh.

"Do you recognize him?" She tied off the thin rope. "From the Cabal?"

"He's from the Guild, Lily."

"What?" Her fingers fumbled on the rope. "Another one?" In a stuttering confession, she regaled him with the vision she'd experienced from the blood of the man she'd shot upstairs.

"This shit just got real. Guess the Cabal and Guild have mixed it up." Jake jostled his cell phone in her bloodstained hand. "Call Ric at the house. Tell him what happened and to get Elizabeth to meet us there in four hours."

She gave him a critical squint. Why the hell was Ric in her house? Lily dialed home.

"Yo, Falbrookes," a man sounding awfully like Jake answered.

"It's Lily Falbrooke. Ric McAllister?"

"Lily? Damn, girl, it's nice to hear you. Yeah, it's the Ricster."

"Tell him to shut up and listen."

Brothers. "Jake and I are in trouble."

"Go on." The too-friendly voice sobered.

She told him what'd happened. "We're hitting the road now. Jake's stable." Jake motioned for the phone, and Lily handed it to him.

"Prepare everyone for Lily and the Twilight collection's arrival—" The phone dropped and he collapsed against the seat, eyes squeezed shut.

Lily fisted his shirtfront. "Don't leave me now, damn you." She found a discarded bottle of water and patted water onto his flaming cheeks.

"Then don't slap me to death," he rasped out. "I'm gonna sleep it off." Like that, he zonked out.

Spying the phone, she picked it up. "Ric, you there?"

"Yeah, flower child."

"He's dead to the world."

"Good. It'll help ease the pain. Make sure he's not bleeding anymore. It's only his shoulder, right? He's had worse."

"Yeah." Jitters unsettled her. She wanted him in the hospital, not spending hours on the road. She clicked off, checked Jake's wound, satisfied the bleeding had slowed, and then reclined his seat and secured his seatbelt.

Over four grueling hours later, Lily parked the SUV on her half-circular driveway in the San Jose foothills.

She'd pulled off the highway every hour to check on the wound, to give Jake painkillers and lunch, but he'd slept most of the way. He griped about a bullet to his foot, a smack on the head, and now a shot in the shoulder being bad for a Guardian's abilities and rep.

Her legs nearly buckled as she stumbled out of the high-rise SUV.

"Whoa there, flower child." Strong arms caught her against a solid steel body. A distinctively McAllister face framed by the same dark hair, albeit much shorter, the devastating smile, the clear and perfect blue eyes, missing the dimples and beard scruff met her troubled gaze.

"Ric, I presume," she said as she pushed off his muscled chest.

"You're a sight for jagged eyes." He grinned and jetted to the passenger side.

Ric and Lily half-carried Jake into the house and fumbled him onto the living room couch. Elizabeth quickly assessed his condition.

"How bad?" Ric asked.

"Bad enough." Elizabeth cut off the rope and peeled away Jake's blood-caked T-shirt, revealing the arrow remnant preventing the wound from bleeding out. She shot a quick appraisal at Lily. "You learn quick."

With Lily's aid, Elizabeth worked to ease the arrow out. The last inch gave way, and Jake roared and writhed on the couch. A pea-green tinge colored the blood seeping anew out of his wound.

"No. No. No." Elizabeth plucked the arrow shaft out, not caring if she hurt Jake or not. "It's poisoned."

"What?" Ric raked his hair, leaving it a chaotic spikey mess.

"Drawing the arrow through activated it." Elizabeth dumped out her nurse's bag, rummaging for a syringe and a vial. She injected Jake's shoulder. "I don't know what kind of poison it is. This antidote should slow the spread, but we need to get him to the compound clinic."

Lily knelt on the floor and clasped Jake's feverish hand as Elizabeth worked her bag of tricks to wrest the poison from Jake's body using herbs and poultices. She felt his life seeping away and it immobilized her. "Is he dying?" She caressed his pasty forehead.

Elizabeth rose, stretched her back. "It's out of my hands now."

Ric leaned over Jake. "You can't stop now!" Frantic, he clawed Lily's arm. "He's not dying because of you. Fix him, Elizabeth!"

"He's not going to die, not after everything we've been through," Lily said through gritted teeth. "He swore to protect me as my First Guardian. I'll be damned if I'll let him off the hook." Pain stabbed her forehead and a flush zipped up her neck. Her head throbbed and stars floated in her vision. A cut on the palm of her hand stung anew.

"Lily?" Her name floated in a distant land.

Lily's knees weakened, and she felt herself falling.

CHAPTER TWENTY-THREE

Jake stirred in the large bed, pulling the covers up to prevent the frigid air from causing serious damage to his balls. The room was too shrouded to tell the time. No clock on the nightstand, and his watch and cell had disappeared. After fourteen hours of unconsciousness—from his last wakeup alert from Nurse Ratchet—he felt as if he'd slid down a Tahoe mountain on his back. He elevated his shoulders to scrutinize the palatial room, but pain lanced through his skull and he sank onto the plump pillow. Weak and listless, at least he lived to tell about it.

Was Lily okay? He sensed vague snippets of her thoughts, but nothing concrete emerged from his brain sludge. Despite the fact that no one would give him the 411 or take him to her, the vague link was a relief.

As much as he tried, he couldn't get her out of his head, literally or figuratively. He should walk away from her. Save her from him, save him from things he didn't want to confront. But after spending the night with her, making love to her, he knew one night would never satisfy him. He needed a lifetime of her touch, her taste, her all. The realization left him reeling.

"You did this, Michael. You set the wheels in motion and drove us together," he groused.

A bang rattled the door in its frame before the door swung inward.

"Jake, you awake? Alive? Dead?" Ric asked.

"Barely." He winced as he shifted to his side to face the door. Elizabeth had patched the arrow wound, but it pained him if he leaned on his left side. The pain was minor compared to the poison hellbent on killing him, judging from the burn in his muscles every time he moved a limb.

Ric sprawled in the wing chair beside the bed, his large frame dwarfing the delicate antique.

"Help me up. I want to see Lily." He tossed the covers aside and swung one leg over the edge of the bed. "Elizabeth refuses to let me up."

"And I take my direction from her on healing matters."

Jake was too weak to move on his own and he gave in, for now. "Then tell me how our *Flower of Tara* is doing."

"Asleep and safe."

"How safe if neither one of us are with her?"

"Dude, we're in the highest level secured suite on the Guild stronghold." Ric waved his arms to encompass one of several plush bedrooms in the East wing dedicated to high-ranking Guild members. "Why aren't you in the healing center? Why're you here if you've been displaced as First Guardian?"

Jake rolled his eyes. "Elizabeth wanted me nearby to keep an easy eye on us. They didn't want Lily in the less secured healing center." He paused to catch his breath, realizing how easily winded he became. "Second, I'm still her Guardian."

Standing, Ric tossed his head back in a gloating laugh. "Guess you haven't heard. Niles appointed me Guardian. Your ass is on the chopping block."

Before Jake got a word in, Ric rushed away. "Duty calls."

Jake settled on the bed and drew the covers over him. Part of him dreaded the Guild tribunal, a destruction of his life as he knew it. Another part experienced an outpouring of unexplained jealousy and bitterness over being displaced as Lily's Guardian. Relief washed over the rest of him. Lily was growing on him too fast, and he refused to allow those feelings to strengthen. He had to cut the cord before it was too late to walk. He had to get her out of his head. How the hell was he supposed to accomplish obliterating her when every breath he took was like inhaling the essence of her very being? Maybe Elizabeth had a Lily purging potion.

His brother was right. His ass lay on the block two ways to Sunday. Ric and his middle brother Liam would have to take his place guarding Lily...if she allowed it. If the Guild allowed it. On top of that, Liam trusted no one in authority. Not since he was forced to desert his position guarding a hoity-toity psychic who'd compelled him to use his touch telepathy to learn secrets from certain Guild members, then forced him to play dirty pool with the laws of the Guild. Rather than turn her in and live in fear of retribution, he'd abandoned his position and earned dereliction of duty charges. He confronted the charges and beat them down, but the Guild tribunal had reduced him to an entry-level Guardian for two years, and he was serving his last months.

Not five minutes had elapsed when the door emitted a duo from the upper echelon of Guild management. He shot a questioning glance at Niles, the only one he trusted.

"Ah, you're awake." Niles Nevin, a Guild Elder, smiled warmly. His Irish brogue was apt to beguile those who didn't know his sharp wit and keener tongue. He preceded Elder Philip Sheehan into the room. Niles slanted his head in a knowing manner. "Glad to see you alive and well."

Philip remained silent, his gaze scurrying around the room, digging into every corner.

"Gentlemen. What do I owe the honor?" He made no pretense of sitting up—even if his body allowed—instead he paid close attention to the body language of the two Elders, especially ticking time bomb Sheehan. The man he trusted less than a terrorist wielding an Uzi. Philip betrayed a study in disapproval...and undisguised hunger.

The jackass in question swept his arm toward a locked door connecting the room to Lily's suite. "We've just had the immense honor of meeting our newest member and thought we'd pay the man who brought her among us his due respect."

Jake's left eyebrow peaked. Niles nodded imperceptibly. "You're welcome." Sheehan didn't give a rat's ass about his well-being.

"Did you see the Twilight ring or *my* chalice?" Philip's cultured smarm sent Jake's tolerance levels into overload.

Arctic air swept over him from the wintry gaze and he hauled the comforter to his chin. "Did *you*?"

"Philip tried to rip the ring off her." Disdain dripped from Niles's words.

Body thrumming, Jake bolted upright, shocking his system. "You son of a bitch."

Niles laid a hand on Jake's knee. "Calm down. Lily retains her heritage."

Philip smirked. "I merely wanted to ensure its authenticity. The ring supposedly has irrefutable markings on the inside."

Niles leaned a hip on the edge of the bed. "How are you feeling?" His genuine concern touched Jake like a smooth Irish whiskey. Niles had been another father figure to him since he'd joined the Protectorate at eighteen, and the older gent treated him square in all matters.

"They tell me I'll live."

"Why aren't you in the healing center?" Philip demanded.

Niles gripped Jake's arm, halting his scathing comeback. "Elizabeth makes the rules about healing. You know the Guild can't situate Ms. Falbrooke in a common room."

Philip slashed the air dismissively. "Or perhaps Jake's compulsion and telepathy need proximity?"

Damn it. How'd they find out?

"Yes, McAllister, we know you inflicted an illegal and immoral act upon an extraordinarily powerful psychic." Philip smirked.

Jake held his wrists out together. "Then take me away. Let's get it over with."

"There's no need for spite." Philip jingled coins in his pocket, aggravating Jake's last nerve. "We haven't discussed how to penalize your transgression."

"Banishment, forfeiture, and penalties are the prescribed punishment," Jake replied. "What else did you have on tap? Torture?"

"Jake," Niles admonished, unable to hide his knowing squint. "We've gone decades since any member has compelled another without permission. The old laws may be overly taxing in light of the current threats to the Guild. We need to make sure Ms. Falbrooke is well guarded. We need time to gather the council and investigate our options." Niles's slight nod kept Jake's tongue in check.

Philip stepped away from the bed and stuck his hands in his jacket pockets, jangling more irritating coins.

"Where's the chalice and the collection?"

A newfound wariness slithered through Jake's battered body, and he tugged on his earlobe. *Where is the collection?* "Haven't seen it." *True story.*

"We know it's on the grounds." Philip plucked at his pansy-ass pink tie. "According to surveillance cameras, Ric carried in an unidentified backpack."

Jake schooled his grimace. "The last I recall, I blacked out in a poison-induced coma."

"Did Lily find the pieces in Tahoe?" Philip turned interrogator.

"You'll have to ask her."

Elizabeth entered the room, a whirlwind in her black turtleneck and charcoal slacks, uncharacteristically dressed for a funeral. He hoped it wasn't for his funeral. "Out, both of you. While he's in my care, you'll answer to me."

On cue, Philip scowled and Niles shared telling eye play with Jake. Without argument, Philip departed.

Niles lingered behind, giving Elizabeth a hug. "Thank you for taking such wonderful care of my boy."

Elizabeth stepped out of Niles's embrace, blushing as she straightened her sweater. Single Niles and widowed Elizabeth seemed touchy feely friendly. Jake smothered a grin. Pain devoured his shoulder as he adjusted himself on the bed. At least his foot and the nape of his neck had quit throbbing. Small favors.

Elizabeth checked his healing wound, poking and prodding as if she were slicing daggers into his upper arm. "It's healing well."

"May I speak to Jake in private?" Niles asked. "I won't be but a moment."

Elizabeth turned on Niles. "You have my approval to visit anytime. Not that other buffoon."

"I couldn't agree more about him. Thank you for your

trust." Niles gave her a loving smile that almost had Jake rolling if not for the fact he was as weak as a newborn. Niles, the consummate bachelor, struck by the arrow. In his case, Cupid's arrow.

"I'll be back with your dinner in ten." Elizabeth rushed from the room.

"She's onto you." Jake grinned, jerking the covers up for the umpteenth time to ward off the Icelandic air.

Niles winked. "I hope so."

"Is Lily okay?" His gut twisted and turned.

Niles slid the side chair closer to the bed and sat. He rolled up the cuffs of his long-sleeved dress shirt, exposing ripped forearms. For all Niles's fifty-six years, he'd maintained the trim, muscular body and the thick reddish brown hair of a thirty-year old. Twenty years of service as a Guardian on top of ten-plus years of combat training kept his physique in top form. Jake hoped he looked as good when he hit middle age. If life let him live beyond the week.

"She was exposed to a small amount of poison when she helped Elizabeth take out the arrow." He held up a hand to forestall Jake's agonized glower. "She's recovering." Niles never held anything back from Jake.

Desperate to see her, Jake knew it was futile to ask. "Is she suffering?"

"No. Just weak, powerless."

Muscles twanged in his neck. "She's not powerless with that sapphire on her finger."

"The ring's not speaking to her right now," Niles explained. "It's possible the poison's interfering with her abilities."

"Christ. More fuel for the Guild tribunal." If he hurt Lily again, he didn't know how he'd survive.

"She'll figure it out once she recovers. There's no power greater than her new bond to the ring, according to the ancient texts." Niles' confidence was heartening, but it did little to assuage Jake's rankling guilt.

"Who else knows what I did, or about the collection being here?"

"Elizabeth, Philip, Ric."

"You know Philip's connected to Michael's death and Randy's disappearance." Jake told Niles about the vision Lily had experienced in Tahoe and the dead, missing intruder. "That asshole needs to be banished from the Guild for starters. Certain other members want Lily out of the picture too."

Niles shook his head. "No, they want her in their pocket."

Rage laddered up Jake's chest. "They'll find a way to get rid of her, man. Don't go stupid on me or I'll believe you want her in your pocket."

Niles waited for Jake's tirade to end. "Good. I wanted you to say it. That's a drop in the proverbial bucket of trouble. You and Lily need to get out of here and fast."

CR&SO

"North Pole, anyone?" Nestled in a massive four-poster bed and elevated on goose-down pillows, Lily bundled the jacquard comforter over her shoulders. Elaborate wrought iron scrolls crowned the top of the bed in the lavish room that made her tiny San Diego condo look like a closet. San Diego was so far from her reality it seemed like the life of her alter ego. The visions she'd experienced in her poison-induced delirium stuck to her like a fungus. Were they from her past? Second sight? Sinking into the pillowtop mattress, she recalled the most vivid one.

He came to her, gloved his firm body around her soft curves, and intoned indecipherable words she strained to understand. Birds screeched from towering trees, eclipsing the sound of their breathing. His arms became her safe haven, protecting her from the world, his mind linking to hers a mental balm, a rope of strength she didn't need but welcomed. She breathed him in, and his woodsy, spicy scent suffused her lungs to draw upon later. A balmy, soft breeze lifted his hair, fluttered a pine needle upon his shoulder. She flicked it away and he caught her hand, pressed a kiss on her palm, turning her legs boneless in a sea of desire.

"When we're alone together, we'll rule the world."

She smiled. "You have high hopes."

"Realistic hopes."

Voices sifted through the woods behind them, and they sprang apart. She spun toward the crunching footsteps, and when she glanced back at her protector, lover, and the heart of her soul, he'd vanished, leaving the barest hint of his presence tickling her mind.

Jake? They'd never been in the woods together at either her house or here at the Guild compound. Must've been Tahoe. Or wishful thinking?

Ric finished scanning the room for audio and video bugs, a twice-daily chore since he trusted no one in or outside the Guild. He shot Lily a heart-stopping grin. *Damn, he looks so much like Jake.* The biggest enigma of her life.

"The air-con helped prevent the poison from spreading." Finally answering, Ric sat beside her on the bed.

"So I'll freeze to death instead?" He tugged the covers up for her, and she awarded him a wan smile. Bedridden *and* a sitting duck, at the mercy of the Guild on their territory. She wanted out so bad the acid of distaste teased her tongue. To top off her week of crap, she was no closer to finding concrete evidence to nail her father's killer. Who was the tall man who owned an athletic bag emblazoned with a red circular logo from Juliana's vision? One of the bounty hunters in Tahoe? One of a million men in the world. A sinking dismay streamed welcome heat into her frigid limbs.

She snatched her purse off the nightstand, needing a link to her father, and noticed for the first time the sword pendant she'd clipped on the zipper was gone. "Did you see a tiny sword? I had it hanging on my purse. Dumbass Sheehan didn't believe it was a priceless artifact and steal it, did he?"

"Don't remember seeing it."

"Son of a psychic bitch. I must've lost it in Tahoe. This week just keeps getting better and better."

Ric scraped the wing chair over the floor alongside the bed and studied her with a heavy dose of wariness. After all, she did almost cause the death of his big bro.

"Why can't I see if Jake's okay?" she asked, not content with Elizabeth's earlier brush off. Bewilderment about their nebulous relationship anchored her down. Part of her wanted to race away from him. Well, her hormones ruled the other part with the helping hand of her heart.

"He's fine. He'll survive."

"Will they let him keep his position?" She looped her finger around her gold chain, afraid to touch the lucky charm that hadn't granted her much luck lately. *Oh, wait, I'm alive.* "I'm sorry, Ric." Lily stretched out her hand. "I didn't ask for this."

He took her hand and squeezed gently, not letting go. His hand, so like Jake's, was eerily and oddly comforting, like a little piece of Jake in her palm. Like the little piece of Jake flitting in and out of her brain, she reminded herself. Ric had explained that Jake kept checking on her. Nothing more. No stealing her thoughts, no reading the slew of emotions she had a tricky time naming.

"Not your fault, flower child." He squeezed her hand again, picked up a drumstick and tapped a solo on the bed. Earlier, she'd learned he used to play drums in a high school rock band.

"Don't I pull a skosh of weight?" *Even if I don't belong to the Guild?* She resented Jake violating her head to hell and back. Yet she understood he'd done the nasty to protect her, and she couldn't refute that his invasion helped fracture the cavern of her lost memories and hidden abilities.

"It's not exactly a cake walk." Ric drummed another silent riff on his thigh. "Other forces are battling against you both. The Guild's on high alert for threats, giving no amnesty, no quarter. Rules are rules."

"No kidding." Teeth clattering commenced, and a more mocking retort failed. He wasn't telling her everything. It boded ill toward her place within the Guild.

A contemplative hush filled the room, fighting for a foothold against the chaos of her new reality. The chilly air very nearly crackled.

There was so much Lily didn't know about herself, her legacy, her family, the McAllisters. She needed answers to the myriad of questions formed and not yet gelled jumbling her brain. She was positive she could get Ric to spill his guts. Elizabeth had hovered over her for the last two days, but Ric fawned over her as if she was on death's doorstep. Was this what it meant to be the Flower of Tara, the most powerful psychic on planet earth? She stifled an indelicate snort. To have a gang of Guardians helicoptering her to death?

"Ric?"

"Hmmm," he said, his voice drowsy.

"Hey! Sleeping on duty is against Lily's law." She slapped his arm, hitting stone beneath his New Orleans Saints sweatshirt.

"I got one eye open."

"Which one? The one in your pants?"

His eyelids slowly lifted, his eyebrows following toward his hairline. "I have my work cut out for me."

"Care to share?"

Ric reached over and tipped up her chin. "Look at me." She did as requested, her cheeks roasting. "I meant, you've got a lot to learn about ESP."

"So everyone keeps pounding into me." Lily pushed away from him and propped her head on her hand to view him better. "How can I trust you?"

"You tell me. You could've offed me with one eye blink if you really didn't like me."

The weight of the Twilight ring bogged down her listless hand. She loathed the idea of the dangerous and powerful ring, the troubles it had caused her family. According to legend, the Twilight collection was supposed to grant luck. What kind of freaking luck was killing everyone off? Was she next? "Yeah, I'm so evil and powerful."

"Naïve maybe." He raised a forestalling hand. "Don't take it ass-backwards."

"I know I'm an idiot psychic, Flower of Tara, what-the-hell-ever."

Ric stuck a finger over her mouth. "Shhh. Don't alert Nurse Ratchet." She shut her mouth, very much wanting to bite down on the digit he removed before her mouth took a trip on the freedom train.

"Go on," she encouraged.

"Since your clairvoyance and telekinesis are emerging, you'll feel evil in the air around you. You'll feel the imprint of emotions. You'll sense so much more than you ever imagined. If I was an evil, horny hottie trying to get into your bed, you'd know it the minute I crossed the line."

"Anyone I loathe for any reason will dissolve into the ether without me lifting a finger?" Okay, now who needed a trip to crazy town? "Cool. I got this." *Mental smack upside the head.*

Ric chuckled. "You'll learn to control your telekinesis. Right now, your power's useless since you don't know how to use and conserve, and the poison messed you up."

"How do you know so much?"

"Our mother was telekinetic. Although I'm clairvoyant, different from you I think, I've studied all psychic abilities. Guardians are required to know in order to guard our charges better, to know what we might confront in our adversaries. I blocked Philip from harassing your head."

Conveniently, she'd conked out just before Guild Elders Niles and Philip the traitor paid her a visit, and Ric deflected their worst ambitions. Studying her ring and the scratch Philip left behind on her hand, she was sure she wouldn't have let him escape the room unscathed. Apparently, he'd tried to rip the ring off her to authenticate it. He'd failed and it pissed him off, which plunked him on top of her growing shit list. *Enemy number ninety-nine.* Awake and recovered, she could've tangled the negative electromagnetic energy waves he emitted and dumped him onto his knees.

Ric's body slackened in the chair, and she nudged him awake, hard. "If you're my new Guardian, then guard."

"No one can skate past the locked doors, the cement walls. If someone tries, the alarm sounds."

Relief zipped through her. "Then work with me here. I have priceless artifacts a boatload of people want, and I don't know what the heck I'm doing."

"You *are* someone everyone wants."

Exasperated with her current state, Lily asked, "Am I stuck with a Guardian for the rest of my life?"

"You could do worse than the McAllister brothers."

"You three are close?"

"Best friends. After our parents died, we left New Orleans to live with our aunt and uncle in San Jose. We resented it at first since my dad shunned anything to do with the Guild, but Mom came from a family of psychics. She relented and stayed in New Orleans and out of the Guild. Jake, Liam, and I were kicking off our diapers when we showed first signs of psychic ability. Dad and Mom agreed we'd be Guild instructed and given the choice to join after we turned eighteen. Coming to California stuck us in the fire pit. My aunt, uncle, and cousins are all involved. We bonded as more than brothers at a time we didn't know if our parents had been murdered or if it was an accident. It's why Jake and I got into the PI and securities biz."

"The Guild or Cabal didn't kill your parents, did they?" A sickening thud hit her torso and she held her breath.

"No evidence." Ric shrugged, emitted a deep ponderous sigh, and leaned over her. "Car pileup on the freeway."

"I'm sorry." Her wrapped hand stung, the pain radiating up her arm. Why did she feel like someone had fished her out of the bay after the tide had battered her on the rocks for days?

Ric pressed a light kiss on her forehead, his lips both firm and soft. Although the kiss was innocent, she sensed a strange lesson from it. There were greater things in store for her, now that she'd run headlong into her heritage. A bizarre tickling energy fizzled between them.

He drew away, scratching his red lips. "Dude. Dial it down. I need my lips."

The sting she caused tickled her forehead like a prolonged static electricity shock.

"Do you feel the bioelectricity?"

Stunned speechless, she nodded.

"Your first lesson. Think what you can do once you master it."

CHAPTER TWENTY-FOUR

Jake tugged on his boots. Niles stood to his left, frowny reproach masking his usual stoic expression.

"You can't up and take Lily out," Niles said for the fourth time. "You're barred from her room."

A steel door separated his room from Lily's. "Ric will let me in."

"He's under strict orders to allow no one in but Elizabeth and Guild Elders."

A river of fury flowed through Jake, streaming over the banks. He needed to see Lily, needed to get her out of the compound. Too many people in and outside the Guild had an uncomfortable interest in her and the collection. It was time to bail and get her to safety, no matter if she kicked him to the curb later. Getting her to a safe haven was his top priority...even if his heart had other plans.

"Not all the poison's out of your system." Niles swung him back to the present. "You'll need to hole up and rest or you're dead in the water."

"Elizabeth left my scrips behind." Jake tied his boots. Teeth clenched against his canvas of pain, he jammed his T-shirt into his waistband.

Niles began pacing the geometric-patterned rug. "All hell broke loose when Lily introduced herself and the collection. Everyone's on guard. Everyone wants her, the collection. There's backstabbing right and left. Alliances are forming, marriage proposals are streaming in—"

Jake snaked a hand out and wound it around Niles's wrist. "Marriage? Whose marriage?"

"Lily's. Who do you think?"

"Are you yanking my chain? We're not in the 1500s." His grip tightened, Niles flinched. Jake released him and sent his mentor an apologetic nod.

"Lily needs you to guard her. She needs Ric to guide her clairvoyance and help her regain her telekinesis. He's better at training. She trusts you—"

Jake snorted. "Doubt that."

"Leverage what you had, make her trust you again." Niles waved to dispel the aura of malice that'd stolen Jake's known world and tossed it into the tar pits of hell. "Elizabeth and I will do whatever's required to secure yours and Lily's future."

His and Lily's future? What future? Adrenaline pumped through every limb of his body. After lying in bed for two days and thinking of nothing but Lily, he knew he'd never walk away from her. She'd seeped too far and too fast under his skin. Would she accept him after what he'd done to her? Did she hate him?

"You're not going anywhere now, so let's sit. We need to talk." Niles's low ominous tone fueled another sprout of dread.

"I'm taking Lily out tonight." Jake settled on the bed. Adrenaline leaked out of him, and he knew he wasn't setting foot outside the door. He'd be useless to her, and he refused to jeopardize her any further. Another night's rest was on tap for both of them.

"Tomorrow's soon enough." Niles shot him a mock stern glare. "Listen to your superior."

Jake managed a tight smile. "What's happening to

the Guild? For six months, the air's smelled bad. Guild members are being offed right and left, or lured into the Cabal. Now Cabal members are infiltrating our ranks."

Niles resumed his straight-backed pose in the chair beside the bed. "The Guild's imploding. Everyone wants their hands on Twilight. One group wants to replace all the directors. Another wants the Guild to ally with the Cabal. Another wants to break down the Cabal. It's a fractured mess. There are very few members left to trust."

"So this has been the intent of the Cabal ever since they began picking off and recruiting our members?" For six months, darkness had crept into his world, one inch at a time. Multiplied assignments, more peril, more threats to his wards. "How long have you known? Why wasn't I told?"

Niles exhaled in capitulation. "The Guild had to understand what we were dealing with before we alerted the Guardians. Most of you tend to go off half-cocked at the slightest provocation." He leaned back in the chair and flexed out his long, lean legs. "You were subtly swayed to get to know Michael—"

A sardonic laugh burst from Jake. "You think I don't realize that now?"

"I'm surprised you didn't mention it."

"Who can we trust?" He braced himself for the answer, already feeling the tidal pool of shit rising above his and Lily's necks. They had to dodge the waves and remain alive to help. *Simple enough. Right.* Sweat formed on his brow. He rested against the pillows piled on the bed, toed off his boots, and they thumped onto the marble floor.

Niles poured a glass of water from an insulated pitcher and handed it to Jake. "You okay?"

He drank half the cold water in one gulp. "Been better. Tell me who I can trust."

"Me, Lily and Ric. The Guild may be manipulating Elizabeth, so keep her off the grid."

"Damn." Jake didn't know what else to say about his imploding life. "What's the real story behind the collection's worth?"

"The sapphires supposedly bring health, wealth, and wellness to the McKenna family. The stones also ward off evil and bad luck, aid psychokinesis, telepathy, clairvoyance, and some say astral projection, although no one's ever verified occurrences of astral projection." He chuckled. "Throughout the ages, the family has believed if they let go of the collection, especially the ring, they'd suffer untold devastation. Prophecy also foretells that anyone who tries to use the stones for gain or splits up the collection will suffer untold devastation."

"The damn collection has destroyed Lily's family. I say we destroy it for good."

"You want to put Lily in peril if the prophecy is true?"

Jake grumbled a slew of curses. "What's the deal with the chalice?"

"Apparently, there's a missing legacy book containing recipes of potions one must drink from the chalice to aid in psychic luck. Any psychic can benefit from it, hence the reason the chalice has been separated from the collection."

A book? The journal Lily mentioned? "This is some freakass medieval witchery. How many more wrenches do we need tossed in our path?"

"It's the reason Michael never wanted to unearth the collection."

"But he didn't know its location…and he'd never do anything at the expense of his life or the life of his daughter."

"Come on, Jake." Niles slid his finger around the collar of his shirt. "He took the hit to protect Lily and left no readily available evidence behind as to its location. What does that tell you? He didn't want her to find it. He was trying to diffuse the situation with Randy and Sheehan and get them off the case."

"But she did find it."

"That's because you cracked her open, and she remembered the location of her mother's hidden journal. Plus she'd already found the safety deposit box key."

"Shit." Jake groaned.

"It was bound to emerge eventually."

"We could've thwarted the threats to the Guild first." How will he ever live with himself if something happened to Lily over ancient artifacts that spelled disaster for the Psychic Guild, positioned the Cabal in charge, and possibly changed the makeup of the psychic world? Did he just dump them all on the path of a bullet train traveling straight to hell? How had a murder investigation flipped the Guild on its ass?

How was he supposed to deal with a woman who possessed more psychic ability than he ever dreamed of wielding? True telekinetics were extremely rare, and none had surfaced in the Western Guild territory in decades, although some possibly skirted the Guild, like his mother.

Niles studied him long and hard. "Did you think you weren't born for greatness yourself? You were meant for this task, to help and protect Lily. To love her, if love is in your stars." The rug under Niles's feet muffled his footsteps. A hush deadened the room except for the ticking of the ornate hand-carved clock on the fireplace mantle and the hiss of the heater. "We need to keep her hidden. Eventually no one will care you broke Guild law by compelling her as long as you keep her safe." Niles stopped, a kaleidoscope of emotions grooving the lines on the bridge of his nose. "You and Lily can reform the Guild."

"It's that bad?"

"Yes."

Jake didn't appreciate being the one man with what seemed the soul of the Earth resting on his shoulders. It didn't take a divine bolt of lightning to tell him why he'd penetrated Lily's mind and compelled her. Nor did it take an explicit directive from Heaven to tell him his heart was chained to the one woman who had the ability to destroy him as well as save him. Only if he kept her alive, kept everyone from stealing her Twilight...stealing her...stealing his heart and soul, the heart of his mind.

CHAPTER TWENTY-FIVE

Crackling static electricity woke Lily from a fitful sleep. The lamp on a dark wood dresser across the room threw a puddle of yellow light a few feet from the dresser. She peered between the satin curtains tied to the bedposts. Heat radiated into the room for the first time in two days.

"Ric?"

Silence drowned the air. Drowsy from the comfort of the bed, her head listed to the side and sleep claimed her again. When she reawakened, gray light angled through the half-closed draperies over the window to her right.

A thud rammed the door to her private living room past the bedroom, startling her fully awake.

Wary, she scrunched up her knees and hugged them to her chest. No reason existed for her heart to knock against her ribcage. *Not.* Her trust meters had conked out the day she'd buried her father and again the day Jake betrayed her in Tahoe.

Jake remained a thread or two winding in her head, but she'd gotten used to his telepathic wings and kept her thoughts from strolling down private lanes. Even welcomed his comfort at times, despite her best efforts to run and hide in her own head.

Muffled voices rose from the hallway. Energy

renewed, she rolled out of bed, tested her strength with a few eager steps. Satisfaction coated her wariness like antacid and she rushed to the door to eavesdrop. Self-reproach didn't bother to swim ashore. After all, it was her room and she was the second coming of the Guild. *Mental snort-fest.* The brass handle on the door rotated, and she hopped to the side, pretending to fiddle with a large vase of flowers on the sideboard table.

The door swung open, and she fumbled a pink rose onto the floor as Philip Sheehan preceded Ric into the room. *Why the hell did the Guild allow this man so much power?*

"Ms. Falbrooke, how lovely to see you again." Philip extended his hand. When she didn't take it, he settled on an old-fashioned bow.

Lily locked her arms to her sides. Ric poised a hand on the gun at his waist, parroting a mad-dog mask, a shadow of Jake's familiar annoyance.

Not one to overstep cues, Lily's guard mounted along with prickles on her nape. "Hmmm," she gave Philip a wicked smile, finger on chin. "Am I to believe your visit is happenstance? Seriously, if you want the chalice, why don't I just give it to you?"

"Ah. It's wonderful to know our Flower of Tara is smart and beautiful." Philip jingled coins in his pants pocket. "May I offer my congratulations on your claim to the Twilight legacy?"

Ric penetrated the clashing will of minds. "To what do we owe this honor, Philip?" He took up Lily's right wing.

"Where's the chalice, McAllister?" Philip didn't let the dust settle. "I'd love to view the entire collection."

"The *entire* collection's safe and sound." Ric winked at Philip.

Was he scamming her and working for Philip to hunt

down the chalice as evidenced by the contract Philip had handed her at the restaurant? Ric had had every chance to steal the entire collection when he'd carted her half-dead body into the compound. He didn't know the chalice she'd found in Tahoe was a fake, or that the real one resided in a San Jose safety deposit box—clues she'd derived from cryptic notes in her mother's journal. Her ace in the hole. *Where's my clue jar when I need it?*

Lily didn't appreciate the eye play between the two men. Suspicion gauges began cranking overtime.

"Lily, go back to the bedroom," Ric commanded in a voice so unlike him it took her aback.

"Think again." Her insides seethed.

Ric reached to grip her upper arm, but she side-stepped out of his reach. "Keep your hands to yourself, *Guardian*. Someone better talk or I won't be responsible for what my untrained powers will do." Emphasizing her point and using her untried telekinesis, she floated the flower-filled vase to the middle of the room and slammed it to the floor. The vase shattered in a million pieces, porcelain shards pinging the floor. Pink, red, and white roses scattered, a meadow of color chasing the porcelain bits. Expensive Persian rugs lapped at the spilt water.

Triumphant, she gave herself a mental high-five. Wearing the Twilight ring seemed to grant her energy, or else her long-dormant psychic powers were staging a scathing comeback. Telekinetic energy harmonized with the random presence dancing in her mind.

"Ms. Falbrooke," Philip's low voice beguiled. "We mean you no harm. I'm here merely to retrieve that which belongs to...Guild members at large. To give it due honor in a setting where all can appreciate it."

"Kiss my ass." Lily gleefully watched a red rash pepper Philip's neck and face.

Stiff as a three-day-old corpse, Ric turned on her.

"The chalice legally belongs to Philip. He hired me to retrieve it. Sorry to do this to you, Lil babe." Grinning wickedly, he clenched her wrists behind her back, tying them with a nylon zip strip. "For your protection."

Stunned, Lily stiffened. "You son of a bitch." She twisted her wrists. "Does Jake know you've flipped? Are you all on the same side?" She explored her mind for Jake, discovering only a barren wasteland. Had Ric bypassed her house alarm and ransacked the house? He had the means and now the motive. Ric crammed a wadded ball of cloth in her mouth. She wanted to cry, rage, throw knives, but all she mustered was a frosty, aberrant revulsion.

Ric left Philip guarding her and determined steps led him into the bedroom. Seconds later, he returned, her backpack in hand. He emptied the pack on the loveseat, and the chalice tumbled onto the floral cushion. Thank her lucky shamrock, her mother's journal didn't join the chalice on its way to Suckers 'R Us.

Why didn't Ric just cut her ring finger off and give it to Philip, too? The minute she got the chance, she totally planned to maim Ric, then escape the asylum forever, no stopping to collect her two hundred bucks at GO.

Philip cast his wide-eyed avarice on the chalice. Ric handed it to him, and Lily thought he'd come on the spot. Ogham, an ancient Celtic script, etched the base of the chalice. She hoped it spelled disaster for Ric and Philip, if nothing else.

Stroking the chalice, a lustful smile set deep brackets around Philip's full lips. "It's magnificent." He snaked his arm around her rear and fingered the sapphire in the ring, touched her bound hands, and grazed his thumb up her arm.

"You got what you came for," she said around her muffle. "Now get out."

"Jake?" Philip's eyebrows winged up.

"Don't worry about him," Ric retorted. "Beat it."

Philip withdrew a fat envelope from inside his suit jacket and tossed it to Ric. He retrieved the discarded backpack and tenderly placed the chalice inside a secure pocket. Stepping in front of Lily, he dipped his head and planted a gentle kiss on her lips. Before she could bite down, he'd inched away. "Lovely Lily McKenna Falbrooke, it's been a pleasure." He sauntered out of the room as if he lorded it over the castle.

Ric secured the door. For a moment, he appeared indecisive before he slowly withdrew the cloth from her mouth. Lily spat at him in disgust. Pent up tears slid down her cheeks, and he thumbed them away while her eyes shot shards of glass at him.

"If you ever touch me again, I'll kill you."

"Don't do me any favors. If I release you, are you gonna take me out now?"

A smile slid across her face, slow, deadly. "What else do you want from me? Planning to kill Jake so you can have it all? Or am I up for sale to the highest bidder? How powerful is Philip? Is he man enough to handle my powers? Are you? Is anyone?"

"Zip it." He jerked her wrists and cut the plastic strips. She swung her arm and slapped his cheek, and then returned to the bedroom. A molten hot fury threatened to turn her to ash. Whatever psychic powers she'd buried, whatever memories she'd hidden in the unreachable pockets of her mind, her identity and her role in the here and now just got real. And she no longer gave a rat's ass about her fear and wariness in discovering the lost life she'd buried.

With stiff, jerky movements, she started tearing the room apart. Ric told her he'd hidden the box containing the jewels and her mother's journal prior to Philip's first visit. She tossed exquisite art objects off the dresser and onto the bed. A decorative ceramic trinket box clanged against a lamp. She struggled to push the ornate dresser away from the wall.

Ric tried to jostle between her and the bureau. "Stop. You'll hurt yourself."

"Screw you. Where's my journal and the collection?"

He strutted to the bed, reached behind the headboard, and the sound of duct tape peeling off the wood shredded Lily's last lonely nerve. She stomped around him and snatched the journal and small box out of his hands. She trailed her fingers over the leather cover of the book, feeling at one with the text, channeling her mother, channeling elusive serenity and wisdom. Wings flapped in her head, excited and wary. Energy swelled, her barriers soared, locking Jake out completely.

Tipping up her chin, she said, "Get out." Art objects on the dresser whirled, struck Ric on his shoulder, and crashed to the floor in angry ruins. Ric departed, leaving Lily floundering in a universe of epic confusion.

Welcome home, telekinesis.

CHAPTER TWENTY-SIX

Unable to trust Ric or anyone else in the Guild compound for that matter, Lily knew it was time to talk to Detective MacKenzie. If she couldn't trust him and Juliana, then she was doomed in more ways than one. The more she thought about it, the more she realized she could investigate Sheehan from the inside if she remained behind and prolonged her recovery. But the cops needed to know her plans before something else happened to her. She found her cell stashed in the nightstand drawer with enough juice to make one call. Once she lost power, she opened the doorway to the marbled hallway to the exclusive wing of the mansion.

"Are there visitor rooms I can meet with outsiders?" she asked Ric. The Guild didn't allow non-Guild members to enter the mansion. She gave them credit where credit was due, but in this case, it didn't suit her.

"First floor by the entry."

"Am I allowed to meet anyone?" she asked, bitter sarcasm stealing her voice.

"You're not a prisoner."

"I guess I'll be leaving instead." She tested him.

He tapped his gun as if he'd stop her by any means. "I'll need a release from Elizabeth and Niles. For your protection and health, that is." He landed a scowl on her and she upped it a glower.

"Sounds like a prisoner to me. In a half hour, I want an escort to a private visitor room." She slammed the door on him, charged into her bedroom, changed her clothes, and tried to arrange her unruly hair, finally tying it in a loose knot. She found the wall safe he'd shown her and reset the combination, hoping his prior instructions were accurate and he hadn't led her on another Benedict Arnold McAllister lying spree.

Ric escorted her down a rear staircase to the visitor conference rooms in the front of the opulent mansion of gilt, carved pillars, marble floors, and stairs fit for royalty and their lousy guards.

She toyed with the idea of running for it, but not without her legacy. No matter how much she loathed the death sentence the Twilight collection had bestowed upon her family, the minute she had possession of it, she knew she'd never let it fall into another person's hands. It destroyed her family, rather than helped them the way the prophecy read, but she refused to allow their deaths to have been in vain by giving up the collection. One way or another, she'd find a way to end the hard-on every damn antiquities dealer, collector, or nefarious asshole had for the collection. And she'd die before she allowed another person to manipulate her and her psychic abilities. The ring bore the weight of enormous proportions in multiple ways. Yet its weight around her finger gave her more confidence and insight than an ocean of vodka and Wikipedia.

Ric dumped her in a small conference room, sparse by comparison to the other lavish rooms in the mansion. Four chairs sat around a small table, and a credenza hosting bottles of water and glasses sat against the far wall. Not one window let in a peep of daylight.

"Is the room bugged?" Not that she believed he'd fess up.

"No. It's against the law."

She rolled her eyes. "Like that ever barred the Guild."

Deep lines tunneled Ric's forehead, the same way Jake's forehead wrinkled, as if unsure how to handle her demands. "I'll keep your visitors off the logs if you want anonymity."

She touched her parted lips, surprise reining in her retort. "You'll do that for me?"

"You're not a prisoner. But if you think you can sic your cop friend on me, think again. You don't want Sheehan on your shit list. He doesn't want the whole collection, just the chalice, which is his by right. No charges will stick to me."

The menace in his voice gave Lily pause. It seemed forced and fake, as if he was putting on a show. As if he was a pawn.

"I'll fetch your guests. Lock the door and don't let anyone in until I return."

Five minutes later, she opened the door, and Juliana Westwood rushed in, arms around Lily so fast, she had no time to blink. When she did, her gaze landed on the delectable chisel-faced Alex MacKenzie toting his badge and a growling grimace. Ric shut the door behind them and Alex locked it.

"How bad is it?" Juliana released Lily, her face a study in distress. Alex rested his hands on her shoulders. "Sorry, you remember Alex, right?"

"Yes. Thank you both for coming." A gun peeked out of Alex's shoulder harness, granting her a dash of relief. "Please sit. I don't know how much time I have before Jake goes on a rampage hunting me down."

Alex spun around the room, cop eyes searching for any threats. "Are you safe here? Are they holding you against your will?"

"According to Ric McAllister, I'm free to leave. I still have my gun. They didn't take that from me, so I guess I'm not a prisoner."

Lily explained all that'd happened to her from meeting Philip Sheehan in San Francisco to her suspicions about Jake, Ric, and every other member of the Guild. "Sheehan now has the chalice. Another fake, I believe. It's only a matter of time before he figures it out."

Alex furiously thumbed in notes on his smartphone, then called the Tahoe sheriff's office and discovered no reports of two gunshot men. "I'll have Sheehan brought down to HQ for questioning."

"Sheehan may have masterminded the kill, but he didn't pull the trigger." Exhausted from her constant fury and worry, Lily pressed her fists onto the table as if to hold herself topside. "Any number of Guild members fit my father's killer's profile."

Juliana squeezed Lily's hand gently. "Do you remember if they all attended the funeral and wake?"

"In hindsight, I saw pretty much everyone now that I've met them here. Sheehan, Niles, Ric McAllister. Not the two men we shot in Tahoe, though. But they were both average height and on the thick side. Haven't met Jake's other brother Liam yet. Apparently, he's barred from the compound and Guardian duties. Hell, maybe it was him."

"Are there pictures of all the members anywhere?" Juliana asked. "At the funeral, I scrutinized every man, as did Jake from a distance. None of them rang a bell."

"I haven't seen any."

Alex paced the small room. "We need to get you out. McAllister's not fulfilling his so-called Guardian job."

"I gave him the slip once or twice." Lily winced. "I haven't exactly been very helpful."

"You didn't trust him. I don't blame you. I had the same issue with him at first." Juliana tapped Alex's wrist and stopped him from stomping a canal through the shaggy gray rug. "Alex, I need to join the Guild now. I can help Lily from the inside, do some touch telepathy and mind-reading—"

"Are you insane?" His mottled red skin prepared to explode blood all over her. "*She's* not safe here. Why would I leave you here?"

"With you as my Guardian," Juliana finished belatedly.

"Nope. Niles said no one's joining until they stabilize the threats from the Cabal. We're taking Lily with us. I can protect her if McAllister can't."

Lily spread her hands on the table, tracing the patterns of woodgrain to steady the storm brewing inside her. "No. I'm here already. I'll work the inside while you work the outside." She held Juliana's gaze. "My psychic ability is coming back."

A twinkling animation accentuated Juliana's flawless complexion. "Are you kidding me? You wait until now to tell me. Cough it up. What can you do? Let's devise a plan of action based on your abilities."

"I'm clairvoyant. I see visions from the energy people leave behind. Or blood." She unloaded about the incident in the Tahoe loft. "It's random. I can't focus enough to trigger it."

"That'll come in time with practice and as your ability emerges." Juliana pursed her lips. "That's not all?"

Lily bit the inside of her cheek, wanting to take a bite out of Jake McAllister instead. "Jake broke into my head and opened my blocks. It's against Guild laws, and he's up crap creek without a paddle. Once he heals, they'll boot him out of the Guild."

"Good riddance," Alex said. "He had no right to

violate you like that. I never trusted him. You shot him for a reason, Juliana."

"It was an accident. He scared me. Plus, you don't understand the circumstances with Lily. He's protecting her." Juliana defended the enigmatic McAllister brother. "She may still be repressing if not for what he'd done."

"There's more I won't go into, but get this." She focused on a pewter *fleur de lis* bookend on the credenza. Clearing her mind, she imagined the bookend flying across the room to smash against a tall metal *verdi gras* vase stuffed with silk flowers. The bookend clanged into the vase, toppling it onto the floor. Autumn amber, purple, and burgundy flowers and grasses spilled in a heap at the foot of the sideboard.

"Oh. My. God." Juliana clapped. "You're telekinetic. I've never met a telekinetic."

"The McAllisters' mother was the last telekinetic the Western Guild had their sights on. Until now." She sat, scribbling invisible doodles on the table. "I'm the reason everyone wants the Twilight chalice and this ring." She dug the Twilight ring out of her front pocket and set it on the center of the table. "I've found the collection, or at least part of it." She slid a key on the table toward Alex. "You need to hold onto this safety deposit box key for me. The box holds instructions to use the chalice. And this key," she dropped another key onto the table, "opens the box containing the real chalice." She slid a piece of paper toward Alex. Her trip to Tahoe and the journal had coughed up more than she'd imagined. "Here are the bank and box numbers. If anyone gets their hands on these two, they can manipulate a lot of psychics without baiting them with money or death." Alex touched the keys, as if afraid they'd ensnare him into the looney bin of psychics. "Can I trust you to keep this safe? I don't know who else to trust."

"You don't even have to ask." Juliana gripped Lily's arm, the blonde woman's eyes blistering into Alex's nervous glance. "Let's talk strategy."

"I'd rather talk about getting you to a safe house." Alex slashed his hand through the air. "I don't like this, Lily."

"I need to kill this obsession inside the Guild and the Cabal once and for all. I can only do it while digging from inside the pit of vipers." She twirled the ring on the table. "I need to figure out once and for all if I can truly trust Jake McAllister."

A dense hush descended upon the room, raining unspoken words of a certain magnitude.

"You're falling in love with him, aren't you?" Juliana asked softly. Alex plastered himself against her back and lovingly massaged her shoulders, caressed her neck.

The love on his face nearly undid Lily. *Will Jake ever look at me with such respect and love?* An unconditional look without desire for what she held in her possession or the arsenal of her mind? Did she want to test the waters further, or run away before she toppled in too deep without a life jacket?

CHAPTER TWENTY-SEVEN

A calming energy cocooned Lily under the thick comforter burying her on the plush bed. Fearing the more intense dreams plaguing her since Jake had cracked open her mind like an egg, she found it impossible to sink into a deep sleep. She flung out an arm, relieved Elizabeth had turned the thermostat up after declaring her out of danger from the insidious poison of indeterminate nature. A weak glow of light angled under the door to the living room.

Active and excited, Jake flitted in and out of her mind. She missed him, but a high price tag accompanied that sentiment. She couldn't afford to lose herself in him without an infinite amount of trust.

Again, something else stirred within her. At first, she thought it was Jake's presence times two, but it felt as if another being lived within her mind. *Meet the new Lily McKenna Falbrooke. Telekinetic. Clairvoyant. Whatever. How many personalities do I have?*

She dangled her legs over the side of the bed, and shunted thoughts of Jake to a corner to concentrate on her surroundings. While keeping her ears peeled for sounds from beyond the bedroom, a quick survey of the room reassured her. Yet, a strange fizzing energy whipped the air.

"Going bonkers now?" Ants crawled up her back, like tiny McAllister psychics on the prowl.

"Ric?"

Silence.

She dashed to the hall door, pressed her ear against the hardwood. Dead silence. The lights in the room winked out. The door alarm beeped as the backup battery kicked in. Door locks snicked and the door opened, crashing against the interior wall. A black-hooded figure rushed into the room, and shadowed her as she raced into the bedroom and slammed shut the interior door.

Subconsciously, Lily screamed for Jake, knowing they had no direct telepathic link, at least none she knew how to leverage. She hoped he sensed her fear and confusion. Flattened against the wall, her heart banged like a jackhammer attempting to drill through her muscles and skin. Forcing her concentration on her paltry telekinesis—her bioelectricity—she inhaled deep breaths to temper her heart.

Too late. The door to the bedroom sprung open. It thudded against the wall, the doorknob jammed in the drywall.

"Ric? What do you want?" She scrutinized the dark figure in the doorway, all wizard-like in a shroud. He tossed back his head, the hood falling off.

Philip Sheehan. Traitor. Thief. Murder suspect.

"I'll bury you if you come any closer." She expected Ric to materialize, but no one tailed Philip into the room.

Frantic, she attempted a compulsion with telekinesis, but Philip had already incapacitated her. She sought Jake in her head, but his faint presence evaporated.

"Save your psychic abilities for later, my dear Lily." Philip dusted a finger across her cheek. "In your weakened state, the power of the Twilight sapphire can't help you sense my hidden talents."

"What might those talents be?" She stalled him. *Sociopathic pain in the ass?*

Philip cradled her chin. "The Guild believes I'm a telepath with mind reading ability. However, my particular talent of separating one from her abilities is quite effective, don't you agree?" He pinched her chin, released her. Desire danced among the silvery flecks in his eyes. "It takes one loose thread, one hole, one chink to allow me in to tear a mind apart."

"How can you cut me off from my powers?" Lily's thoughts revolved as fast as her heart galloped.

Puffing out his chest, he said, "A simple pinprick into the core of your mind enabled my entry and my command to curb your powers. Everyone has a flaw, including you, my beautiful flower."

She implored Jake in her mind, but her windswept landscape gave no quarter.

"Time to go. Scream and I'll kill you where you stand. Got that?"

Not believing for one second he'd kill her, she nodded and racked her brain for an escape hatch, or a plan to out Philip as her father's murderer. He withdrew two zip strips from his pocket, tied her wrists together, and then tied her to a bedpost. "Now, where's the *real* chalice?"

Lily swallowed down the lump of panic in her throat. Was the chalice all he wanted? "Ric gave you the chalice."

Philip's lips compressed in a thin line. "He'd have you believe so. I bet Jake doesn't know how his own brother betrayed him yet again. The Guild tasked Ric to guard you. What does he do? Abandons his post and steals from you, from the Cabal. From me."

Had Ric seriously betrayed Jake? Or were they working in tandem? Thinking was worth only so much, a picture worth a million words. She no longer trusted her own intuition where it revolved around the McAllister brothers. She'd do well to avoid them...once she doused this particular fire.

Philip swished his arms angrily as if to dispel an attack. "We're wasting time. Where is it?"

His stride ate the distance to the credenza by the door. Expensive art objects she'd sacrificed earlier crashed to pieces onto the marble floor.

Lily tried to dismantle Philip's mind control, but for every fiber she pulled apart, it revealed a flaw, and his telepathy braided tighter. She concentrated on the power denied her, to no avail.

Cursing under his breath, Philip blustered closer to her, and she now saw her mother's journal and the box of jewels cradled in the crook of his arm. Perspiration dotted the nape of her neck.

He tossed her a pair of jeans, a sweater, and her sneakers, untied her and waited for her to dress. While he watched her out of the corner of his eye, her clumsy hands shook, and it took her eons to change her clothes.

"You should have taken your friends up on their offer to leave with them yesterday." He clucked his tongue and grinned. "Your last mistake."

"Screw you, asshole." She spat in his face. "You do know one of my friends is a cop and they have all the names of the Guild members I suspect are my father's killer. Including yours."

"I'm only here to get what's legally mine. I paid for the authentic chalice, and I will obtain it by any means."

"Kidnapping is a felony, no matter how you slice and dice it."

"Don't fret yourself. Once you hear my offer, kidnapping won't be a word in your dictionary. Once I give you the evidence you need to nail your father's killer, you'll be thanking me."

Lily sucked in her stomach.

"And once I give you the evidence to prove your mother and brother's accident was *no* accident, you'll hand me the world." Philip seized her arm. "Now let's go." His unyielding fingers numbed her forearm. "One final ability I've kept in check," he chuckled, "is the discreet art of compulsion. Your precious Jake isn't the only one who practices the lost arts."

Her feet shifted forward as though they had their own command center, and her brain gave the order to tighten her throat.

One nightmare replaced another, as more of her tenuous world disintegrated.

CR§O

Ric yanked the zipper on his backpack, hefted it over his shoulder as Jake met him outside the door to Lily's room. They were both dressed in solid black, more than ever looking like twins. Remorse pricked Jake. He didn't want Ric involved, but choices weren't flinging themselves at him like bikini-clad women on the white sands of Mexico.

Ric cracked open the door to Lily's wing. "Clear. Niles locked down the wing. Elizabeth won't make rounds until morning before she heads to the office." The recessed backup lights pooled dim puddles of yellow on the white hallway floor. As the door opened all the way, Jake knew shit had gone ass-end wrong.

"Was Niles shutting power down?" Ric asked.

"Not that I'm aware." Needles of adrenaline jabbed holes in his veins.

Jake raced to Lily's suite door and glued his ear to the panel, listening for signs of an intruder, for sign of life, for Lily. Nothing but cold, dead steel. "What the—" He turned the doorknob and inched open the door.

The room had met the eye of a tornado. No sign of Lily.

Ric rushed into the bathroom. "She's gone."

Jake rounded on his brother. "How'd she get past the locks and the alarm? Or you?"

"Shit. I was gone for five minutes." Ric slammed his fist in the wall. "I set the alarm, locked the third lock only Elizabeth and I have access to. There's no way she got past that without help."

The wall safe door hung ajar. Jake thrust it open to find the safe empty. "Where's the real chalice?" A deep sense of dread multiplied those needles throughout his body.

"In whatever safety deposit box Michael hid it. Can you feel Lily?"

Jake scrubbed his chin. "No." How'd his brother know what he'd done to her?

"You know what they say about denial being a river." Ric grinned.

"Bite me." Jake was never able to slide anything past his youngest brother. "How'd you guess?"

Ric's grin sobered. "I sensed something in her clairvoyance. Put two and two together. "

He'd deal with the ramifications of his actions later. "Let's go. I sense her enough to track her."

"Someone cut her off?"

"The question is, who has that ability in this day and age?" Jake drilled his sight out into the ebony night. He wanted his twilight back, his sunlight, the light of his entire being.

CHAPTER TWENTY-EIGHT

Lily tugged the nylon zip strip binding her wrists behind her back. She tried kicking Philip and earned a fist to her right jaw, a new round of throbbing pain decimating her head. His compulsion ability was pathetic, lasting mere seconds in bursts. His telepathy on the flipside was strong, blocking her access to her own abilities and Jake.

Outside the mansion, he shoved her in the backseat of a sedan and blindfolded her. It took a half hour to reach their destination, which could be any part of San Jose, the surrounding towns of Silicon Valley, or possibly farther into the foothills from the compound toward the coast. Lily bided her time, conserving her energy for when he unbound her, and waiting for him to slip up and confess that he had killed her father.

Once the car stopped and he shut the engine off, he removed the blindfold and guided her through a large Spartan living room, home to a brick fireplace, a couch, and entertainment center. Devoid of decoration, whites and grays brought the kitchen into the 21st century, a gourmet six-burner gas stove the focal point on a center island. Still no clue as to her whereabouts, the darkness surrounding the house offered zilch. One of two doors at the far end of the kitchen led them to a basement, which meant an older home.

Phillip didn't utter one word as he prodded her down the stairs, into a small basement room, and then blocked the doorway. He was so silent, Lily wondered if he needed his entire concentration to keep up whatever mental block he'd placed on her.

A carpet remnant covered the glossy, brown-stained concrete floor. One tiny frosted window close to ceiling height graced the outer concrete wall. The air smelled dank, musty, unused. A faded southwestern print futon was shoved against a wall with an old scarred oak coffee table in front of it. An open doorway to the left led into a pint-sized bathroom, which included a shower, pedestal sink, and toilet. Fluorescent tubular ceiling lights lit the space.

The room didn't attempt to mimic the over-the-top Guild headquarters. However, Philip had attempted to make it serviceable. A stack of new towels, sheets, blankets, and pillows lay on the futon, and he'd stocked the bathroom with a new supply of drugstore brand toiletries. A pre-meditated abduction charge awaited him.

The key clicked in two new door locks, and Philip abandoned her without a word. Lily listened for exterior sounds, but nothing fed the machine of her desperate curiosity. Sharp slivers of frustration and fear pierced her. Philip had effectively blocked her powers, her strange one-sided telepathic link to Jake gone the way of her family.

"Damn it." She stamped her right foot. Why had her father—everyone—waited until now to clue her in on her identity? Why had she resisted trying to regain her memories and abilities? Why had she avoided the truth? Now her phobias and inabilities trapped her on a spaceship hurtling toward Earth. Her mind roiled with bits of space debris, trapping a meteor shower between her ears.

Lily's cheek stung where Philip had smacked her. She wanted to rub it, make the pain disappear, and kick his sorry ass into next week. She sank onto the coffee table, pressed her mind for a connection to the ring, to Jake. Hell, she'd even take Ric over Philip.

"Damn it all to Sunday! Jake, where are you?" she murmured under her breath, not wanting to offer clues on a silver platter if Philip had bugged the room.

The locks clicked again and the door swung inward. Philip filled the doorway, his suit jacket and tie gone, shirtsleeves rolled up to expose his dwindling summer-tan arms.

"What do you want?" Lily locked down her mind. She figured she better learn his full intent and derive a plan from the information she gleaned rather than hit him half-cocked.

He shut the door, locked it. Pinching her chin, he tipped her head up. His smile was both loving and somewhat lustful.

"I want you, beautiful Lily McKenna, Flower of Tara." He caressed her cheek, and Lily fought the revulsion threatening to overtake her calm facade.

"Well, I don't speak moron, so you can't have me."

"Oh, but I already do have you."

Focusing on his exotic violet-gray eyes, she tried to dig through her repressed memories, searching for anything that might clue her in on him. "You have the chalice. You got what you really want." What did he know about the Twilight collection, the abilities of the chalice, and the legacy book locked up in a bank vault?

Philip smiled his patient smile. "There's much you don't know, Lily McKenna. Much I can teach you. We can have everything we've ever dreamed of at our disposal. We can rule the Guild and the Cabal both. We can rule the world, you and I, if we wanted to reach for the stars."

Lily shook her chin out of his pinching fingers. He knelt in front of her. She slid backward on the table, and he followed, a lion ready to pounce.

"No thanks." The words spat out like glass. "I'd rather spend my life alone and powerless at ground zero for sinkholes."

"Unfortunately, that will never happen." Philip smelled of acrid sweat. The stench churned Lily's stomach. "Why just today, the Guild received five offers of an alliance or marriage. Not one offer is good enough for you."

Holly hell on high! Marriage proposals? "What the...we're not living in the dark ages. No one marries me without my permission. And why do you think *you're* good enough? Is your wife into polygamy? It's the 21st century. You should join it." *Delusional asshat.*

"Leave my wife out of it. I have no intentions of marrying you. This is a business arrangement, pure and simple. I may not possess the powers these high ranking psychics do, but not one of them have what I possess."

Hands still tied behind her back, Lily mentally twirled her finger by her right ear. "Right. Not one of them has resorted to kidnapping and theft."

Philip leaned in, his mouth mere inches from hers. "Quite true. However, I'm referring to the fact that I *own* the chalice. It was stolen from me and I have proof." His voice lowered to a stage whisper, "And the fact that I'm a McKenna by blood, with the same lineage to the Kings of Tara as you enjoy. I may not be *the* McKenna Flower of Tara, nonetheless, my claim is defensible."

How was that even possible? Was he high or tricking her? "Prove your claim."

"Ah, Lily. I knew you'd ask for proof. In due time, I'll show you our family tree. Suffice it to say your mother and I were third cousins."

The odor of whiskey permeated Philip, not unpleasant, but unwelcome. Alcohol and kidnappers were not a mix she wanted to confront. Inwardly searching for her source of power, she met a blank wall with one tiny fissure. Pushing on the crack, she felt for the feathery sensation she would've killed for to get rid of earlier. Only a barren coldness toting a headache met her feelers. *Come on brain cells, work for your next meal!*

"Don't hurt yourself," Philip chastised.

Another round of shock suffused her. Putting the brakes on her thoughts, she asked, "Did you kill my father? Did you shoot the arrow at Jake?"

He laid his hand on her knee. Warm and heavy, his hands were smooth, his nails manicured, distracting while she conjured up an escape hatch. *Manscaping at its finest.*

"As I've informed you, I don't do my dirty work. You've already witnessed two of my transactions."

She bit. "The man who broke into my Tahoe cabin?"

"An idiot best left dead, I'm sure. He let you slip through his fingers. Haven't heard word one from the man."

Cold, lifeless fingers. "Ric McAllister?"

"What do you think?"

Had Ric arranged to shoot Jake? Why would he handle Philip's business, especially against his own brother? Unless a fat payoff sat in a pot at the end of the rainbow. Unless she dangled in the center of a Guild and Cabal setup and they were all working together.

Suppressing more tremors, she recalled Ric pumping information out of her. What had she done? Philip's wide smile was all the answer she needed. She had to force herself to stop fidgeting and spur him to split a vein. Her stomach gurgled, and she fought the nausea, not willing to grant Philip the satisfaction of witnessing how his words affected her.

"Did. You. Have. My. Father. Killed?"

He chuckled, a sadistic gleeful sound. "I wished I'd done the deed myself."

The man Juliana Westwood pictured in her vision appeared taller, more muscular, more like Jake. Or Ric. "I need water."

Her jailor stood and ambled to the door. "I'll prepare a tray with your dinner soon. You won't stay in this room for long. I know it's hardly fit for a rat. Just a brief stop in your destiny."

Silent, his leather dress shoes made little sound on the concrete floor, and the locks clicked her into her own little pokey. Dropping her head between her knees, she warred with the raging nausea threatening to unhinge her. "Son of a freaking bitch." Philip hadn't harmed her, so why was she stirring the pot on her weaknesses? *Get a grip!*

She lifted her head, feeling a fraction better. She wrangled with the zip strip tying her wrists together, needing to access the supposed power of the Twilight stone since she couldn't reach the bioelectricity in her head. Did Philip believe she needed visual contact with the ring, hence the reason he kept her wrists tied? Why hadn't he pried the ring off her finger? What was his deal? It made as much sense as an ice sculpture in the Sahara. Maybe the Twilight collection was nothing but a pile of priceless jewels and the rest an epic lie. *Welcome to Clueless City.*

"Well, here goes nothing." She envisioned the sapphire, and the star in the center sparked to life, just a sting of electricity against her hand. Swiveling her left wrist, she pressed the ring into her palm, the vacant stone dead against her skin. She worked to separate the tiny fissure in her brain, trying to find her memories, her bioelectricity. Nothing. She concentrated on breaking the links on the plastic zip strip one by one, watching them in her mind's eye stretch and pull apart. Again, zilch. Hunting for Jake, she pushed against the crack again. An oil-drill began an excavation in her head. Ignoring the tortuous pain, she pressed the ring harder into her palm.

Two prongs on one side of the main stone broke skin, and she ripped it along her flesh, drawing blood, sticky on her palm. Smearing blood on the sapphire jolted electricity up her arm. Feeding off it, she kept the ring pressed into the cut.

A pulsing, feathery awareness welcomed her. *"Jake!"* she mind-screamed.

"Lily." A faint male whisper reached her.

"Help me." Relief loosened her tight shoulder muscles.

"I'm here for you," the voice grew stronger. *"I won't let harm come to you."*

"Get me out of here!" She lifted off the coffee table and stomped around the small room.

"In due time."

Frustration rooted her feet to the floor, and she banged her aching forehead against a wall. "Jake?"

"Don't fret about your bond with Jake. Prophecy foretells his death this night."

Philip Fucker Sheehan.

Lily sank to her knees. "No! You can't kill him." The external force rocketing her psychic abilities to the Milky Way exploded in her skull.

A soft chuckle grated against the itchy nerve endings in her head. *"I won't have to, my lovely flower. He'll die by your hands. Tonight."*

CHAPTER TWENTY-NINE

Losing his link to Lily felt like someone ripping out a piece of his soul. Jake couldn't deny it any longer. Lily was a part of him and probably always would be. He didn't know how to handle the eerie bond, or lack thereof. And now Ric was driving him insane with his happy-go-lucky, I told you so attitude. He was about ready to lose his shit.

"I'm next, you know," Ric literally crowed the words.

Jake shot him a withering glare meant to shrink his own stupid denial. "You're messed up, little brother."

They sped down Highway 17 toward downtown San Jose, Ric driving Jake's Corvette while Jake tracked the glimmers of hope zipping in and out of his head.

"Dude, if you could blunder upon a highborn psychic and fall in love, it's gonna happen to me. The writing's on the wall." Ric flicked Jake's heart.

"Who said I was falling in love?" Jake thrust Ric's hand off him. "Cut it out or you'll find your sorry ass in the middle of the highway."

"While you've been hiding from your destiny, I've been hunting mine."

Ric accelerated past a van sliding down the highway at a mere seventy miles an hour. The Corvette glided past the slowpokes, Jake's eye constantly on the radar detector.

"Helluva job you've been doing there," Jake replied. "You're great at securing ancient artifacts, but a woman? You suck. What was the last one's name...Wendi. The one before...Heather."

"Suck it. At least I try."

A growing unease circled Jake's heart. He'd always told himself he didn't need a steady woman in his life. He lived for the moment, played the field, did what he wanted, when he wanted. He was the best damn First Guardian on the planet. He still had a lot of service to give. Why chain a wrecking ball to his ankle?

Even with their psychic bond temporarily severed, he knew he was fooling himself. Even if she wasn't the Flower of Tara or a feisty, repressed psychic, he knew the writing was on Cupid's wall. He'd fallen in love with Lily. No bond necessary to drill that into his head, heart, and soul. He'd win back her trust, earn her love, and learn to accept that she was more powerful than him, a scary place he avoided like the plague. Speaking of head, a tiny breeze awakened his telepathic receptors.

"Slow down. I got a hit."

Ric downshifted and swerved the car to the shoulder of the highway. "We on track?"

Jake held up a finger. Ric waited, drumming the steering wheel.

Anger coated the knots in his gut, hardening them. "Someone's screwing with her."

"Meaning?"

"Another telepath. A strong one." He paused, scratched his jaw. "Get off 17. Head to the Almaden area."

The star-studded velvet sky showed signs of a dusty lilac dawn. A crisp, fall morning had forced him to turn on the heater a while ago, but Jake now found the air stifling. He dialed the temperature down to sixty. Five miles back, he'd received strong sensory surges. He once again sensed a tenuous link to Lily, as if a strand of her fiery red hair was winding around his finger.

They sped down another endless suburban street lined with well-maintained two-story houses. The car crawled along at thirty miles an hour, up one hill and down another. Enough speed to stay abreast of Jake's tracking.

Jake fisted his hand, pinched his earlobe. "She's close. Just can't pinpoint a location."

Ric drove the twisting neighborhoods. Houses lit up as the occupants readied themselves for another workday.

"Hold up." Jake grabbed the steering wheel.

Ric slammed on the brakes, tires squealing. The car jolted to a stop in front of a dark two-story Tudor.

Adrenaline pumped into Jake. "Son of a bitch. The link's crapped out. I can't tell if she's trying to break through or another is interfering." He wanted to roar his frustration for the world to hear. "I need to concentrate outside the car."

Jake climbed out of the low-slung car and slammed the door behind him. The garage door of the house across the street began to roll up, creaking in the silent pre-dawn. The light on the opener glowed on a white SUV parked in the garage. A woman stared at Jake.

He waved to her and rested his hand on the roof of his car, hoping he hadn't startled her. The last thing he needed was some hyped-up-on-coffee woman calling the cops on a lurker in the dead of dawn. Ignoring her, he focused on his tenuous bond to Lily. Normally, he didn't have to focus to feel her link. It just existed…until she'd learned to shut him out. *One more nail in his Guild coffin.*

The SUV's engine caught and churned, breaking Jake's fragile concentration. He swore under his breath and hiked down the street, finding a trio of birch trees in another yard, the house dark. A spattering of amber leaves crunched underfoot as Jake stepped into the center of the trees.

"Lily, where are you?" He rested his forehead against the white bark of the largest birch, clinging to the trunk.

A light breeze rustled the bare branches, a handful of early fall leaves twisting and dancing to the lawn. A dog barked, ceased as a porch light flicked on next door. The early morning air penetrated Jake's sweatshirt, skating a chill up and down his body. A balmy breeze scraped his mind, and he clung to the tail end.

"Come on, sweetheart." He tightened his grip on the tree trunk, unmindful of the new day evolving around him.

He tumbled into the abyss of warmth and light, and the world dissipated. Heart hammering, he followed the burgeoning lifeline to Lily, sinking deeper into his center. His telepathy blossomed, and he rode the wave toward the beach. He propelled his mind along the questing link. Lost in concentration, Jake's body ceased to exist, and he became the link, roaring down the path of bioelectricity. He was the link. The link was him.

Then it slammed him...a tidal wave of electrifying power. He dove into the curl.

"Lily! Can you feel me?" Jake flung his words down the tunnel.

"Jake?" Faint, but unmistakably Lily.

"Tell me your location."

A dizzying, euphoric heat drenched him. Weak and untrained, her mind held back. He felt tender tugs on the fragile strand, a link severed, another knitted together. It wasn't enough! Who was screwing with her? Frustration sliced at his gut, leaving simmering acid behind.

She battled an unseen foe, drawing on her power,

losing it again. A tug inhibited Jake's concentration. Endorphins popped in his veins, and an explosion in his head was imminent. Ignoring the pain, he recovered his slip. *"Take it. It's all yours."*

Another forceful heave, and hope tangoed with his fear and frustration. *"You're doing it!"* Euphoria adrenalized him. *"Darlin', I'm here for you. Work the link to open your mind."*

Pea-soup fog descended in his mind. The loving, ethereal light surrounding him shifted inky black.

The welcome power circled the drain.

Gone.

CHAPTER THIRTY

Lily worked at snapping the invisible chains barring her telekinesis and tried to draw on her pathetic link to Jake. His telepathy kept flowing into her brain, ebbing, each time stronger, and lasting longer.

Night gave way to an inevitable dawn, but the basement had retained night's chill. She tried to wrap the velour blanket around her with her wrists tied. Quaking, she lay on the bed, curled on her side, knees huddled to her like a fetus. She wanted to rest, needing a momentary escape from her empty, aching head. Giving up wasn't an option, but exhaustion bogged down her limbs, and she didn't know how much more she had to give without rest. Even if it meant kissing up to rat bastard Sheehan for freedom's sake, she'd escape on her own merit and not rely on rescue. She rubbed her cheek against the pillowcase, trying to massage her throbbing head, her itchy eyes. When she got out of her jam and hell earned its minion back, she planned to train her brain to work with her emerging abilities to prevent her situation from happening again.

A familiar intrusion breezed through her mind. Jack-knifing upright, she centered her fragmenting mind. Thrusts of power forced the crevice open wider, allowing a fraction of her power to escape and hunt for her link to Jake.

"Lily! Can you feel me?"

Her heart contracted. *"Jake!"* She mentally shouted.

His telepathy gushed in and broke apart Philip's vise. Her walls sprang wide open like an oyster shell, leaving a pearl-sized remnant behind. Welcome warmth relieved her ravaged head and queasiness.

Jake's power continued to seek and destroy while hers took comfort from his bond fueling her. One excruciating telekinetic command later, the zip tie disintegrated in a heap of nylon bits on the bed, freeing her wrists.

Heat gutted the last frigid fragment of Philip's control. Would the dickhead know his telepathy had faltered? Rising off the bed, she stretched and worked her stiff arms. No time to waste, ideas formed.

"Use my telepathy to enhance your telekinesis!" Jake's voice left no room for argument.

Struggling to bind the threads of her psychic ability to Jake's telepathy, she managed to connect to him, staggered backward under the strength of his bioelectricity. He mentally encouraged her to accept more, to strengthen her own telekinetic receptors. She grabbed the power again, concentrating on destroying the locks on the door, painfully ignoring the exhilaration buzzing through her.

Suddenly, the door to the room exploded inward and slammed into the wall.

Lily's link to Jake disintegrated. Frustration created a cacophony of energy inside her, teeming for liberation. Slinking under the futon, she visualized the gas line, similar to every house she'd lived in. In her mind's eye, the six dials on the gas stove turned to the ON position. She concentrated on mentally turning the dials.

Minutes flew by as she waited for gas to build. She smelled only the dank, moldy air of the ill-used basement. *Please, let it work.* Was she wasting her time for a massive payoff headache? She banged her shoulder against the leg of the futon, hardly feeling the added pain. "Concentrate, Falbrooke!" Again, she envisioned spinning the dials on the stove.

The faintest hint of gas infused her nose, and joy streamed through her. She hoped the basement and the sturdy futon protected her. Not like she had much choice.

A tiny flame ignited in her skull, one little flame to end Philip Sheehan, wherever he lorded over the house. The flame winked out. "Come on! Come on!" She tried again, focusing on the ignition on the stove burner. A spark. A flame. Incineration.

An explosion rocked the house's foundation in a deafening boom. The roof and walls creaked. Windows shattered upstairs. A crescendo of noise deafened her. Dust clogged her nose, clouded the air. Inwardly cringing, all she could think about was the movie *Carrie.* But she lived to think it.

CR⁊O

Jake pounded his fist on the smooth tree trunk. An explosion boomed and lit up the dawn a block north, an amber red glow in the brightening gray sky. His link to Lily shattered and his heart skipped a beat. About to let fly a deluge of brain waves, he felt the familiar tweak on his core. It enticed him toward the scene of chaos in the northern block. The bond grew stronger, more resilient.

Dogs barked, houses lit up, and doors flew open. People poured out of their homes. Jake jogged back to the Corvette, and they headed north. The bond to Lily strengthened, and Ric drove toward the scene of destruction, a burning house with a section of an outer wall missing, debris blanketing the yard.

"She's here. I feel her." The moment the words tripped out, the bond unraveled. Alarm dipped in and clawed Jake's heart.

The car rounded the corner behind a fire engine. The red lights of a police car lit up the two-story houses, flickered scarlet splashes on the windows, mimicking splatters of blood. Wailing sirens woke up anyone who managed to sleep through the blast. Fire licked one side of the two-story house, dancing around the front outer walls, now a pile of sticks and dust on the front lawn.

"No!" Jake banged his fist on the doorjamb. Was Lily in the house? Was she okay? Another pluck on his bond thrilled him, and he closed his eyes to concentrate, slowing his heart and letting his senses do their magic. "There's another telepathic bond. I think it's Lily. It's traveling fast to the west, I need to follow it." He spun on Ric. "Stay here..." his voice choked up, "in case."

"Be careful, bro." Ric thrust open the door and they traded places. "Things aren't what they appear."

Two minds tugged at his. He had little choice but to follow the strongest. Its lure was too great to ignore when the other bond unraveled as fast as he tailed it.

He raced the 'Vette down the deserted dawn streets. The farther away from the decimated house he drove, the stronger the bond. Another two miles of twisting streets led Jake to the upper hills of San Jose where the houses sat farther apart on larger, more secluded lots among dense foliage and mature trees. He refused to think the worst, thought only of finding Lily alive and well at the end of the intangible trail. If he was too late...if he lost her, he didn't know what he'd do.

The last lingering stars winked out, giving way to sunrise. The sun peeked over the top of the Eastern hills on the other side of the city, painting the sky with strokes of gold and amber. A reflection of light off a window tugged Jake's peripheral vision. He approached a driveway off the main street leading up a slight incline to a dark house visible through a small forest of trees. A twelve-foot high wrought-iron gate with a Triskelion symbol drew Jake's eye. He downshifted, then hit the brakes.

Something familiar about the house and grounds set off a new shitstorm in his gut. He parked his car near a stand of cedar trees outside the fence and darted to the open gate, shutting it with a quiet snick behind him. Morning birds trilled in the trees, and a mild breeze set the ambiance for the day's weather. It boded well for a positive outcome. Positive thinking was all he had.

Yet, an apprehensive chill chased the breeze up his back. He stepped in a thicket of oleanders and concentrated on mentally calling Lily. An answering tug freed a finger from the claw gripping his heart. A second awareness on the other side of the house rattled his already shaken mind. *What the hell? She can't be in two places at once.*

In stealth mode, he rushed to the back of the too static house, checking for tangible and intangible traps. In a neighborhood of multi-million dollar homes, the house boosted two levels and sat on at least a half-acre lot. The driveway curved to the rear to a detached three-car garage. No lights glowed anywhere in or outside the house, not that lights were necessary as the sun razed the dawn.

Jake withdrew his gun. Crouching low, he hiked up the slate steps to the porch beneath an archway, hiding in the shadows against the beige stucco walls between shuttered windows. He knocked a foot on the dark walnut door and waited thirty seconds. The doorknob turned freely. He cast one last sweeping glimpse over his surroundings, then snuck inside the house.

Not a stick of furnishings filled the house. Not a speck of dust on the tile kitchen counters, the sensation of evil hovering in the air its sole occupant. The vibe prickled over his skin, overrode his faint bond to Lily. In fact, he hadn't sensed her since he'd stepped foot inside the house.

Not ready to give up the strong lure that'd carried him there, he sprinted forward, his boots soundless on the Spanish tile floors. Closed blinds covered every window. Opening the doors, he found an empty pantry, closet, and bathroom as he worked his way around the kitchen. One final door remained. The trigger on his gun clicked loudly.

Jake flung open the last door. He met a dark stairway leading down to the lower level. The source of evil emanated from the first floor. Still no sound eclipsed the thundering of his heart in his ears. Not that he expected the electricity turned on, he flicked the light switch on the wall. Nothing. As he took his first step down, a presence like a cat on the prowl snuck up on him. He spun on his heels, his gun trained at a man's heart.

A freeze crackled through Jake. An inhuman darkness swam in the familiar eyes. Before Jake could react, a tornado of action stole the air from his lungs, and shoved him down the stairs.

CHAPTER THIRTY-ONE

Lily spit out dust, slapping drywall debris off her arms. She swiped her sleeve over her face and wrung out the crud from her hair. A piece of plaster crashed onto the ground. The air settled, and she crawled out from under the futon, the room thankfully in decent shape.

She high-fived the air. "Telekinesis is alive and kicking." The door at the top of the stairs dangled on one hinge, leaning toward a far corner of the unfinished section of basement.

Jake's presence in her head had evaporated in the explosion. Is that what Philip meant about her destroying Jake? Was he in the house? Had she wrecked everything? The one man who mattered the most? *No*. Jake was too smart to let Philip catch him. "Hell to the no." She forced her thoughts onward, forced her heart to level out before she lost it.

What if she'd destroyed the Twilight collection? Maybe it needed a permanent address in the ash pits of hell. It had brought too much death and destruction to her life.

Too many variables to twist her up if she didn't get her rear in gear.

She bolted up the stairs to the door, exerting pressure

to pry it open. Where would Philip hide the journal and collection? Lily racked her brain. She didn't know the house, and he may've hidden it anywhere, if it wasn't a useless pile of rubble.

Lily raced into the remainder of the kitchen, skirting the small fire burning near the gas intake line. The outer wall had blown out, exposing the room to the outside world. Shrill sirens filled the air, and dawn emerged, stealing the cloak of night.

Whispers skated through her head, too indistinct to discern. Her previous link to Jake and Philip had disintegrated when the house blew. Sunlight blazed off the star in her ring, and an answering sliver of light lit the living room. Lily slung kitchen cabinet pieces and furniture in her mad scurry through the debris, heedless of the ruins scraping her palms. She sucked in gas and smoke and nearly coughed out a lung, but refused to let it stop her.

She stumbled onto something soft and rigid at once. She nearly sank to her knees in a blithering pile when she spied Philip's body and the man who'd used Jake for bow and arrow practice in Tahoe. A wood pillar pinned the two men to the floor. A piece of windowpane stuck out of Philip's neck, blood slicking his hair black. The other man's face had frozen in a shocked stare, his mouth moving silently. She tried to lift the pillar off them, but it was too heavy. Time remained for first responders to rescue them before the fires spread out of control. One good thing about having minimalistic furnishings...there was little to burn.

"Where, Philip? Where'd you hide what didn't belong to you?" Fresh air poured in and the smoke had thinned. Still, her eyes and nose stung.

An idea popped into her brain sludge, and she touched Philip's neck, cringing as her grubby fingers slicked over blood. She'd barely cleared the sludge when the imprint of his life impaled her, the final moments of his death: his lust for her abilities, an old anger, a woman he'd loved once—one he vowed to avenge—her mother, Rose McKenna Falbrooke laughing with him at a family gathering. Stunned, Lily glommed onto the image. *Philip's young, distinctive eyes slurped up her mother, his desire uncontained on his face, in his he-man protectiveness with his arm snaked around her waist. In her early-twenties, Rose sipped a glass of champagne, an adoring gaze directed at Philip. He leaned in and kissed her. Laughing, Rose pushed him away and said, "Later. When others can't see us."*

Lily's heart careened. Her mother and Philip Sheehan? A cousin? Oh. My. God. What did this mean? Had her mother dated Philip before she'd met her father at her twenty-third birthday party?

Another vision, hazy at first. *Philip's mottled face, punching Lily's father in a barroom brawl. Rose yelling and trying to break it up. Older than in the first vision, Rose screamed at Philip to leave them alone, she didn't love him, it never would have worked out for them. It was wrong of them to be together, and he knew it. She loved Michael, always had, always will.*

Heat assailed Lily's shock but she didn't release the vision. Couldn't. Had to see it to the end. The last few scenes of Philip's life clanged against her skull. *He'd smelled gas and hurried into the living room. Had he kicked the fireplace gas on? Did he have a leak? He slung his arm over his mouth and nose, breathing into his sleeve and reached inside the chimney. The Tahoe man stormed the room shouting, "Get out. It's gonna blow."*

Lily fell backward on her heels, the building heat suffocating her vision. Gauging the spreading fires and the clear space around the fireplace, she pulled her sweatshirt over her mouth and nose and crawled forward, remaining below the tendrils of gathering smoke. She hopped up on the hearth and stuck her arm up the chimney. Wrapped in the leather satchel and hanging on a hook in the chimney's interior, Lily found the journal. Relief loosened the hold on her heart and she let herself breath. Lifting up on her toes, she barely reached the leather pack. She yanked it off another hook and held both for a few joyful seconds.

Red lights bounced off the neighboring houses, like slashes of blood spraying the windows. Sirens quieted and firefighters descended upon the house. Lily staggered out the hole where the front picture window in the dining room used to reside and tumbled onto the front lawn. She sputtered and sank to her knees. Shouts of emergency personnel escalated as they converged upon the house. Fire sizzled and smoked as water sprayed down upon it.

"Lily!"

She swallowed the bitter taste of death and destruction in her mouth. "Ric?"

He scrambled toward her, charging through a line of first responders who'd surrounded her. Ric lifted her up, and she sagged against him, pressing her face to his chest. "Can you walk?"

"Jake? Is he alive?" She managed to croak out. "Philip said he'd be dead by tonight."

Ric combed the gritty, tangled hair off her face. "He's okay."

"Are you sure? I can't feel him in my mind. Is he here?" Frantic, she pushed against Ric.

"No, flower chick. He went after you, felt another link, thought it was you." He called Jake on his cell, received no answer, and it rolled to voicemail.

Sudden horror hijacked Lily. "You set me up." Slapping at his chest, she shoved out of his arms. "You gave Philip the chalice."

"It's not what you think. I knew the one you brought back from Tahoe was a fake. The real chalice has a marking on the bottom the fakes are missing. Since you found another fake in Tahoe, we knew your father had stashed the real one elsewhere. It was all a set up to flush Philip out. We needed to keep you in the dark in case he was reading your mind. We figured he'd try something, but not while you were on the compound, and not after we restricted his access. He conned his way past security somehow." Strength leaked out of her limbs, and he towed her back into his embrace. Relieved, she wanted to feel his solidness, hoping to reconnect to Jake through him.

"If Jake wasn't chasing after me, who's he chasing?" Lily's pitch elevated, her knees weakening another notch.

"I don't know." His sudden flinty eyes, hiding his emotions, undid her completely.

⋘⋙

Jake landed hard on a black-painted concrete floor. He lay on his back, flexed his legs and arms, assessing his injuries. Other than a parade of encroaching bruises and a new hammer factory in his head, he lived to tell about it.

Quiet steps descended the stairs, and Jake sprang up, only then realizing he'd lost his gun. He delved deep into his subconscious, deeper into his core, and hit iron walls closing in on him.

"Sorry, pal, but your psychic abilities are too risky to let loose on the world." The familiar suave voice with the Irish accent floated from the silhouette on the stairway.

Thoughts banged against the sides of his skull. Randy Campbell? Was he hallucinating?

"Campbell?" Jake sounded raspy as he struggled to

work through the barriers shielding his mind from himself.

Silent, the figure jumped down the last few steps in the all-consuming darkness. Wall sconces flared to life, pooling light in a swathe beneath them. One light above the man's head gave Jake his answer.

Son of a bitch. Randy Campbell. He'd caused Michael's death. The one chasing them, the cause of everything happening to them. Jake knew it as much as he knew the sun now blazed upon the house, driving the darkness of night into the madhouse.

"Hello, Jake." A sly smile curled the corners of Campbell's lips. Bare-chested and barefoot, he wore only a pair of gray sweatpants. Stamped on his chest was the Psychic Guild's logo, a Celtic knot wrapped in a heart, except it was upside down, the heart bleeding drops of blood spearing toward the waistband of his sweatpants. The sign of the Cabal. Campbell held Jake's gun trained on his heart.

"What kind of whacked shit are you playing at? You don't belong to the Cabal. You slammed them at every opportunity. You accused them of luring your girlfriend into their shit and killing her when she refused to cooperate. Rhiannon, wasn't it?"

Campbell puffed out his chest. "No pretenses here. All a front to play both sides of the fence. The Cabal's rising and there's not a damn thing you can do to stop them. Once I get my hands on the Twilight collection, I'll officially cut ties to the Guild. By then, there'll be a bunch of pansy-ass psychics who won't be able to read their own minds left."

"You son of a bitch." Jake sneered. "You've orchestrated this whole fucking mess."

"Michael opened doors for me." Campbell rocked back on his heels. "I'd have gotten away with everything if you hadn't taken something of mine."

"What? Your one-way ticket to hell?"

The asshole stepped closer. His gaze flared in black triumph, not exhibiting an iota of humanity. "Hell sounds mighty fine with the *McKenna* flower," his tone dropped several octaves. "I've been imbedded in her mind for ten years, biding my time, waiting for the right moment to take back what's mine."

A thorny vine wrapped around Jake's heart, tightening with each loop. Where was Lily?

☙❧

Ric and Lily moved out of the firefighters' way, and away from the nosey neighbors circling like excitement vultures. A black body bag on a stretcher encased Philip's body. Paramedics carted the other man to an ambulance.

"We need to find Jake," she said.

"I don't know where he is. My clairvoyance isn't a GPS. He's not answering his cell." A dark shadow descended over Ric's face. "He was linking to you. Is he still there?"

"We linked for a while, then it became intermittent. Now he's gone."

"Completely?"

"Not totally. I feel him, same thing since he violated my head." Lily touched his cheek, soothing the ticking in his jaw.

"We can work with that. Concentrate. Envision Jake, draw from every source of energy inside you. Think positive."

Braced against his chest, Lily shut the world out and envisioned Jake's smile, his delectable dimples, his hot as sin body. Mostly, she focused on the feather playing hide and seek in her head, a tickle here, a scrap there. When she found the end of a thread to Jake, she eagerly followed it. Excitement swamped her as she mentally traveled toward the man she had fallen irretrievably in love with, beyond comprehension.

A sledgehammer crashed down and smashed the trail to smithereens, jolting Lily out of her trance.

Hands on her hips, Ric held her upright on her wonky legs. "You found him?"

A tear slipped down her cheek. "Lost it. I'll try again." Trying everything under the sun, she couldn't locate the trail again. A cold dead hollow met her, colder than the black holes in her head.

CHAPTER THIRTY-TWO

Campbell had bound Jake's wrists and ankles and left him sitting on the cement. Struggling to break free, Jake scoured the long, expansive space for a knife or cutting device. Walls, ceilings, and floor were all painted black. Ebony boards covered windows along the right wall. A king-sized bed butted against the wall to the right. A freak-ass altar stood on a black stone slab at the foot of the bed. An object lay on top next to a small basket, but Jake couldn't make it out from his distance. The room was almost as desolate as upstairs, not a personal belonging in sight...until he spotted a familiar athletic bag with a red university logo on the other side of the altar. The same athletic bag he'd seen in Juliana Westwood's vision, in the cargo hold of a dark SUV above the road where Michael Falbrooke had lost his life.

Unnerved by the strange twist of events, he flung off his confusion as mental light bulbs winked on. "Where's Lily?"

"Safe from you."

No matter what Jake did, he couldn't regain his telepathic link to Lily. If he put his all into it, he might forge a link around Campbell's block, but it might incapacitate him. He couldn't risk it. First, he needed answers to play out the game.

"Will you give me the goods on your plans?" He modulated his temper, not wanting to trigger Campbell's rage.

Campbell cocked his head and remained silent for a long moment. He skirted Jake, checked his bindings. Jake grunted as the ropes dug painfully into his wrists.

"Since you won't see the light of day again," Campbell said, straddling a wooden chair he'd dragged five feet away from Jake. "I'll toss you a bone." He smoothed his hand over his tattoo. "Ask away."

"Where's Lily?"

"Don't stew about our lovely flower. My partner Philip Sheehan's taking care of her until I snag her."

"You two are working together?" Jake spat the words out like razor blades.

"Let's just say I coerced him into joining the Cabal once I discovered he was seeking the chalice, setting in motion his lust for the Twilight collection. He was the perfect stooge and salivated to take my expert direction." Tapping his head, he said, "And my manipulation. Like feeding candy to a baby. Unfortunately, he wasn't supposed to move on her yet. But your precious Lily alerted the police yesterday." He shrugged his hands. "He panicked, took her to our temporary safe house."

Jake gritted his teeth. "If he so much as hurts a hair on her head, you're both dead men walking."

"Don't worry, that idiot couldn't protect his own ass. He won't touch her. Either way, he's a dead man."

Lily must be at the Westside house where he'd left Ric. Had the explosion killed her? Pain and terror nearly immobilized him. He worked at loosening the rope and tried to engage her telepathically again. A fissure existed but a stone blocked it. It might be Lily closing him, Sheehan, or Campbell out. "You never joined the Cabal yourself, why? Telepathy not strong enough for their needs?" he baited.

"I never took you for a fool, McAllister." Campbell settled in the chair as if watching a movie. "The Guild's going down. Soon, it won't exist. The Cabal will rule and psychics won't have a choice. They either die if they use their talents in the open, or they join the Cabal."

"What does your pipe dream have to do with you not joining them, or the Twilight collection?"

"Simple, really." Campbell traced his tattoo, stroking himself as if caressing a lover. "Once I have Lily and the collection with the *real* chalice, I'll be the deciding factor on which group lives and which one dies. As you can see, I'm favoring the Cabal. The Guild's too tame for my tastes."

"You plan to hold Lily captive for the rest of her life? Dude, you're insane."

"You'll be dead, why do you care?"

Fury melted his glacial horror, and Jake lost his shit. "Then what are you waiting for? Kill me now."

Campbell strolled to the altar. He picked up an ancient jewel-encrusted dagger, blood staining the blade rusty brown, and wiped the blade on his sweatpants. He carried the basket back with him. "Ric will be joining you soon. Two Guardians. One stone." He laughed at his attempt at humor.

Was Campbell stupid enough to allow both Jake and Ric in the basement together alive? *Well, hello, stupid-ass.* Eagerness tempered the anger vibrating in his insides, and questions vaulted to the forefront again. Campbell stepped closer, sharpening the blade on a whetstone. He slicked the dagger blade down Jake's hair, short of cutting. "You're a smart Guardian. No wonder Falbrooke hired you to guard his precious daughter. I honestly never dreamed we'd come face to face again."

"Seriously? Did you expect to hide forever?"

"No. I expected you dead. I expected Lily sitting at my side."

"You'll never have her." Jake kept poking at the block in his mind, digging through Campbell's telepathy holding it hostage.

"She's already mine. Along with the chalice, the *Codex of Infinite Wisdom*, the ring, and the powers they'll bestow upon her telekinesis."

Rolling with the conversation, Jake concentrated on a weak point in Campbell's plan. "Lily hasn't found the chalice or the legacy book. Do you think after all this you'll gain her cooperation, especially with the Guild coming down on your every step?"

"I've already forged a connection to Lily." He dangled a familiar sword pendant and a pair of women's sunglasses in his free hand, and dumped a pile of mementos at Jake's feet: a hair band, a tiny silver moon and stars ring, several snapshots of Lily and her family, a rainbow-colored shoelace, innocent belongings. Items Lily probably never missed throughout her life.

Campbell was also a touch telepath, possibly with the same coercion ability Jake wielded. He could control Lily's actions forever...now that Jake had flayed her mind open for the taking. Jake dwelled inward to break down the steel walls in his skull. His head hammered, ready to explode, payment for his betrayal. As fast as he splintered the foundation of his steel cell, Campbell patched it...until Jake found the one tiny hole the man was unable to plug. The fissure in Jake's mind fragmented, and a rush of Lily's thoughts deluged him. He drilled through the crack and bombarded Lily's mind with his predicament, his location...his strength and love.

A sinister smile wrenched at Campbell's mouth. "Games, Jake? Haven't we gone beyond such pettiness?"

Despite Campbell's smug arrogance, sweat popped onto the lunatic's forehead.

Jake fed the link to Lily, opening up more than he wanted, but he had no time to control the hamster wheel of thoughts. He sucked in thinning air. The sensation of a steamroller flattening him forced out a tortuous bellow. He sensed Lily trenching a path toward him. Every second that crawled by, the path seemed to lengthen. Jake's power slipped, power he'd never recoup if he didn't stop Campbell from destroying his mind, or killing him before he saved her. Air diminished as the agony in his head exploded.

ⒸⓈⓄ

Searing pain and stark terror doubled Lily over. Ric grasped her waist, holding her steady. Jake's thoughts overwhelmed her, and she separated out two coherent splices from the chaos. "Jake's been captured. It's…Randy Campbell." Shock immobilized her.

Ric's face bleached of color, and his fingers stiffened on her hips. "We need to haul ass." Lifting Lily off her feet, Ric spun her around, and they beelined for Philip's late model sedan, scattering the last lookie-lous. "Did he feed you a location?" He hunted for keys in the off chance Philip had left them in the car.

A black SUV screeched to a halt across the street, and Niles Nevin stepped out. Ric snatched Lily's hand, and they raced over to him.

"Give me your keys," Ric shouted. "Jake's in trouble." Without a second's hesitation, Niles tossed his keys to Ric.

As soon as her butt hit the passenger seat and she belted in, Lily shut her eyes. The throbbing receded, and Jake's thoughts clarified for a second, then vanished. The thoughts were too muddled, but distinctly Jake.

"Something cut him off. I think he's in the foothills near my house."

"Randy's a telepath and touch telepath. I don't know if he has the same ability to coerce, though. Let's not rule it out."

A vision struck Lily: Jake sitting on a floor, revulsion riding his gaze to a scattering of small objects on the floor. Sharp stabbing daggers sliced through her head, growing in number and intensity as his thoughts blitzed her.

"Oh. My. God." She banged her fist on her thigh. "He's the one who stole my sunglasses the day after the funeral. And he has my dad's sword pendant!" She massaged her scalp, spurring her mind to work faster to decipher the mystery, to view the man who held Jake captive. An odd *déjà vu* swirled in her chest, and she urgently needed to see his face.

Once they cleared sight of the emergency vehicles, Ric gunned the lumbering SUV out of the neighborhood.

"If he stole items from you, then he's been using them to keep tabs on you with touch telepathy. Have you felt manipulated?"

"I don't know. Maybe." A new round of panic settled in her roiling stomach. Psychic ability was for the birds if she'd have to suffer nausea every time she used her abilities. She may have to invest in a pharmaceutical company or buy a cage at the zoo.

"I think you're too strong for him. Do you think he's been reading your mind?"

Lily sucked in her stomach. Was Randy the second presence she kept feeling? "If he was, then he knows my every thought, including where the real chalice and the legacy book are hidden. He knows who has the key." She grabbed Niles's cell off the center console.

She dialed Alex MacKenzie, and he answered on the first ring. "Alex, it's Lily Falbrooke. Where's Juliana?"

"Eating breakfast with me. Why?"

"Don't let her out of your sight. I've got a lead on my dad's killer, and I think he's been in my head for the last week or so." She gave Alex a nutshell version of the situation. "If that's the case, he knows you have the key. He'll do *anything* to get it."

"You need to leave this to the cops, Lily. Don't try to track this bastard down," Alex commanded.

"I can't. He's luring me to him using a telepathic compulsion." As much as she tried to deny it, she knew Randy, not Jake was sucking her to his lair. The closer they traveled, the sharp stabbing lessened in her skull, and the lure became a hunger she had to slake or she'd wither up and die. The craving to find him, see him, touch him ate at her like an insidious fungus, leaving her jittery.

Alex tapped the phone on speaker, and Juliana brought her out of the abyss she was careening into. "Alex is placing an APB on Campbell. We'll find Jake," Juliana said. "Build your mental blocks. I know you can do it."

"It's too late," she wailed. "Once Jake broke them down, I haven't been able to build them back up except in spurts. I have no clue how much this asshole's reading." Part of her hated Jake for what he'd done to her, despite knowing deep in her heart her walls needed to fall before the ten-year long war inside her ended.

"I know, honey, but concentrate freeing your mind, easing each thought out one by one until nothing's left. Then work on building each wall up one by one."

Ric jerked the car around a slowpoke on the road. Lily's head bonked the window, and she lost cell contact with Juliana.

"Sorry," he muttered absently.

The bang on the window knocked a little sense into her, and she mentally thrust the compulsion away. She realized she hadn't given Ric directions, but he was traveling the path her mind mapped. "Um, Ric?"

He pinned a wide, stricken gaze on her. "You're projecting outward, Lily. Like a radio frequency, and I'm riding your tail. I can't shake you off. Whatever he's doing to your head is triggering my second sight."

She squeezed his taut arm. "It's helping. Just keep driving."

"You have to stop pushing him away. It's the only way we'll find him...and Jake." He clamped her hand in his, damp with sweat. "Keep contact with me."

The SUV climbed into the hills near home. Too near. Every block they drove closer to the man invading her, the more Lily's yearning amplified until she was practically salivating for release, fidgeting in her seat, her legs pressed together tight. "He's peeling me apart like an orange. I need to shut him out."

Perspiration dripped off Ric's pasty temples. "It's taking everything in me not to pass out. Double-edge sword here. Don't shut him out yet."

"Let me drive," she demanded, blood pulsing in her ears, warmth trickling between her breasts, slinking lower to the V of her thighs. Mentally, she screamed at the torture, the walls begging to ascend, begging to let Jake back in, dying to lock the stranger out.

"I can make it," Ric rasped out, hunching over the steering wheel. "Keep the link open."

He turned left on a street a block past her house. From the corner of her eyes, she saw sunlight slash the windshield of a car to her right. "There!" She pointed up the hill, recognizing Jake's black Corvette and a house hidden behind groves of cedars and fir trees dotting the property, surrounded by a wrought-iron fence. The gate welcomed, beckoned, forming a new layer of ice across her bare skin.

Ric stomped on the brakes and jolted the vehicle to the side of the road at the bottom of the driveway. He slammed the SUV in park, his hand slipped off the gearshift, and he slumped onto the steering wheel.

"Ric!" She shook him, checked his pulse, and he listed to the left against the door. His pulse thumped dull against her fingers. "Thank God. Damn it," she wailed. Before she could utter another word, a slightly nasally voice deluged her brain.

"Come to me, my love."

Jake? Confusion ran roughshod across her scattered emotions. She silenced her thoughts, but the voice drilled deeper, turned vaguely familiar.

Not Jake.

"Everything you want is here with me."

Someone else. Who? *Think, think!*

"I can offer you the world."

The voice touched a button in her brain, and his face rolled into her mind's eye.

Connor Finnegan. The man she'd bumped into at the pier after her lunch with Philip Sheehan. *Well, hello, mystery and mayhem.*

CHAPTER THIRTY-THREE

Lily hated abandoning Ric to follow the intangible trail toward the two-story Spanish house, situated less than a mile from her father's house. The snare remained powerful, even though she still had physical control over her body. Had Randy Campbell aka Connor Finnegan tracked and controlled her movements since she'd arrived in San Jose?

Ducking below shuttered windows, Lily jetted down the hill to the backyard, the mental connection tempting her to the unlocked back door, then inside the bare kitchen. An open door revealed a stairwell to a lower level. A mental force compelled her to the doorway, and she stumbled down the stairs in her haste.

She banged her already tortured elbow against the black brick wall and stars flitted in her vision. Unsteady on her feet, her gaze zipped from one dark corner to another until it settled on the bare-chested stranger beside an odd ritual altar. No sign of Jake. The vague presence dissipated, and a sense of release rolled down her arms.

Since he'd loosened the reins on his link to her mind, the stranger's familiar muscled chest, lean waist, and six-pack abs no longer dripped fire into her hormones. His fine-chiseled bronzed face, full lips, and aquiline nose no longer ranked at the top of her most beautiful men in the world list. Instead, his appearance caused needles dipped in disgust to scorch her skin. An inverted Guild tattoo covered his entire chest, the trinity knot bound in a heart, so like the tattoo inked on Jake's back. Drops of red blood dripped off the Celtic knot.

"Lily McKenna Falbrooke, Flower of Tara, what a pleasant surprise." He stepped toward her. She flustered his hair with a stray thought to test out her telekinesis and he stuttered to a stop. "Awesome. Your telekinesis is reemerging." He smiled, parading straight white teeth. A too gorgeous smile. Too perfect. Too fake.

"Who are you? Where's Jake?" He still held fragile control of her in her weakened state.

He moved into her personal space. "Like games, my love?"

"I'm not your *love*." She planted her fists on her hips, unable to take her eyes off his tempting visage. Shaking her head hard, she wanted to swab out her brains with bleach to vanquish the false desire turning her into a love-struck idiot.

"Lily." Silent, he drank her entire length in, as if she were a fine brandy to a thirsty alcoholic. "Don't dismiss truth. Your mind is your reality. It's where we both live."

Unable to budge a muscle, confusion swirled thick, snarling cobwebs in her head, battling against his manipulation. She knew him somehow, had felt his presence on and off, always believing her lost memories were the culprit. Had he delved into her head randomly for ten years? Elusive and just shy of intrusive? Is that how he knew she was telekinetic?

Muffled sounds stemmed from beneath the stairs and spun her back to the moment. She searched for the source of the noise in the dim recesses of the long room. She reached for her connection to Jake, slicing cobwebs that knitted faster the more she diced them up.

"Lily!" Jake's voice drifted from a faraway place. A seed of his telepathic presence from an alcove underneath the stairs emerged.

In a showman's play, Connor whipped his hand in the air and severed the intangible cord leading to Jake. Limbs freed from Connor's control, Lily surged forward. He didn't try to stop her as she bounded around him and found Jake beneath the stairs, duct tape over his mouth, hands and feet bound and tied to a steel support pillar. Her gaze devoured him, hunting for signs of external injuries. She wanted to kiss him and never let him out of her grasp again. Almost losing him about killed her. No matter what he'd done to her in the guise of protection, she knew they'd find a way past it. If he wanted her, that is.

Searching for a skosh of Jake's telepathy, Lily butted minds with Connor. His presence nauseated her, her token for the invasion. His telepathy retracted a fraction, and she mentally advanced an inch, then he swooped in and gained three inches. They parleyed back and forth for what seemed eons, and she quit caring that her head was ready to launch into orbit. Was he screwing with her for shits and giggles?

As Jake struggled to loosen his bonds, his eyes implored her to get out. She reached forward to pluck the tape off his mouth, but Connor yanked on her arms, binding her within his strong embrace. He carried her away from Jake. She kicked at his shins, but it was like kicking a tree trunk, and she earned sore heels for her effort. He set her in the center of the large space between a king-sized bed and the stairs leading up to the kitchen. Nowhere to run, nowhere to hide. Not a weapon in sight. Only her mouth. Not always her preferential weapon.

"Did you kill my father?" she asked.

"The old man killed himself. I just facilitated his demise."

Lily seethed with a storm of anger, fear, and loathing. "Why the ruse with the chalice then?"

"You're a smart woman. I'm sure you'll figure it out."

"To expose him, confuse him, flush me out of hiding? Hoping to break down my mental walls?" She ground her teeth.

"Nailed it about Michael." He slid his thumb into her hair above her ear. "Like I said, you're a smart woman. Your father's singular goal was to protect you and the collection. Honestly, he just didn't know how. How do you think he could protect you if you didn't have full access to your psychic abilities? I gave him ten years, and all he wanted was to hide you and your mind. His time expired."

Ten years? That little tidbit is worth the price of admission to the inquisition. "You're a piece of work. What about Sheehan? You two working together? By the way, I killed your bud earlier this morning," she taunted him.

Ignoring her, he angled his head in Jake's direction. "Unfortunately, McAllister butted in. He broke through your mind before I put my spin on your brain. As for Sheehan...of course, we were working together. He's my pawn in the Guild, keeping the heat off me. The more the merrier hunting the chalice and the Twilight collection. You saved me the trouble of killing him. Good job." A smirk eclipsed his smile. "He had his own motives as you've figured out. In love with your mother, was it? Third, fourth cousins?" He shrugged, and Lily had to fight to keep her eyes off his toned pectorals flexing into the shrug. "If you hadn't killed him, I would've taken him out later."

Lily swallowed a pocket of air threatening to cut her

off from reality. "What do you want, Connor, Randy, whoever the hell you are?"

"Real name's Connor Finnegan. I never lied about that. I hid behind the name Randy Campbell once I shoved my Finnegan identity into a temporary holding cell. The cell doors are open now."

"What reality do we share?" *Bring it to my level, pinhead.*

"You and I belong together. We always have, always will. Don't you remember? The time we spent alone at Tahoe that summer, the promises we made, the love we declared. The secrets we shared."

"What secrets do you and I share? What promises?" More lies trying to fake her out.

With gentle fingers, he tucked her hair behind her ears, then cupped her cheeks in both his long-fingered hands. "I've waited ten years to touch you again."

Lily froze, squinted. "What's your angle? I don't know you from Adam." She wanted to know what he knew, how she knew him. Could she stall him long enough for Ric to wake up, for Detective MacKenzie to storm the scene?

"I'm hurt you haven't lugged the memories of us out of your dead zone." His full lips twitched, and Lily had the faintest urge to press her lips to his in a way she'd done once before.

Whoa, what? She blinked the urge away. Thoughts of him flip-flopped in her head, trying to emerge, trying to hide, revolving around the two instances she'd met him recently. Oh, yes, he was the man who'd prevented her from becoming roadkill on the Mt. Hamilton road. Pain burned behind her eyes, another riot of agony.

"Shall I make it easier on you and tell you?" Connor asked, lines forming a V between his eyes. "I hate that you're in pain."

"Then get the hell out of my head."

His tongue clicked in his mouth. "Little flower, you treat me like the enemy I'm so not."

Lily changed her tactic, her face softening, trying to catch him off guard. "Then enlighten me, Connor. I don't know what's real and what isn't. Please." Managing a tear, she sniffled. He allowed her to move her right hand, and she laid it over his heart, feeling his steely muscles, fighting the urge to jab her fingernails into his skin and the other urge to sift his hair...the way she used to. *Oh. My. God.*

Memories soared back. Not all, but certain memories she'd blocked for a decade.

The summer boy from the lake house. The twenty-one year old she'd fallen in love with when she was eighteen. The boy who'd pledged everything to her, his love, his life, promises to honor and cherish her forever. The boy her father told her emphatically to stay away from. What eighteen-year-old girl listened to her father when it revolved around love? Connor had usurped all her time that summer, and she'd fallen madly in love with him, on the verge of facing the world as a young adult. Until her mother and brother's fatal accident on the lake and her memories and psychic abilities died in the wake of the tragedy.

"You remember," Connor whispered reverently. "Lily, I've never stopped loving you."

Trembling with a tangle of emotions, she rested her cheek on Connor's upper arm. "I remember." She wound her arms around his neck. "Connor. Oh, God, Connor. I remember. I'm so sorry I left you."

He stroked her hair, his touch a tingling wash on her neck, reminiscent of a time she had loved him with her entire being.

"Shhh. I know you didn't do it intentionally. It was the accident."

"Why did you wait so long to come to me?" Lily tightened her arms, refusing to let go of him again.

"You didn't remember me. Your father refused to let me visit you. So I waited until you needed me."

The eight legs of confusion spun more webs, muddling memories with fantasy and reality. "How did you know I'd regain my memory? Or remember how I wanted to spend my life with you?"

"I'm a patient and hopeful man." Connor kissed the top of her head, his breath moist against her scalp.

Lily turned her cheek against his chest, his spicy cologne infusing her nose, so similar to Jake's it puzzled her. She glanced away, and a small pile of familiar objects caught her attention. Belongings that had mysteriously vanished one by one over the last ten years. *Ten years!*

Shock shredded the cord stringing her mind to Connor's mind. She thrust against the fraying threads, prying them apart. His arms stiffened around her, and the threads reknitted. Did he know she battled against herself? She loathed the constant intrusion, like a rave in her skull, and wanted to boot everyone out—Jake, Connor, even herself, for a brief blissful moment of oblivion. Would he end up killing her through his mind control?

"Stop, Lily. You'll hurt yourself. I'm too strong for you. I don't want to hurt you. I've risked my all to keep you alive, haven't I? I saved your hide at the crash site. I handled the dead man in Tahoe. I watched over you and made sure no one else threatened you."

Tamping down a sneer, she shook back her head, muzzled her thoughts. "If you love me, why bind me? Why treat me this way? Let go and let's talk rationally. Remind me of our love, our promises, and secrets. I need your help to remember." She rose on her toes and grazed her mouth over his. Connor tried to take more in the parting of his lips, the press of his tongue between her lips, but she drew away, smiling slyly. "Later, love."

Another fiber frayed off the cord, and she kicked it out of the way before Connor fused it with the others again.

"What do you want?" Lily pressed, hoping to force him to confess his motives and goals.

"I want you, us as one again, everything we had. You had my heart and soul that summer, just as I had yours. You planned to take the Twilight collection and the chalice, your birthright, and we were leaving to start our life together. Do you remember?"

A barrage of memories clouded her mind: on the lake in a boat, Connor held her in his arms. They made plans to run off together after summer ended, to develop their psychic gifts, to form a business to help others. To steal the chalice and the *Codex of Infinite Wisdom* from her mother, Lily's birthright. It wasn't really stealing, he'd said. *Codex of Infinite Wisdom*. The name jolted her. *Oh. My. God. We'd planned to pander the powers of the chalice and the book.*

"The accident happened and you lost your memories. I couldn't compete with a blank slate. It killed me. I loved you so much and you didn't know me." Devoid of emotion, his tone flattened as if reciting from a book.

He triggered a tempest of mistrust. She believed his words, saw them in the memories popping up, but his intent had changed since that summer. Or had it? Had he misled her all along? At eighteen, a world without the thumb of her parents had beckoned. It promised freedom and a love she'd never experienced. He represented her everything, her present, her future, her all.

A scene snaked in her mind: his father, a roundtable of men and women in the late afternoon, the sun a golden orb resting on top of the lake, striping coral and pink light onto the surface of the rippling waters. They'd coached him on what to do, how to handle Lily. Lily had hidden behind a trio of fir trees just beyond the deck wrapped around the turret of the Finnegans' Tahoe cabin. *A puppet master. A set up. Lies. All lies!*

"Is your father still alive?" she asked.

"Doesn't matter. I don't belong to the Cabal and haven't since I discovered my parents were using me...and you. I'm my own man."

"Liar!" She prodded his shoulders with all her might and it was like shoving a boulder. "You're just feeding me lies, the way you did that summer. All anyone wants is the Twilight collection and its powerful, priceless properties to benefit the psychic world. To benefit you!"

The sudden realization that he'd always been a part of her kicked her where it counted. Most recently, she'd mistaken him for Jake. Anger and devastation cut more threads, and a new memory blasted out of the black hole in her head, more devastating than the lies and secrets Connor had fed her in those long-ago moments. The world spun black and she wilted against him.

Lily crumpled to the ground on a carpet of fir needles, tears creating tracks of ruin and humiliation down her cheeks. Connor had faked her out. He didn't want her. He wanted her for her psychic abilities and her birthright, playing to his father's fiddle.

"Lily?" Connor rushed to her, kneeling on the ground to embrace her. "Are you okay? Did you fall?"

Lily cringed away from him. "Back off. You lied...about everything." She clawed his face, raked her fingernails down his cheeks.

"No, babe, it's not what you think." He gripped her wrists in his long, slender fingers, holding her from digging holes in his skin. "I love you, Lily."

"What do you love more? Me? What I can do for your precious Cabal? Or the legacy that belongs to my family?" She jumped up, slapping at his hands reaching for her.

"You. Only you. Like we promised one another." He tried to embrace her.

She butted against the trunk of a small dying pine tree, brown needles raining upon their heads. "Don't touch me!" She clamped her hand around her wrist over her lucky charm bracelet. "Would you want me if I was an ordinary girl, no powers, no priceless heritage, nothing special?"

Connor's hesitation gave her the answer she hated to hate. Arms extended to the sky as if wielding the powers of a mystical sorcerer, she rained pine needles down upon them. She bolted toward the lake, passing the con artists he called family sitting on the deck, planning her future as if she were a child rather than a new adult of eighteen. As if they owned her.

Panting, she paused on the shoreline of the lake, the waters lapping over smooth rocks to her toes. Spinning in the direction of her family's cabin, she assessed her options. Needing to escape her ruined life, she wanted to run home, but Dad had gone into town to meet a client, and Mom had taken Kevin out fishing in their speedboat. She flew down the dock and hopped into the top of the line sport yacht Connor's father had paraded around all summer.

He followed, spewing words she refused to hear. Her mind roiled, her untapped telekinetic receptors surging and contracting, ready to loose cannons out unto the world. Only Connor knew she had telekinetic abilities. Her parents didn't know she possessed more than clairvoyance in her psychic makeup. How could she have been so stupid to trust him with the most sacred part of herself?

As she flung herself onto the driver's seat, rummaging

for the hidden key under the cushion, Connor's thoughts and emotions inundated her, his mind connecting to her the way they'd practiced all summer. Head pounding from the effort, she forced his thoughts and emotions, his control to the wayside. He was too powerful. Although he'd never exerted such power over her, she knew he had the ability. They'd played games to see how he could control her and how she used her telekinesis to break his control. The time for games had ended.

She shoved him with all her strength, and he stumbled backward, landing against the backrest of the passenger seat. "Get out of my head and stay the fuck out."

Connor withdrew his feelers from her, and his grip on her arm felt like the talons of a monster. "You're not going anywhere. Not until we hash this out."

"There's no more to hash out. You played me. I'm done with you. Game over. Go back to your shyster family and find another idiot to screw over." Through her swimming vision, Lily spied her family's red speedboat streaking past the horizon, headed toward their dock a few hundred yards down the shoreline.

Lily invoked her telekinesis, ready to fire one of those mystical cannons on Connor if he didn't release her arm, but he pushed harder against her building pressure. They engaged in a tug of war of mental might until the ultimate clash unleashed a barrage of psychic energy outward, traveling blindly across the surface of the lake in the direction of the speedboat approaching them at a few knots per hour. In surreal horror, the boat picked up speed. Too close to shore! She screamed and screamed, her voice drifting into the woods.

The boat accelerated to unimaginable levels until it slammed the fuel station between the Finnegans' dock and the Falbrooke dock. An explosion rent the air and flames mushroomed toward the sky. Birds took flight from the trees and swarmed across the lake, taking Lily's life with them.

Lily slumped to her knees, conking her head on the console between the two seats, allowing oblivion to capture her worst nightmare.

CHAPTER THIRTY-FOUR

Visions, words, and a catalog of emotions subsumed Lily, and she lost herself into the vortex. Memories emerged from the sludge, and the chaos trampled them. A familiar comforting seed ascended to the top and expanded, drilling through the dregs of helplessness. The moment kindled, and the memory struck the match. Truth detonated into a firestorm.

"Lily! Come on, wake up."

Dad? Mom?

Connor?

"It's Jake. Burn this asshole down. Come on, darlin'."

Jake McAllister?

The vortex swirled, carving her memories into crumbs. The voice called to her like a bobbing buoy in a stormy sea. Love and safety accompanied the voice, and Lily harbored the most precious seedling on earth.

"Lily, darlin'. Don't let Connor get away with this. Don't let him take everything from you. Break through his control."

Lily dug deep for the one true bond no one could ever sever. The tie she knew existed the moment she realized she had fallen for Jake McAllister. The bond of true love.

"You stoop to save a man who betrayed you?"

Connor's voice grated past her thoughts. "Remember his crimes, then rethink your alliances. Dark and light are entwined within *us*. A perfect balance. You can't refute that. We're destined for each other. You've known since Tahoe."

Tahoe? Mom, Kevin. The accident...she'd caused. The memory of that fateful day blasted the voices in her head, smashing the bands imprisoning her mind. Molten anger flowered and met her tormentor.

"Pot. Kettle." She flailed her arms wildly. "You've raped my mind for a decade. God knows what else you've done. Because of *you* my mother and brother are dead." *Because of me, they're dead.* "You destroyed my entire family."

She tumbled into the safe place of her mind again. *No!* It wasn't safe. Not as long as Connor lived.

"Did you never think I'd remember the truth and detest you? Did you snort stupid dust? You want *me* to ally with *you*?" Bile stung her throat as she rose from the bed where Connor had laid her down after she passed out.

He twined her hair in his fingers, cupping the nape of her neck, his thumbs caressing her prickling flesh. She rolled, hauled up her knee, and smashed it into Connor's crotch.

Bellowing his rage and pain, he slammed her head against the headboard. Screaming, Lily writhed beneath him. Visions flickered in her mind and she quit moving. A river of calm flowed over them and Connor's grip relaxed.

"Trust only the man of your dreams," he repeated the words her mother once spoke in her ear. He nibbled on her ear lobe, his breath hot on her skin as his lips slid down her neck. She shivered with a familiar awareness, and heat trickled into parts of her accepting his words. More lost memories vaulted to the forefront: Connor keeping her safe and secure, giving her small gifts of love, making slow love to her on a bed cushioned by fir needles in the Tahoe forest.

The visions turned cruel and biting: Jake causing her father's accident, befriending her father, stealing his business and usurping her father's claim on his home. Jake's steadfast quest for the chalice. Ric's possession of the chalice and aiding Philip Sheehan. Jake dragging Lily into his maze of deceit to coerce her, against the laws of the Guild. The Guild existed to serve Jake in their quest to control the true Tara descendant for their own quest for power.

Connor embraced her, his strong arms tender and comforting. Epic bafflement jumbled her mind, and she clung to him, her cheek against his chest, the beating of his heart barely perceptible. His skin was feverish, searing her flesh, but she didn't want to let go. Now that Connor was her dream made flesh, returned to her, she would never give him up, never run from him again. Never lose the cerebral link to him.

Doubts niggled at her. Why? Why did her thoughts keep shifting and dancing like leaves in an autumn breeze?

A faint shouting crammed her skull. Lily dismissed it, glaring past Connor's shoulder at the traitor beneath the stairs sporting wide-shocked eyes that beseeched her.

Connor dropped his arms and laid his hand over hers, his heat toting a telling magnitude of weight. "Let's destroy the man who tried to split us apart."

Following him off the bed, Lily squeezed his fingers and smiled up at the handsome face that had replaced the young man's face of his early twenties. She pressed her mouth to his, tasting home on his lips, and leaned against his hardness. Hot-white passion zinged toward her nether regions. The strong yearning to strip off his sweatpants nearly unraveled her. The screaming in her head dialed up another notch, and she faltered. Fire lanced her skull.

Connor clutched her shoulders. His mental magic mushroomed, dampening her warring powers, dialing down the screaming of the other. Lily rubbed her temples, quieting the voices.

Not long enough.

The other man roared, thunderous agony echoing between her ears. She sank to her knees, dragging Connor down with her. Pain jarred up her legs from the contact with the concrete floor. The other man punched holes in Connor's mental prison encircling her brain. Thoughts and memories tumbled like rocks in an avalanche. Whose memories? Whose thoughts?

"We kill him now." Connor picked up a jeweled dagger off the floor. "Then we'll be free to be together. Forever. You'll finally be mine the way we were destined, the way we promised each other. I've waited long enough. Haven't you?"

Blurry faces of two familiar men danced in her vision. She shook her head to dislodge the fuzz, trying to discern their identities and reality from illusion. A gleeful chuckle echoed in Lily's head, and the other one rebuked it. She wanted to join in the dance with the two men who wanted her above all else. But strange sensations subsumed her from the inside, and she mentally tried to kick them out.

"Lily, wake up," the other shouted. She arrested his voice, his thoughts, and followed the path to his heart. It beat for her mind, her soul, her heart. It beat only for her.

Jake McAllister. The real man of her dreams.

The mental door creaked open inch by excruciating inch, tearing apart her prison. Horror swamped her. She schooled her expression, bolted her mental doors. *Holy hell in Crazy Town!*

What had she almost done? Shudders rolled up from her toes. She lunged to her feet, a rapturous smile spreading her mouth wide. Destiny in her grasp, she'd play it until the end. The dark side of the Flower of Tara would prevail. *I will own you, asshole.*

The flower in her mind blossomed like a rose in the summer sunshine. Connor shrieked and rounded on her, growling like an angry bear. In one split second of his inhuman rage, she found the strand of his telepathy and knifed it in half. Lily erected another barrier to prevent him from penetrating her again. Exerting her newfound telekinesis, she coerced him to raise his arm, the one holding the dagger, and stabbed it into his chest, once, twice. Connor's bellows deafened the dim, musty room. A third plunge, not deep enough to cause internal damage. A fourth time, closer to his heart. Not deep enough. Connor sank to his knees, fighting to maintain his control and stop her intangible revenge.

Clarity winked on like a new light bulb in her skull, and Jake screamed. *"I'm almost loose. When I say go, run like hell."*

Connor could no longer concentrate on her bond without releasing Jake from his mind control. Lily gave herself a mental fist bump amid her internal battle against Connor, forcing him to stab himself again and again. Blood slickened his chest, its metallic tang drenching the air, spots of deep rust dripping onto his gray sweatpants.

Wild thoughts invaded her. Connor couldn't exert more energy and maintain their connection. Another flare of triumph buoyed her up. Lily's mental power expanded until she totally severed his bond. Perspiration dripped between her breasts, proving she was alive and feeling the normal human reaction.

Connor possessed an odd inward mask as if looking in upon himself. Just in case, she strengthened her internal shield, and battled to maintain her manipulation while she searched for a rope.

Knocking sounds arose from beneath the stairs and she spun toward Jake. Flinging off his bindings, he staggered up and faltered toward her, his gaze drinking her into the depths of his soul. She feasted her sight on him, but she'd lose her depleting mental abilities if she obeyed her heart and ran to him. Anxious, she glanced at Connor who sat transfixed, still warring with himself...with her.

Jake reached her, a welcome brush of his hand over hers, a quick squeeze, the most precious look of love she'd ever received from any man. "Are you okay?" she asked.

"I will be." Jake wiped his slick face on his shoulder. "Another couple minutes and the fucker would've permanently reduced me to a blathering idiot. The question is, are you okay?"

She touched his cheek, a sweep of her fingers. "Now I am."

As Jake stretched to seize the drooping dagger from Connor's hand, an icicle snapped apart in her mind. Connor shoved forward and plunged the dagger into Jake's chest.

The world turned red. Lily's heart stopped, a silent scream forming in her throat. "Jake!"

A torrent of psychic energy unleashed upon the room. The altar slammed onto Connor's head, steamrolling him to the granite slab, bashing his head once, twice, three times, until he stilled, his face a bloody pulp. Lily crawled to Jake, lifted his shoulders onto her lap, and cradled him, tears obscuring her vision. She found his steady pulse and heaved out a breath she didn't know she held.

"I'm sorry. I'm so sorry. Jake, Jake, can you hear me?"

He opened his darkening eyes, and she wanted to drown in his piercing gaze, in the sapphires that matched her Twilight. "You did it."

Lily held him close, inhaling his scent, cleansing the stench of blood from her senses. "*We* did it."

"I'm spent. Think you can call me a ride to the hospital now, *Carrie*? First, can you kiss me? I need your lips—"

Her quaking lips on his quieted him. The too brief kiss adrenalized her, dislodged the crumbling mountain on her shoulders. "Do you have a phone?" she asked.

"No need. I think the cavalry's arrived."

Before she could blink back her surprise, footsteps thundered above them and stomped down the stairs. Ric and Alex MacKenzie.

"Yo, bro." Ric jogged to them, phone to his ear calling an ambulance. "How bad?"

"Other shoulder. I'm good."

Ric shoved his phone in his pocket and took Lily's hand. "Randy Campbell?"

"Connor Finnegan." Lily stifled an epic sob of guilt, sorrow, loathing, and relief. "It was him all along."

"What? Who the hell is Connor Finnegan?" Ric squeezed her hand so hard she flinched, forcing him to let go.

"Long story, bro. It's his real name. Campbell's a fake name."

Ric scratched his chin. "He killed Michael, not Sheehan?"

"See the athletic bag." Jake pointed to the bag near Connor's prone body. "It's the bag Juliana envisioned inside the SUV the night of the accident. I bet we'll find the nail gun in it." Lily pressed a pillowcase against his wound to staunch the bleeding. "Tell me about Sheehan."

She gave Jake the Cliff Notes version of her escapades at Philip's house.

"You knew this Connor asswipe?" he asked, jealousy

flicking across his face.

A flush worked up Lily's neck. *Ten years of stupid.* "He's been haunting my head for years. I thought it was my own psychic powers trying to awaken."

They waited for the ambulance, and she recited the history between herself and Connor. Alex MacKenzie's thumbs flew on his smartphone, taking her statement. "After I met Jake, I mixed him and Connor up." Another hard knot twisted in her gut among the others loosening for the first time in a week.

"I stayed clear of your head, Lily, except to check on you at the compound. You have to believe me. He must've manipulated you all along."

"I never would've figured it out if you hadn't gutted my walls."

Jake beat his fist on the concrete. "And Connor and Sheehan would've never linked to you if I'd played by the rules. Sweetheart, I'm so sorry. I didn't think of the implications. I only wanted to protect you from this insanity."

"But Connor's been there all along." She scratched her scalp, wanting to scratch away the remnants of Connor's mental strands. "He would've forged a deeper connection eventually. I think he may've kept my memories from emerging. You only rushed along the process."

"You're being generous." He choked up. "I almost got you killed."

"I feel like an idiot. I had visions of Connor and thought they were you." Her turn for the waterworks.

"Lily, don't." Empathy schooled the jealousy graying his pale face. "You had no way of knowing he'd coerced you through all those years of suppression."

Lily's gaze swept the room, until it froze on her belongings, a small insignificant pile of enormous proportions.

The paramedics arrived and attended to Jake, diverting her from the ramifications of her new life. Alex handed her a phone. "Tell Juliana you're safe before she shows up here."

Taking the phone, Lily strode to the mementos representing her life. "Juliana, I can't thank you enough for everything you've done."

Juliana scoffed. "I had a couple visions. No big deal. You did the dirty work. I'm so glad you're okay and you found the killer."

"Without Jake opening my head, I don't know how I would've done what I did to both Sheehan and…Connor. God, Juliana, do I have a story to tell you."

"You remember everything now?"

"More than I want to. Can I call you later? Girlfriend therapy?"

"I'll always be here for you, Lily. We'll work through the issues of your mind together." Juliana laughed. "I have a lot of experience, ya know."

"Not with telekinesis."

"I know a great paranormal psychologist. Remember Brian Miller from the Institute? I'll hook you up."

"Deal. Love you." She clicked off the phone.

Without touching her stolen mementos, she absorbed each one, remembered when she'd first noticed it missing. Innocuous items, but memorable. Each time an item had vanished, she'd scour her house, hunting for it. Her ex, Daniel used to tell her she was scatter-brained, and not always in such nice terms. She'd known better.

She refused to allow anyone's mind to ever screw with her again. Gazing upon the man whose intense eyes refused to stray from her, she offered him a tentative smile. He held out his hand, and she weaved her fingers in his, refusing to ever let her heart go.

CHAPTER THIRTY-FIVE

Lily touched the engraved chalice on the marble pedestal. The sapphires studding the base gleamed. The overhead recessed lights bounced off them, creating blue stars on the ceiling.

"Finally, the real deal." Using a microfiber polish cloth, she wiped a fingerprint off the rim. Ric and his securities company had retrofitted a windowless alcove attached to her suite on the Guild compound to hold the Twilight collection with top brass security. Lily strolled to the marble-topped console in the walk-in vault and traced the ornate gold necklace, matching earrings dripping in diamonds and precious gems, and lastly, the ring. The wall vault behind one of her mother's castle paintings housed the *Codex* and her mother's journal.

Once she'd located the safety deposit boxes containing the real chalice and the *Codex*, she knew she had to place the collection on display, if only to Guild members and their visitors. A sliding steel wall at the far side of the room revealed an impenetrable window, which allowed viewing during specified times. Ric had keyed the security pad with Lily's fingerprints and retinal prints. Under her domain now, no one else was allowed in the room or in her wing, other than the McAllister brothers, Elizabeth,

Niles, and a few trusted Guild members.

She cast her gaze upon the castle painting, wondering about the strange herbal concoctions and prophecies mentioned in the *Codex*. Prophecy maintained that the potions enhanced any psychic's abilities. She held no immediate craving to enhance the abilities she still needed to get a handle on. "Maybe later...in another decade," she announced to the empty space.

Lily left the secure room and thumbed the biosensor. The air was noticeably warmer in the adjoining living room, and she rubbed away the goosebumps on her bare arms, pushing up the strap of her slinky black dress. Rustling sounds from her office obstructed her heartbeat for a second. After a shakedown of Guild directors and an ouster of several members linked to the Cabal, the Guild allowed very few members inside the compound without a trusted Guardian escort. One mystery at a time...and she had a law firm to run. Let the Guild take care of the Cabal once they restructured and weeded out the troublemakers. Until then, she planned to divide her time between her house in the foothills and life on the compound to keep her finger on the pulse.

"Lily, is that you?" Elizabeth's voice floated from the office. "It's a warm evening. Let's eat outside on the back terrace. Jake's building a fire."

"Thank you. I'm starving." Relief cascaded down her arms. Although she was an orphan now, her new family surrounded her each day: Elizabeth, Jake, and the other McAllister brothers, Niles, Juliana and Alex. Although she missed her father more than she had words to describe, she felt incredibly loved. Now, she needed to get her best friend Marisa up to San Jose and her family would be complete. "My next step in world domination." She fist-bumped the air.

She strolled into her office, the mahogany desk in the

center covered end to end with the items from Connor's lair, organized by year stolen. The items had provided Connor's link to her, allowing him to watch her every movement, hide in her head, and shadow her.

Each item had disappeared from her life throughout the last decade, from the butterfly barrette she'd worn as a six-year-old, to the black-leather studded wrist band she'd worn as a teenager, to diamond earrings stolen earlier in the week and so much more, including her father's wedding ring, which Connor had used to trick her. She leafed through the stack of papers ranging from articles of her birth announcement, to articles about her mother's death, her high school graduation announcement, to her father's obituary. Disgust filled her empty stomach. She had loved Connor once, planned to spend her life with him. *Stupid eighteen-year-old love-struck girl.*

There was one man she trusted implicitly now, no matter if he'd unwittingly tricked her...for her own good. A good that returned the memories she'd fought to regain for ten long years. A man who'd protected her and watched over her at the expense of his life. No doubt remained that she loved Jake to the heart of her soul. Never believing she'd fall for another man so soon, so fast and so deeply, she couldn't deny her attraction to Jake...everything about him vastly different from the others, vital and connected to her real self.

The edge of the handkerchief he'd lent her at her father's gravesite peeked out of her purse. She'd meant to return it to him, but had a hard time bringing herself to give up that tiny, innocuous piece of him. Smiling, she stroked the fine cotton before fisting her hand around the handkerchief. For some odd reason, she knew it meant the world to Jake.

She left the suite and practically skipped down the

stairs to the secluded back patio surrounded by the forests of the Santa Cruz hills. The sun had plummeted into a hazy dusk, creating a murky glow through the darkening woods on the balmy night. Candles flickered on the tables and planter walls, a twinkling field of fallen stars. White fairy lights dripped from the trees like spikes of lightning. In the center of the round patio, Jake bent over a blazing fire in the firepit, the flames dancing toward the clear sky. The glow of the candles filled her, and she strolled down the flagstone pathway to a secluded wrought-iron bench on the left. A gravel path led into the woods toward a hidden electronic fence surrounding the compound.

Jake's booted steps thumped on the stone, echoing the excited thump of her heart in her ears.

"It's beautiful out here. Thank you for doing this." His tantalizing cologne filtered through her senses before she opened the welcome gates of her mind to him. Lily wallowed self-indulgently in his scent and senses, in the fullness around her heart. "What did the Guild say?"

He brushed against her back so close, the heat of his bare skin ignited the waiting cinders inside her. Lily tapped her foot, her heel clicking on the flagstones.

"Under the unusual circumstances," he nuzzled her neck, his warm lips doing delicious acts of sin across her bare shoulders, "and after your approval and acceptance, they'll absolve my indiscretions, expunge my file."

Lily's knees swayed, and she spun into his awaiting arms. The scent of leather layering his heady cologne infused her. Bare-chested, he must've quickly donned his leather jacket to build the fire at Elizabeth's demand. She smoothed her hand over his warm skin, feeling his heart quicken. "Will you remain my Guardian?"

Laughter rumbled inside him, vibrating against her palm. "Full-time. They trust no one else."

"My one and only?"

A growl worked up his throat. "Only you, Lily. Now and forever."

She gazed upon his gorgeous arrogant face, his hair loose and free. At least he refrained from saying his psychic abilities were stronger than hers and she needed him to guard her mind. The idea of Jake always at her side sent her pulse skittering with a mixed bag of excitement and relief.

"I bet they're scared shitless of me." She snorted half in jest and halfway knowing she possessed untold and untapped power. The Guild hadn't had a telekinetic on its roster for decades.

"Hell, yes, they're running scared." He kissed her forehead. "Of you and of anything happening to you." He wrapped his good arm around her, his hand held possessively against the small of her back, needing her touch as much as she needed his.

"What if I don't approve of absolving you of your crimes against me?" she asked ominously, her lips twitching to smile.

His arm stiffened. She giggled and the tension fled his arm. "Lily, darlin'," he murmured. "Don't tease me. I need to know you want this." He tensed against the length of her. "You are my compass, my twilight, my everything. If I'm not your Guardian, your everything, I don't know if I can stand it."

Silence reigned until all Lily heard was the pounding of her heart in her ears and her mind shrieking joyfully.

"What do you really, really want?" She wedged her leg against his thigh, and his hand drifted down to hold her leg against him. She wanted to straddle him on the spot and sink her being into *him*. "By the way, I have a nice soft bed upstairs all to myself."

Jake groaned, and his dark mask of hunger almost

liquefied her to the stones beneath their feet. "You, Lily McKenna Falbrooke. I want you."

Molten desire gushed through her veins, happiness nearly propelling her heart out her ribcage. "I love you, Jake McAllister." Together they were whole, the sum of their parts. No other would ever come between them and their psychic minds.

His mouth descended, and she melted into his soft, firm lips devouring hers in the most indescribably passionate kiss. His tongue parted her lips, and he plundered the inside of her mouth, tasting of whiskey and love, his thoughts racing into the open and welcome cavern of her head.

"You are all I want, enchantress of my heart," he mentally said. *"I love you now and forever."*

"I accept you, guardian of my life, guardian of my heart, my soul, my mind." Lily recited beautiful and apt words her mother had written for her father, copied in her journal. *"I want only you."*

"Does this mean you're not evicting me?" he breathed into her mouth.

She couldn't imagine her life without Jake, nor did she ever want to. They had so much to learn about one another, and she was eager to delve deep. "I guess I'm stuck with you." She handed him the handkerchief. "Remember when you loaned me this?"

Jake studied the snip of cloth. "The cemetery. I thought you'd burned it."

She play-pinched his arm. "I wanted to keep it, but it felt important to you."

"My mother had them made for my father. Each of us brothers took a couple after the accident."

"Then I'm glad you have it back."

"Thank you." He kissed her neck. "Later, I'm going to see what color underwear you're wearing. Your disorder in your orderly world." He slipped her strap off her right shoulder.

"Bingo." She slipped the strap back up. "And who said I was wearing any?"

"Drive me any crazier with talk like that and I'll take you here and now." He nipped her shoulder.

She angled her head to give him more skin to tease. "I aim to please."

Footsteps thudded on the walkway. "Oh joy, this what I've got to look forward to from you two love birds?" Ric asked. He stood near the firepit, a wan smile belying his teasing words.

Lily returned his smile, thankful once again he'd not been hurt when Connor mentally knocked him unconscious. A grim expression clouded the teasing joy on his face in the amber glow of the roaring fire.

Jake snuggled Lily inside his jacket, fused so close she felt his heartbeat inside her. "What's got you so bent? Please don't tell me I have to kill someone else riding my tail." The teasing words fell flat in the wake of her guilt and sorrow. By the end of the week, she'd have to visit a shrink to deal with the ramifications of her little killing spree.

Ric laughed, wooden and detached. "No. Forget it. Tonight's your night."

The deaths of Sheehan and Connor snipped at her heart. Though they'd harmed and had meant to harm her and everyone she loved, she didn't know if she would ever survive the fact that she'd used buried psychic abilities to destroy them. While researching her family tree, she discovered Philip Sheehan had told the truth about being a distant cousin. Since her memories had returned, she understood why his odd violet-gray eyes had tripped her heebie-jeebies—the same color eyes as her maternal grandmother, dead over twenty years. Yet, no records existed to prove his claim on the chalice or if he and her mother ever had a fling. Regardless, his and Connor's reign on earth had ended.

Lily awoke each morning with nightmares of Connor and her part in killing her mother and brother. But Jake held her close to his side to quell her phobias and absolve her sorrows, vowing to never let anything happen to her, vowing to love her forever for as long as she wanted him. In time, she'd come to terms with her headfirst fall into adulthood that fateful summer in Tahoe. One nightmare at a time.

Every time she thought about her capabilities, it instilled a mega dose of fear in her. She definitely needed to take a road trip with Juliana up to Oregon to visit their old doctor, Brian Miller, and learn to control her powers. That is, if Jake and Alex took time away to accompany them. No way would either über protective caveman allow Lily and Juliana to journey alone.

"Maybe you and Juliana can coax Dr. Miller to come out of semi-retirement and fly down here," Jake said.

She slugged his arm. "Stop that."

He dipped his head sheepishly. "I'm trying. Connor royally screwed up my head. Yours too. It'll be a while before we can build our walls up again and block each other out."

She kissed his chin. "I get it. We'll figure it out. Juliana and Alex have some tricks to help us."

"Lily?" Ric's soberness so unlike his normal happy-go-lucky attitude rode the air.

"Bro. What's up? This isn't you. How bad did Connor screw you up?" Jake released Lily, linked his fingers in hers, and they sidled closer to Ric, scuffling dead leaves off the pavers.

"I had a freaky vision this morning I can't shake," Ric replied. "Lily, does your clairvoyance give you indecipherable cling-on visions? Mine are usually clear and I recognize the people in them."

Lily clasped his hand in hers and Jake's hand in her other, loving the feel of the McAllisters on both sides of her, her protective wingmen. "Before I lost my memory, my second sight was pretty clear. Afterward, just random impressions I never pinpointed until after an event occurred, then the impressions made sense." She squeezed Jake's fingers. "When your big bro here opened my head with a can opener, and I had the vision in the cabin when I touched that dead man's blood," she paused, chomping on her bottom lip, adding another notch on her kill list, and continued, "It came on sudden and clear. Not much else since then."

"What do you see in the vision?" Jake's unease radiated in his grave voice. "More Cabal threats?"

"Nothing decipherable." Ric shrugged. "Hey, I'm not going to intrude on your date. Third wheel and all."

"Date?" Jake frowned, kinked his head to the left. "We haven't even gone on a date." He grinned mischievously.

Holy eating dessert before the main course. She'd never slept with a man before she'd dated him for a while. "We'll have to remedy that situation." She traced her fingers down Jake's abdomen, inciting a lusty growl.

"I'm formally asking you out on a date. Tonight. Your bedroom," he whispered in her ear, nipped her lobe.

Itching with desire, she forcibly cooled her jets and said to Ric, "You're staying and we're celebrating first. Jake has a new job...guarding me from killing any more creeps." She might be able to banter about the deaths in the light of twilight, yet nighttime remained a different story. Lily met Jake's gaze and gave his pout a conciliatory smile. Their first date would have to wait for the lifetime ahead of them.

He flashed one of his irresistible smiles, one meant only for her, the kind that made her heart stop and dissolve the world surrounding them. *"You're my sunlight, my twilight, my everything light. No one will ever steal my light from me again,"* he said in her head.

DID YOU ENJOY
STEALING TWILIGHT?

If you have a few moments, I'd love for you to leave a review for *STEALING TWILIGHT* at your favorite online retailer or review site. Your review is greatly appreciated!

To stay up to date on Erin Richards' latest happenings, including new releases, sales, special announcements, exclusive excerpts, and giveaways, subscribe to her newsletter at: **www.erinrichards.com/connect.htm**

Catch the Psychic Justice Series from the beginning with *CHASING SHADOWS* and *TWILIGHT RISING*.

ABOUT THE AUTHOR

After lamenting the lack of young adult books to read, Erin Richards wrote her first novel at the age of eighteen hoping to shift the tide. But the only tide she shifted was moving from high school to college. Then everyday life took its toll on her writerly dreams until 2003 when she couldn't ignore the writing bug any longer. By then, she had immersed herself in reading adult fantasy and romance novels. Writing paranormal & fantasy romance was a no brainer and she went on to publish two adult romance novels. But her muse wanted to give that YA writing gig another chance, and Erin finally realized her lifelong dream of publishing a YA novel with the debut of *VIGILANTE NIGHTS*.

Erin lives in Northern California. In her spare time, she enjoys reading and re-landscaping her backyard, even though she hates digging holes...unless she's burying fictional bodies! She also confesses to a fascination with American muscle cars and reality TV.

Please visit Erin Richards online at:
www.erinrichards.com